PRAISE FOR CARISSA ANDREWS

"If you like adventure, prophecies, journeys, excitement and surprises, it's all here and then some."

"Bringing a world to life is a marvelous feat, and with *Polarities*, Carissa Andrew's second book in the series, you get to peak even more into an extra-terrestrial marvel that brings with it amazing characters, and a story you truly don't want to put down."

"Even tho I had several books I needed to read I was unable to move on without knowing the end of this series."

"This is the second book of a series and in it Carissa Andrews is coming into her own as an author. I found that there was a deeper depth to this book, a deepening and fleshing out of the broader story. The characters are richer, more alive and I rooted for them -- often on the edge of my own seat."

D0377241

Original Copyright © 2017 Carissa Andrews

Published in 2017 by Carissa Andrews

Revised in 2018

Cover Design © Carissa Andrews

All rights reserved.

ISBN: 0991055829

ISBN-13: 978-0991055821

DEDICATION

Sometimes you have to lose something before its value is truly appreciated...

To my brother, Scott... I miss you, bro. Give the angels a high-five for me. Hope you're kicking their ass at Uno. ;)

ACKNOWLEDGMENTS

Special thanks to the amazing Five Wings Art Council, who, with financial support from the McKnight Foundation, provided a grant to make Polarities and Revolutions possible. I am both humbled and grateful to have been given their support to continue to write, design, and publish my own novels. Thank you!

POLARITIES

THE PENDOMUS CHRONICLES: BOOK 2

CARISSA ANDREWS

DO NOT BE FOOLED INTO BELIEVING THE POLARITIES OF LIGHT
AND DARK . . .

THEY ARE BUT OF THE SAME COIN.

1

RUNA

I DIDN'T THINK it would be this hard. I really didn't give much thought to how things would be at all, come to think of it. I kind of just hoped taking a leap of faith would be enough to guide me through the rest of what was to come. Boy was I wrong.

My focus softens as I stare out over the undulating mounds of sand, heat radiating in rolling waves. With my NanoTech jacket bundled up in my lap, the absence of the protective fabric allows the small granules to pelt the soft skin of my arms. Each strike is like being burned with hot pokers and reminds me just how far out of my element I really am. I've never felt the unfettered sun on my skin before now. It isn't as pleasant as you might think.

I take a deep breath and close my eyes.

For some reason, I assumed if I did what was expected of me—going into the Tree of Burden, seeking more answers as I was told— I'd have more support than this. More information, or details...not a mostly blank book which refuses to hand over any more of its secrets.

My eyes fall to the worn leather and paper of the Caudex

beside me. Reaching out, I stroke the cover with my palm. I've stared at the same passages over and over, hoping to glean something new. They're burned into my memory now; for whatever good it does me. There hasn't been anything to help me determine my next steps, beyond what Adrian had given me.

What's worse is this crushing pain of being all alone. I miss my friends, I miss Traeton...

Wow, do I miss him.

Once you've gotten used to someone's presence, their absence is an enormous void; almost crushing. With everything that's been thrown at me, I thought I'd be stronger... more *capable* to handle this somehow. What good is being this so-called *Daughter of Five* if it doesn't mean anything? Just words.

How can I be the savior of the planet and bring about any kind of change here? I'm just as lost as everyone else—maybe more so.

I pull my knees closer to my body as my mind drifts back to my happiest moment. The place I go to when I need to escape the harshness of the present. It's becoming a feeble attempt at finding equilibrium to this internal darkness I'm sinking into.

Pressing my fingertips to my lips, I try to recall the brief moments in his embrace. The feel of his breath and the way his hands touched my body; like I was his, and his hands knew it. Those moments between Trae and I weren't all that long ago, and yet it feels like an eternity since I last saw him. Last spoke to him...Last *touched* him. I'd do anything to be with him right now.

I don't even know if he's safe.

The thought makes me cringe with regret. I did what I thought was necessary, but I left them all behind to deal with the aftermath without me. What if I never make it back to them?

Squinting out to the horizon, all that's before me is sand. Lots and lots of it. The landscape is foreign, the region inhospitable. All I have to go on is the sun's location still locked in the sky and impressions I received from Adrian.

I run my tongue over my parched lips, wondering how much longer I can survive without a larger water supply. The tiny pool I discovered has run dry and it's only a matter of time before I dehydrate completely. My stomach grumbles, empty. Time is running out and I have nowhere to turn to. *No one* to turn to.

Brushing the sand off my legs, I slowly pull my NanoTech jacket back on, careful not to disturb my blistered skin as I leave the safety of the rocky alcove. I clutch the Caudex to my chest and trudge through the drifts. The sun blares down, making the suit unbearably hot, but I already know what happens if I leave it off.

I've walked for days, trying to find some sort of clue to why I was left here. Any clues to lead me to my next destination, but all I've seen is more sand. There are no birds, no creatures of any kind stirring…just me and my book. I lift the Caudex above my head, trying to shield the sun from my eyes as I walk, but after a while the weight of it is unbearable.

In the distance is an outcropping of stones, much larger than any I've seen so far. I make it my destination as I continue onward. The ground begins to look more like a vast ocean spread out in front of me.

Keep going, Runa. You're almost there.

Sweat cascades down my back and my legs give out.

"Just a second…to rest."

The Caudex lands in a heap in front of me. Wiping the sweat from my forehead with the back of my hand, I squint in the distance to my destination. It seems just as far away now as it was when I started.

The breeze picks up, sending sand flying around me. The pages of the Caudex flip back and forth furiously, and I reach out to grab it before some of the brittle pages rip. As I do, an enormous set of black claws extend from the open pages, reaching outward from inside the book and into the sand storm around me. With a mixture of amazement and horror, I step back as a muscular black arm follows, then a large black face. As realization dawns, I squelch my scream and scramble back, trying to put distance between myself and the emerging Salamander.

Effortlessly, it slinks out of the Caudex, then stomps from side to side, huffing and hissing at me.

"Stay back. Do you hear me?" I scream at the creature, kicking sand its direction.

A long pink tongue flickers out, as if mocking me for my feeble attempts. The Salamander slinks from beside the book, making its way toward me, despite my protests.

I grab a rock the size of my fist and hold it above my head.

"Don't move or I'll be forced to use this." I warn, unsure if the Salamander has any idea what I'm even saying. Truthfully, it doesn't matter— it will know soon enough if I'm forced to use it.

I quickly scan the open desert around me, watchful of any reinforcements—other Salamanders, juncos—*Videus*. The Salamander halts in front of me, turning its head from side to side, sizing me up. Blue flickers of electricity zap between its toes, making me extremely uneasy.

Whatever you're going to do...do it. I don't have all day.

With a final huff, the Salamander spins around, its tail slamming into my hand and knocking the stone clear out of my grasp. It lands a good ten meters away with a soft thud.

Surprised, I scramble on my hands and knees for a larger stone. The Salamander wastes no time, rushing back to me. Its face is inches from mine and it lets out a shrill cry like nothing I've ever heard. The reverberation sends a shiver up my spine. Instinctively, I cover my ears and lower my head. The squeal abruptly stops and I wait with my eyes squeezed shut for its inevitable attack. When nothing happens, I take a chance and look up.

The Salamander watches me closely, tilting its head to the side. I swear its ice blue eyes see right through me. For a moment, I forget myself and lean inward. The corner of its lip pulls back in a snarl. Then it closes the last few inches between us, its breath foul, like it recently ate something rotten.

Perhaps it did.

After a moment of standing utterly still, it again spins in its spot, and begins to saunter away. When he reaches the Caudex, he nudges the book shut and glances back at me.

"Hey—don't you touch that," I call after the beast, pushing to a stand.

Startled into movement, I rush to the book I'm meant to guard with my life. The Salamander huffs, as if reprimanding me. Confused, I pick up the Caudex, clutching it to my chest and step back, watching the Salamander closely. I cock my head to the side, narrowing my eyes.

"What are you waiting for?" I ask, more for myself than for the creature.

As if understanding my words, the Salamander looks into the distance at the rock outcropping I've been trying to reach —then returns its gaze to me.

"Oh, no...not on your life," I say as a strange understanding settles in, "If you think we are going there together —or worse—you're deluded. I don't care if you came out of the Caudex."

Again, the Salamander huffs. However, this time, he starts walking, leaving me in the full blaze of the sun alone. For a moment, I watch, partly relieved he's on his way. A more annoying part of me is telling me to follow it; that I shouldn't be so stubborn.

"You've got to be kidding me," I shake my head, and take a seat in the sand, "Kani would tell me I was mental if I followed it. She'd be right."

After all I've been through with these creatures, there's no way I'm going the same direction. They have a direct connection with Videus and the last thing I need right now is to be taken over—or captured. The little blue stone around my neck glows brightly, tugging itself toward the Caudex. Curious, I crack open the monolith to see if there's new information. Flipping through slowly, page after page is still blank.

My eyes rest on the two passages which have been there from the very beginning…

In the age of the elders, the acropolis served as the source of foundation for all of Pendomus—long before the invasion of dying Earth. The structure was the most beautiful in the world, truly a spectacular sight. Inhabitants of Pendomus kept the site sacred above all others. When humanity released its scourge upon the land, nature conspired to protect the acropolis, burying it deep within itself. Creation itself split apart into five equal fragments. Each held its own special gift, none more important than the others. They hid themselves away, waiting for the day their gifts could be resurrected to restore balance to Pendomus.

My eyes fall to the five-petaled flower drawn in glowing metallic ink.

The Everblossom is the image used to invoke the five, and key to the one who can reclaim its purpose. Once known to grow even in the most frigid of storms, the Everblossom was finally destroyed when humanity laid waste with their misguided efforts to terraform the planet. All cycles of Pendomus ground to a halt as the planet was locked to the closest star in an attempt to eradicate the new inhabitants.

I shake my head. Of course there was life here before; it has always been obvious to me, despite the history. The trees were examples of that.

Before my eyes, as if being written by an invisible hand, these words appear:

The original inhabitants of Pendomus were known as the Four Pillars. They connected all elements of Pendomus into a cohesive elemental planetary system...Salamanders, Waterbears, AirGliders, and the elusive TerraDweller. Together, they managed and maintained the balance of all things. None was higher regarded than the other, but each was powerful beyond measure.

When humanity reigned down on the planet, it was the gentle Salamanders who were the first of the Pillars to come forth, offering their assistance and making their presence known. Feared for their ability to conjure the element of creation and destruction, they were also the first to be manipulated and eventually, conquered by the humans.

As the AirGliders came to their aid, offering their intellect and support to relieve their comrades, many too were unable to maintain their distinction. Their minds were all too easily corrupted.

It was the Waterbears who were all but annihilated by the covert efforts of those they once trusted, their partners in balance. When the Salamanders and AirGliders were taken, the Waterbears were unaware of the shift in power. As the balance of the Four Pillars crumbled, only a handful of Waterbears remained.

The TerraDwellers remained stoic and centered. Refusing to engage in the initial battles, it was their lack of intervention, as perceived by the other three Pillars, to be the undoing of Pendomus. To this day, the TerraDwellers remain concealed, perhaps biding their time deep within the depths of Pendomus until the evidence of the prophecy's initiation has come to pass.

I lean forward on the book, running my hands over my forehead.

So there is a prophecy.

What does it say? Why can't they describe it here?

I sit back and shake my head. How could any of this be foretold? It doesn't make logical, scientific sense.

"Wow, I just let my Helix show," I snicker at my train of thought.

Logic gets you so far—but it's not everything. There's so much I've seen and experienced lately, and my training and education in the Helix never prepared me for it. Yet here I am, relying on old thought patterns.

The Salamander huffs nearby, then covers its nose beneath one of its paws as it lies down, waiting.

With a sideways glance at the large black creature, I return my gaze to the book.

The Helix was extremely efficient in drumming into our heads not to trust anything unless the scientific facts back them up. Part of me does agree—everything does have a scientific answer, but we just don't have the know-how or tools to understand it yet.

A month ago, I could say with certainty, I had no concept of these creatures of the Four Pillars. So who knows what else could be hidden on Pendomus that no one is aware of.

Though the Caudex doesn't go into specifics of their bodily types, I know I've seen the juncos known as the AirGliders. They were fairly obvious. Though I'm sure Caelum and his cronies really don't want to be seen as the peaceful proponents of thought and reason.

I look up at the face of the Salamander who appears to be studying me closely. Obviously, I've dealt with them; and clearly the Waterbears. Well, *Waterbear*.

I lower the book to focus on the horizon beyond. I have, as of yet, to come across anything resembling a TerraDweller. How will I know one when I see it? What if they're worse than the others? What if I do meet one? Will I come up against something I can't handle?

What makes them so elusive? Are they dangerous?

Most of these details on the Pillars are ones I've heard before. Adrian told me most of this at the waterside of the pond when I had gone through the Tree, though she didn't specifically call them this.

I cast my gaze to the rogue Salamander as it stands up, giving up on me as it starts tromping further and further away from me.

Okay, maybe I do get it. The Salamanders weren't always bad. They were made to be that way—by us.

I glance down at the open pages, and sigh.

Follow her.

The words write themselves on the page, but vanish before I have the opportunity to look again. For a moment,

I'm not even sure it was really there, but then the next sentence follows in its place.

She will guide you to where you need to be most.

I blink to a completely blank page.

Am I hallucinating? It could happen, considering the heat.

I close the Caudex and stand up. With the book tucked under my left arm, I shield my eyes with my right hand. A bubble of energy surrounds the Salamander, much like Tethys' shield does for her.

"Fantastic. The first creature I see in days, and the one meant to help me is the same type of creature who tried to kill me and my friends," I mutter, dragging my feet, but following after it.

I keep my distance, but the Salamander must recognize my presence, slowing its own pace to allow me to catch up. Wind whips a flurry of sand up and I turn my back and close my eyes. In the distance, I swear I hear the Salamander cackling.

Great, one of these creatures with a sense of humor. Just what I need.

I miss Tethys. Without a doubt, I could trust her.

The connection of safety is not evident with this Salamander, despite what the Caudex nudges me toward. Of course, my brain rebels. There is a nagging piece in the back of my mind reminding me trust with Tethys wasn't always there, either. In fact, she was the most feared thing on the planet before I was able to communicate with her. After our first encounter, I had every reason to be scared to death of her.

When I reach the Salamander, I continue walking. The ice blue eye on the side of her head briefly glances my direction and she huffs, looking away as she carries onward.

We walk in complete silence, neither one of us seeming to want to give in to any kind of truce. After a while, though, the full brunt of the sun's heat begins to wear on me. Sweat pools in the small of my back and beads across my forehead and neck. My lips are parched and right now, the only thing on my mind is finding someplace with water.

The large rock outcropping is finally growing closer, but by my calculations is still an hour or two off. *Much too long.*

I feel the stare of the Salamander as her eyes briefly flicking from our path, to me.

"I'm fine," I mutter, more for myself, than for her.

She snorts, but it sounds almost like an indignant laugh; as if she knows something I don't.

I raise my eyebrows and turn to look at her.

"Do you mind?" I say, "I don't appreciate the tone."

For a moment, I'm completely serious, staring into the bottomless blue depths of the Salamander's eyes. We both stop our progress and I bend over, laughing.

I'm completely projecting my own thoughts onto the Salamander, not the other way around.

Her curious eyes watch me, but I laugh even harder. It feels good to laugh—even to have someone to project thought onto, considering I've been alone for a couple of days. I never realized how much I enjoy the company of others—whether inside my head, or beside my body.

"Come on. Let's do this," I say, shaking my head.

My feet feel heavy as I drag onward, training my eyes on the destination on the horizon.

I can make it if I just keep going…

After a short distance, inky black tendrils creep in from the sides of my vision and I drop to my knees.

"I think I need to take a—break," I say, bending forward and clutching at the sand.

I feel my body dropping as darkness takes me over completely.

DRIP, drip, drip.

I lick my lips, trying to find my voice to ask for some water. A gritty, cracked texture meets my tongue, and I open my eyes.

Surrounded by complete darkness, I blink hard, expecting something to change. When it doesn't, I clamber to my hands and knees, feeling around at the space in front of me. Cold, wet, and rocky is the landscape beneath me. I stand up, nearly slipping as I do. Beside me, something growls and I freeze, completely still.

There's something in here with me. But where is *here*?

Suddenly I remember the Salamander, the trek to the outcropping and I take a tentative step back.

"If..." my voice wavers, "...if that's you—please, just...let me know."

There's a scratching sound, then an electrical charge builds beside me. The hair on the top of my head begins to rise and flames burst from the feet of the Salamander. Blue lines of electricity jump from the flames, zapping between its toes, connecting to the arcs from its other feet.

I inch toward the wall, nodding.

At least it's only her.

But how did I get here? What about the Caudex?

I search the ground beside where I was and find it resting a meter or so away.

"Did you bring me here? What happened?" I ask, eyeing the Salamander.

She tips her head in acknowledgment and stomps toward me. Backing away quickly, her head nudges my knee, pushing me deeper into the tunnel.

"Stay back, please. I'm not ready," I say, trying to sound strong, even if my insides are something quite to the contrary.

She continues to advance, huffing and swaying in a strange kind of dance as I continue to edge backwards.

"If you brought me here, that's great and all, but I'm really not in the mood to figure you out right now. So, if you don't mind…" my voice cracks, but I continue, "I'll be on my way from here. Alone."

With that, my foot sinks into a pool of water, sloshing around my NanoTech boot and up to my knee. My boot and trousers instantly turn black, as they start working to expel the moisture.

My parched lips scream at me and without thought, I bend down, scooping as much of the water as I can into my cupped hands. I pull the cold, wet liquid to my lips and drink it in deeply. Over and over again I refill, drinking until my stomach aches and my lips are sated. My belly rumbles with the first ounce of anything hitting the depths of my stomach in a long time. When I can't drink another drop I take a seat against the stoney wall, giving my insides a moment to calm down.

The Salamander sits a few meters away, watching me as I glance up. Its head is slightly cock-eyed and tilted, as her heavy black eyelids slide open and closed.

I take a deep breath and sigh.

"Thank you," I finally say, nodding my head in acknowledgment.

As if appeased by this gesture of words, the Salamander snorts and lies down.

"Why are you doing this?" I ask, wishing I could get a response I could understand.

The Salamander nods to the Caudex on the ground beside me, then toward the darkness of the cavern beyond.

"I don't understand," I say, eyeing her movements, "You know, if you're not here to kill me, I wish we could communicate like Tethys and I do."

The Salamander exhales heavily.

Maybe she does, too.

I walk to the book, opening the pages slowly, just in case. Nothing appears out of the ordinary. There's no new passages, nothing to explain the Salamander's role, or what I'm meant to do next.

The Salamander stomps the ground, sending a blue arc of lightening down the cavern tunnel. The light dims out the further it goes, and I turn back to her.

"Are you telling me there's something I should be aware of deeper in the cave?" I ask, my eyes widening.

In an odd sense, it sort of feels like home. After all, the Haven and Lateral weren't unlike this very cavern.

Fire shoots from her nostrils and into a small circular ring a couple meters away. Though there's nothing inside the ring to keep the fire lit, it does so anyway.

I set the book aside and crawl on my hands and knees to get a closer look.

"How did you— ?" I turn back to the Salamander, but my words cut off as I stare into the darkness of the rest of the cavern around me.

No longer nearby, or keeping guard, the Salamander has vanished.

Once again, I'm utterly alone.

2

TRAETON

HOW DO YOU KNOW if you've lost your moral compass?

Over the last few days, I've considered hunting a man so I can kill him, make him suffer—at least, I think he's a man— more times, and in more ways, than I care to admit. But do I really have it in me to hunt Videus down and extinguish the light from his eyes? Is it bad if the answer is always a resounding yes?

My temples throb in rhythm with my feet as they pound over the wet cobbled stones as I walk this corridor of the Lateral for the hundredth time. I've practically worn a groove in its firm exterior. For some reason, walking back and forth helps to ease the unrest in my soul. All this sitting around isn't doing any good, especially for Kani. Hell, who am I kidding? It's not helping a single one of us.

I step aside as a young boy with light blonde hair and a book clutched in his hand clammers by. He practically trips over his oversized shoes and baggy trousers, but laughs it off heartily as a brunette boy points and giggles.

"Nice one," the brunette laughs, "Ya nearly toppled that guy with the blue hair."

"Well, if I wasn't the one who had to do all the heavy lifting—" The blonde one holds up his book and bops his friend on the head with it as he walks by.

Neither one can be more than ten, maybe eleven, and they bring me back to a time not all that long ago, when I was running up and down these streets with my best friend with blonde hair. Shaking my head, I try to dismiss the uninvited memories cropping up. I'm not ready for them.

It's only been a week since the devastation at the Tree. Mere days since I last saw my best friend Fenton alive. Days since I last saw…

Runa.

Her blue and amber eyes haunt me in my already restless sleep. Sometimes I hear her voice in my mind, smell the soft hint of vanilla in my sleep pack. Thinking about her makes the hole in my chest implode in on itself further. Pretty soon there will be nothing left but a black, sucking void. It isn't fair—any of this. Fenton and Runa should both be with us, and yet…

They're not.

How does a person ever come to terms with this kind of loss? How do you find a way to fill the vacancy of someone you love? I don't believe you ever can. You just find a way to muster the strength to move forward, step by step.

It's been nearly a decade since I lost my father and sister Ava…and even after all this time, their absence still lingers; haunting me into remembering them. Losing them was my fault, too. And here we are—round two for a guy who doesn't learn, I guess.

I turn the corner and walk up the steps to Landry's home.

"Please tell me you aren't self-flagellating again," Kani

reprimands as I open the door. When I stop in mid-stride, giving her a confused look, she merely shrugs, "You have that look again."

"I didn't realize self-flagellation had a *look*," I say, dropping into the small couch along the left hand side of the main room.

Kani takes a seat next to me and pulls her knees in close to her chest. She fiddles with the scarf around her neck, revealing a fresh bandage where Videus had cut open her throat. Lucky for her, the cut was only a surface wound—or I'd be mourning another friend.

"Of course it has a look. My only question is—are you being productive or a pain in the ass?" she says.

I pluck at the tattered edges of the couch's green arm.

"How can you be so nonchalant about all this?" I ask, avoiding her question.

"I'm not. I just don't see how sitting around having a pity party is gonna change what happened," she says.

I watch her movements closely for a moment, and she nervously tucks a strand of black hair behind her ear, then the ends of the scarf. Though her words say one thing, the pain hidden deep in the recesses of her eyes screams something entirely different.

I know the feeling.

"Perhaps you're right. I'm working on it, okay," I tell her.

"Good," she nods, as if trying to convince herself, too.

"Have you seen Landry lately?" I ask, changing the subject.

Kani bites the inside of her cheek, and shakes her head, "Nope."

"He's really gone off the grid this time," I mutter. Part of me wishes I could do the same, but there are answers I need. I have to find out what happened to Runa—see if there's a way we can help her get back to us. Kani thinks she's gone, since the Tree's nothing but ashes. But I have to know for sure.

"He'll be back. You know how he's—he needs to piece stuff together on his own," Kani says, her eyes flitting to the empty chair at his desk.

The main room of Landry's place has become a second home, of sorts. Neither one of us have been ready to go back to the Haven. There's too many painful memories to contend with. I already know it wouldn't feel like home without the others.

"Do you think we should go look for him? I really don't think him being on his own right now is a good idea," I say.

"Give him a couple more hours. If he hasn't contacted us soon, we can go all search party on him. He's probably with Alina, though."

"He's lucky to have her," I mutter before I can stop myself.

"Traeton—" Kani starts.

I wave my hand dismissively, "It's okay. I didn't mean it like that. If Landry's found a way to reconnect, all the better for the two of them. But it doesn't help me—us—find answers."

"It's only been a couple days, Trae. He's just found out his only brother is—"

"I know."

We sit in silence for a long while, listening to the soft hum of Landry's mainframe. It looks weird without the holographic screens lighting up the back wall.

"How do we ever get over this?" I ask, not ready to look her in the eye. She knows exactly what I mean.

"Traeton, life is fragile. You of all people should know that. I hope you know I did— " Her voice cracks and she clears her throat to recover, "— what needed to be done."

"I'm not blaming you, Kani."

"Lucky you," she says, frowning. Her knees drop into a cross-legged position and she stares at her hands as she entwines her fingers and places them in her lap.

"You were put into a difficult position. One you never should have been put in. Had roles been reversed...I would have made the same call. Fenton was compromised and there was no telling what he was capable of at that moment. Videus was already threatening to use Fenton's memory against us and we know he wouldn't have hesitated to kill you when he was ready. Just look at your neck."

"Aren't we all compromised? If Fenton could be taken over, any one of us could be. He didn't even have the eLink connection. But then, I keep thinking, what if I'd waited just a little longer? What if the possession was temporary? What if Videus eventually released him? What if— "

"What if you hadn't put an end to the connection and Videus used Fenton's body to kill us all?" I say, turning to face her brimming eyes, "Would that have been better?"

"Well, of course not," she spits, "but at least we wouldn't be left with this, this— "

"Void?" I offer.

"Regret," she whispers.

"Now who's the one self-flagellating?" I smirk. Kani's face flickers, but remains mostly stoic, "Besides, you heard Fenton. He was proud of you. You made the right choice."

"Yeah, I know..." Kani stands up, brushing off her legs as she does so, "I've been thinking—we have a mission now."

"We do?" I say.

"Damn straight we do. We're gonna avenge Fenton and Runa. Right? I mean, I know I'm not the only one who's been thinking it."

I blink hard, "You're not."

"So, c'mon. I can't keep sittin' around waiting for this hole to heal itself. I need to make an impact. Take some action. Make that bastard hurt as much as…" her voice trails off, but her jaw is set in determination.

"First of all, we don't know if Runa is really gone, gone."

"Trae, I know you want to keep hope, but we've been over this. There's no Tree left. You have to assume the worst and hope for the best," Kani says.

"I agree, but I'm not giving up on her until I have a reason to believe otherwise."

"Alright. Then I have your back," Kani says, tipping her head.

"There has to be something more about Runa, or the Tree somewhere. If she was this important, there has to be more of a record. I know there was supposed to be the caudex thing, but who knows where it is. As for Videus, we don't have much to go on there, either. We have the tiniest bits of intel from when we researched at the Archives but that wasn't much. We need to know more so we can hit him where it hurts. At least now we know if we're not careful, he can take over people's minds and control them. Hell, like you suggested, maybe even if we *are* careful," I say, shaking my head.

"See, I've been thinking about that. Fenton didn't have the eLink hardware embedded like we do. We were running off the assumption the eLink was made mandatory so Videus would have a way to control people's minds. How do you think Videus did take over Fenton?" Kani asks.

"I have no idea. I would have thought if anyone was susceptible, it would have been us; you, me, hell—Runa. I watched him turn people into Labots right in front of us when we were in the Helix."

"So strange…" Kani mutters, beginning to pace, "This is

more Landry's deal than any of us. He's the one who could crack the reasons—*if he were here.* Maybe we *should* go look for him."

"I agree. Landry's our best bet to understanding how Videus does it. If for no other reason, he knows the intricacies of how a ComLink or eLink works. Maybe by understanding better, we can defend against another takeover. In the meantime, though, we know Videus has got his vassalage thing, but we have no real idea where it is. Maybe that's our best start? If we could find the vassalage, maybe we'll get more details on Videus' real plan. At least we'd be helping Runa, too. She wanted her brother found."

Saying her name out loud makes me flinch internally. Thinking about her like she's going to come around the corner at any time makes me feel so damn insane.

Kani nods, "That's a really good point. If the vassalage is a prison, we should be able to poke around, or find out who else he's kept there. His agenda can't just be about some girl and putting an end to her life. There has to be something bigger than that."

"People do strange things when their livelihood is in jeopardy," I offer.

"You think that's it? He feels threatened?"

"Sure...but of what? He's gone to some pretty great lengths to make sure no one even knows he exists. What could he really lose?"

Kani continues to pace for a moment, shaking her head. "Doesn't make sense, does it?"

"None that I can think of until we have more of the puzzle."

"Maybe we need to do a bit more digging into Runa's past, too... Things aren't everything they seem to be with her, either. What if the key lies with her?" Kani says, "I mean, what's up with her paternal code? Why would the Helix not have her father on record? Would they have erased him from the database completely when he died?"

"Your guess is as good as mine," my words fumble out and I stare at a bunched up piece of the area rug.

"Traeton—are you okay?" her question lingers in the air.

I wave my hand dismissively and say, "Let's just focus on this. You're bringing up some great questions. Ones that need answers. I'd rather be proactive, than reactive, wouldn't you?"

"Let's do it," she says, as she moves to the pile of crumpled packs and supplies. "What should we do about Landry?"

"If you pack up, I'll go to Alina's and check on Landry," I offer, nodding at the bag in her hand, "But if he's not ready, we need to be prepared to do this without him."

Her almond-shaped eyes widen, but she nods.

"Good. Give me an hour to convince him. If he won't do it, then we head out tonight. We'll start at the Archives and follow the trail from there."

"Sounds like as good of a plan as any," she says, dropping the pack and walking toward the allayroom.

I clutch the handle of the door, feeling the cold, smooth texture as I walk out with a sense of renewed purpose. Whatever happens now, at least I'm not sitting and stewing. I'm taking direct action and control. Fenton would be proud of that.

Alina's house isn't far. Landry's probably been to see her —but whether he's still there or not is anyone's guess. Losing Fenton was just as hard on him as it was on the rest of us… maybe more so. The two of them always operated more like twins than merely brothers, even though Landry is almost four years older. Sometimes, I even wondered if they shared the same mind; they were that close. I can't even really imagine how this must be hitting him.

I walk up the stone steps of Alina's small house and as I raise my hand to knock, the door swings open. Alina's piercing blue eyes stare back at me from under her black bangs.

"Hey, Trae," she says, clutching at the side of the door.

"Is he here?" I ask, tipping my head at the space behind her.

Alina looks over her shoulder, then back at me, "He's not doing real well. I don't think now's— "

"Look, we're going to the Archives to do some recon. We want to hit Videus where it hurts, and we could really use Landry for this. We have questions only he can answer. I understand how he's feeling, believe me, but— "

"No Trae, I don't think you can understand."

"Can I at least just talk to him? Explain what we're doing, so if he changes his mind he can— " I ask, taking a step forward.

Alina pulls the door in tighter, "I'll pass along the message."

Her eyes fill with sympathy, but she means business. I've known Alina long enough to know not to mess with her judgment. If Landry's not ready, he's not ready. I kinda figured it might be the case anyway.

"Fine," I nod, "Let him know I'll take a ComLink with me, but we won't use it unless absolutely necessary, just in case it's how Videus was able to control Fenton."

"Okay. Good luck, Trae," Alina says, offering a faint smile.

"Yeah..." I say, raising my hand in acknowledgment. The vein in my right temple pulses, making my eye throb. I walk quickly, pressing my fingertips to the vein, trying to get it to relax. I shouldn't let this stress me out.

When I get back, Kani has three packs spread across the table, couch, and counter top in various stages of being filled. She enters the main room from Landry's bedroom with some of his clothing.

"So is he—?" Kani's words cut off as she sees the look on my face.

I shake my head.

"Okay—won't need these," she says, throwing them without care back the way she came.

"What more needs to be done?" I ask.

"We need water filled, food sorted. Do you have an idea of how long you want to be away from the Lateral for this?"

"Who knows? Could be days, could be weeks. It's not like the Archives are far, though. We can always come back if we need to. For now, let's aim for at least a week's worth," I say, stepping past her and looking for the canteens in the cupboards beneath the sink.

"You realize we won't be able to carry enough water for a week," Kani says, raising her eyebrows as I take two canteens out of the cupboard.

"Won't need to. There's a fountain in one of the other sections."

Kani snorts, "Nice of you boys to clue me in on this little tidbit."

"You never asked," I shrug.

"Wonder what else the two of you never told me…" she mutters under her breath, continuing to pack.

I grin, turning away and heading to the stash of tech supplies Landry keeps for times like these.

Kani works at organizing the food rations, while I search for a set of ComLinks. I have no idea if they'll even be tuned into the right frequency—or whatever the hell Landry does to make them active. As leery as I am to use one, I figure it's better to have them, than not at all. Placing two in tiny storage containers, I cram one each into our packs.

"Did Landry say he'll keep in touch with us?" Kani asks, as she zips up her pack.

"Nope."

"Ah," her eyebrows flick upward and she takes a seat, "Then why the ComLink?"

"Just a precaution. At this point, I don't even know if we should use them. Do you think we should bring anything else? NeuroShields?"

"You mean those idiotic wigs Landry invented to scramble Helix tech?" Kani snickers. "No thanks."

"That's a no then," I laugh. I have to admit, they weren't one of Landry's better ideas.

Kani zips up her pack and takes a seat at the table. She kicks her feet up and crosses them at the ankles, "Well, that's me packed. Anything else you need?"

"Don't need much. As long as we have sleep sacks and food, I'm good to go," I say, remembering the last time I'd been in my sleep sack. I'd offered it to Runa and she ended up sleeping beside me. I glance up to Kani's arched eyebrow. She misses nothing, that woman.

"Excellent," she says, "then, let's make this happen."

"After you," I say, picking up my stuff and sweeping my hand out in front of us.

I STRETCH MY NECK, trying to ease the tension from the pack and sleep sack I'm carrying. The throbbing that started in my temple earlier has settled in the base of my head and doesn't seem to want to go away. I finally drop everything.

"Let's rest here for a bit," I mutter, digging through my

pack for the NeuroWand I grabbed before we left. I flick it on, listening to the soft hum as the tech lights up when I wave it over the sore spot.

"Wow. Didn't know people still used those," Kani says, pointing at the NeuroWand.

"Yeah, been getting headaches the past few days. No big deal, just stressed. Landry said to try using this and see if they get better. Well, before he took off to hide at Alina's."

"I wish I had some proper medical equipment here," Kani mutters, "If we were back in the Helix, I could cure you in an instant. You'd never have them again."

"I know. For now, this will have to do," I say.

I flip the switch to shut it off and place the wand in my front trouser pocket.

Humans found a way to eradicate most neurological disorders well before we arrived on Pendomus. Unfortunately, we don't have the resources for all the same technology as the Helix. Wish we did, though. Would make life a helluva lot easier.

"We're not too far, now. Maybe a half hour," Kani says, pacing in front of me.

"Got a bit of nervous energy?" I ask, following her progress back and forth.

"No, what makes you think that?" she asks without stopping.

I raise my eyebrows and smirk, "No reason."

"I'm fine," she says, wringing her hands.

This will be the first time back on the surface since Fenton... I don't think she realizes it, but I've heard her screaming while she sleeps. Regardless of what she says, or her hard exterior, Kani's still dealing with her actions.

"Okay," I nod.

"Why do you say it like that?" she says, her words accusational.

"No reason," I say, shrugging. I close my eyes to rest for a moment, trying to will the thumping still resonating behind my eyes to go away.

With each pulse, the edges of my brain feels like bits are frozen and the ice is cracking.

"Has the NeuroWand helped at all?" Kani asks, her voice sounding so far away.

"No, not really."

"Well, just rest for a minute. I'm not in any big hurry," she says, taking a seat beside me.

"Thanks. I just need a minute to close my eyes," I mutter, pulling my legs in close and resting my head on my knees.

"No worries."

For a few minutes, all is silent, which suits me just fine. Then, Kani begins to hum softly to herself, then she starts humming louder and louder. The strange thing is, the louder she gets, the further away from her I feel. Like her humming is somehow pulling me away from myself, like I'm floating. At first, I feel like I'm high in the sky, floating above dead trees, until gradually, the snow line begins to pull back into patchy areas of green and brown grass. The motion of it is unsettling with the pounding of my head and my stomach rolls.

"Kani, do you mind? That's not helping."

She continues humming.

"Kani?" I repeat, again to no answer, "Please, just stop."

I open my eyes, surrounded by the pitch black only a cavern without a torch can offer; and all is deadly quiet.

Where the hell is Kani?

3

RUNA

S LEEP IS ELUSIVE, but I know I need it almost as much as I needed water. Especially if I'm considering going deeper into the cavern. My curiosity is getting the better of me, wanting to explore. However, without sleep or food, it's a disaster in the making. Even I know that now.

I stare into the fire, my focus softening. The flames lick the air and the heat ripples the stone wall in the background. I still find it strange the way heat can look so much like water when it wants to.

I cross my arms, tucking my hands in my armpits like a petulant child who doesn't want to do what they're asked. There's a lot to consider before setting off. After I get some rest, I'll find a way to take some of the fire with me and explore the tunnel.

Adrian said my next mission will be to find my brother—that it was critically important I do so quickly. By using this as my guide, I can give myself some sort of direction, even if I don't know technically where I'm supposed to go. It makes sense the vassalage would be on this side of the planet, considering the heat I felt when I was transported by the Salamander.

If I could be transported anywhere, why wasn't I sent directly to the vassalage to find Baxten? Then again, maybe they couldn't? Maybe it's heavily guarded. Or has secret traps. Or safeguards against weird, mystical phenomena? Or maybe it's as simple as I was transported to one specific location and I was only shown the mirage of what it once looked like.

I glance down at the Caudex and sigh.

Only time will tell.

The firelight lulls my eyelids to drop shut. The crackling melody of the flames sings me into a soft sleep, but the flickering remains in my mind's eye and permeates my dream-like state.

I don't know how long I've slept before I see the Tree. Ashes are all that remains of the doorway I entered and sorrow strikes my soul. There's no way I would be able to come back the way I left. What if this is the reason I am where I am now? Not because of any greater purpose, but because this was the only other place I *could* go.

Are there a limited number of ways I can leave and return?

The lucidity of my questions makes me pause. This dream isn't like some of the others I've had. In many ways, it mirrors reality all too closely. I turn around in the snow, remembering the scene in the woods behind me as I'd entered the Tree not all that long ago. Regret washes over me and I wish I could turn back time, considering how things have been.

Splotches of scorched ground are scattered here and there, only slightly covered by drifting snow.

What happened once I'd gone? Are my friends safe? Will I ever find a way back to Trae?

~He's gone, you know. Forever.

The words come out of nowhere and I step back, my foot sending ashes flying into the air like grey snowflakes. Even in my dream, the snow crunches beneath my feet and I start to wonder if in some way, I'm really here.

"Who's gone?" I ask, trying to ignore the worry seeping into my mind, "Who are you?"

Hidden in the wind's gentle hiss, a name is whispered.

Fenton.

I blink, trying to understand.

"What do you mean? You're Fenton, or Fenton's gone?" I say, needing clarity.

The wind grows stronger yet, but instead of hearing more, pieces of me break apart, flying into the wind like sand.

When I reconstruct myself, particle by particle, I'm standing inside the Tree, knee deep in water. It's no longer ashes, but whole again.

"Runa," Trae's unmistakable voice reaches into my dream. "I'm here, Runa. Can you feel me, too?"

Even a memory of him sends an eruption of pangs through my heart. I miss him so much. Being alone in this next phase, not having him by my side—it's almost unbearable. In my dream state, the security in remembering Traeton's embrace helps me relax, dropping some of my restlessness.

I open my mouth to respond, but find it missing. Not stuck, nor forced closed.

Missing.

I claw at my face frantically. But the entire thing is blank —just like a Labot.

I wake up screaming, groping at my face and checking for cheekbones and lips. The fire is still blazing in front of me, as if nothing at all has changed.

Somewhere in the distance of my mind, I hear whispers. I can't make out what they're saying. Perhaps they're remnants of my dream, or a wishfulness to return to the safety of Trae. Either way, I must have fallen into a deeper sleep than I realized.

I stand up, brushing off my trousers. There's no point trying to return to sleep. With dreams like that, I'm not going to feel truly rested, anyway.

My stomach grumbles loudly and I sigh.

"Food is going to be a problem, too," I say aloud. If I don't find something to eat soon, I'll starve. It's been a couple days already since my last true meal.

It's such a strange concept, considering I spent my entire life never eating. But there aren't RationCaps here, and as far as I can tell, nothing to eat, either.

"Hello?" I call out, wondering if the Salamander is still nearby, "I could use a little help. Human, here—I need food, too. Any hints on where I could find some?"

If it could bring me to water, maybe the Salamander could help me find food. I wait for a few minutes, but nothing breaks the silence.

"Of course not. Would have been too easy," I say, nodding to myself.

Truthfully, I'm not excited about trusting a Salamander in the first place. This is just as well. I can do this on my own. Somehow, someway, I will find something to eat. I may not like it, but I'll figure something out.

Walking over to the pool of water, I scoop up another handful and drink it in, hoping inspiration will come to me.

In a sudden eruption further along the tunnel, flames

ignite on their own accord in a similar circle to the one the Salamander had lit. Then another one lights up, and another, leading deeper into the cave. The walls around me are cut with deep grooves and not at all the semi-smooth texture of the Haven or Lateral. I look tentatively over my shoulder, and stand up.

"Well, if that's not a sign, I don't know what is," I mutter. "The only question is, is it a good one?"

I take a step forward, then stop.

What if this is a trap? Then again, what if this is what's supposed to happen?

Curiosity finally wins out and I find a little alcove to stuff the Caudex in so it's out of sight. It's far too heavy to carry deep into a cavern, especially if I find myself needing to run. In only a few moments, I'm halfway down the tunnel with no torch, no microLight, nothing but the pits of fire lighting my way.

I already know this could be a disaster, but it's better than waiting around to die. I need to know if there's more here than meets the eye—which appears to be the case. Maybe there's even food hidden somewhere in here. An animal I can hunt, or something growing in the depths. I know enough to realize looks can be deceiving. Obviously, someone has gone to great lengths to incorporate some level of sophistication with the lighting. Perhaps there's more.

"I wish Trae were here with me," I whisper, taking tentative steps forward.

Though I'm sure he'd be telling me that I'm being reckless. Or I should do a better job to look for a torch of some kind. With every step, I'm acutely aware this tunnel is leading me further into the darkness. Should the lights go out, I won't be able to tell which way is out. The absolute abyss of a cave is all consuming, I've seen it already.

"Hello?" I call out, my voice shaking slightly, "Salamander...are you here?"

Sounds of something scurrying over stone makes me jerk my head around. The source isn't immediately evident, but I swear I see a set of long, hairy brown legs pulling back into the darkness.

My hand rises to squelch my surprise.

Whatever it is, their legs are as long as my whole body, if not longer. I shudder and seriously consider heading back the way I came. I round a corner and hear sniffles in the stillness. I stop moving, close my eyes, and listen intently. Cocking my head to the side, the only sound is my breath as I inhale and exhale.

I shake my head, continuing down the path with slow, steady steps.

"Must be hearing things," I whisper to myself, trying to draw in some strength.

I examine every crease and crevasse etched in the stone wall as I pass by, just in case.

The sound doesn't occur again, so I make my way to a large open space inside the cavern. The large circular opening houses a smaller circular stone wall, dead center in the room. I walk to it and look over the ledge. I find myself standing meters above a massive, circular spiral staircase made out of carved stones. From the ceiling, a single beam of light shines in, highlighting the rim of the ring and cascading all the way down to the very bottom, as if emphasizing its importance. Something small and green rests in the center of the floor hundreds of meters below.

Amazed, I walk the circle's edge to the backside, where the beginning of the large set of stone steps becomes evident. Without a second thought, I start the descent.

There are intricately carved arches, like windows in the

stone walls that overlook the center. Smattering of green and blue mosses grow on the stone, evidently hardy enough for the tiny space and beam of light.

Unlike anywhere else in the cavern, the light is powerful enough to illuminate the path without the need for more fires. My footsteps echo softly on the stone and I concentrate on the sound so I don't lose my courage to descend. Walking in circles for what feels like hours, I finally reach the bottom. Without much fanfare, I step from the stairway onto a layer of white sand covering the bottom of this large well-like feature. In the very center is a stone pillar about thirty inches in diameter. Atop the pillar is a patch of the most brilliant green I have ever seen. As I walk closer, I realize what it is.

Grass.

I stand beside the pillar in awe. I've never seen grass before. Not alive, not growing—not even at the Lateral. With a tentative hand, I reach out and let my palm glide over the top. The tips of each blade tickle my palm and make my skin feel alive with a renewed sense of energy.

"Okay, so this is new," I whisper, trying to make sense of what I'm seeing, what I'm touching. "Why are you here?"

As if understanding my words, the grass flickers by a non-existent wind. A flash of metal buried in the sea of green makes me lean forward and pull the blades back. Reaching in, I pull out a large key, like one of the old skeleton keys I saw at the Archives when we were there.

I turn the worn metal over in my hand. It appears to have seen better days. Chunks are gouged in some sections and the tip is slightly warped. Yet, the symbol carved into the end is unmistakeable. Inside a circle is the five petaled flower—the Everblossom.

What does this open?

The light beam begins to vibrate, sparkling with orbs that

break away. I've seen this sort of thing happen before. I close my left eye—my scarred eye—and the vibration ceases.

"Okay, so this is meant for me," I say, nodding. If it wasn't, the light's dance wouldn't be something my enhanced vision could see, surely.

I slide the key into my trouser pocket and step away from the pillar to get a closer look around. Perhaps there's a doorway down here? The second I step back, the light above me is extinguished and I'm plunged into utter blackness. As quickly as I can, I make my way to the edge of the circle, trying to find the wall. My heart races, threatening to make a new home in my throat.

The silence that falls is deafening at first; enough to shock anyone's senses. Suddenly, there's the sound of movement nearby—far too close. My eyes struggle to make out shapes, sense something, *anything*.

Finally, I make contact with the wall and I crouch down into a ball, trying to make myself as small as possible. I cup my hands over my ears, childishly hoping that by shutting out the sounds it means whatever's in the darkness doesn't really exist. For a few minutes, this plan works fine, but then something brushes against my foot, making me scream and bolt upright. My head slams into something large and sort of furry, which is enough for me.

With one hand poised on the wall, I run the circle, trying to find the steps leading upward. My foot misses the first step and I trip, my body slamming against the hard stone. My knees burn and my vision sears white as I catch myself just in time.

Scrambling up the steps on all fours, I try to put as much distance as I can between me and whatever is down here. Unfortunately, something tickles the backs of my legs, as if groping for my calves to make me stop. The sensation sends shivers up my spine and I remember the large legs pulling back in the crevasses of the cave when I first started out on this suicide mission.

The complete and utter darkness is disorienting as I spin in circles trying to get to the top as quickly as possible.

How far do I have left? How far have I gone?

Suddenly, I'm pushed flat against the stairs, as something large rests on my back so I can't stand back up. The warmth of breath beside my right ear gives me goosebumps.

"Please, what do you want?" I cry out, "Don't hurt me."

A grunt meets my reply, then a howl from somewhere else in the cavern.

There's more than one.

I struggle beneath the weight pinning me down, but it's no use. Whatever this is, it's far larger and heavier than I am. Fears of being eaten alive are triggered by my experience with Tethys before I knew she wasn't the Morph. She had slashed open my eye and licked my face, as if she was going to eat me slowly. Luckily, that hadn't been the way of things. But I had no way of knowing any of that at first.

Suddenly, my fear begins to subside.

Am I misunderstanding this, too? Am I assuming this creature is sinister, when it's really something else? Why would the Caudex bring me here, only to have me killed?

No—this is a message sent for me.

The instant my fear evaporates, the creature releases me and light returns. Instead of the beam, however, small torches along the inner part of the stairwell are lit. I turn around to find myself face to face with the largest arachnid I've ever seen. Easily three times my height, its four large eyes are surrounded by tufts of bright red, blue, and green fur. Its mouth is covered by large furry tusks the color of my hair.

Instantly, I scramble backward.

The spider doesn't move, its black eyes watching me without any lids to blink. The white tusks move like a mustache, but makes no intelligible sound beyond grunts and clicking. One large leg raises, then taps the pocket of my trousers where the key resides.

"The key? Are you saying I caused this to happen? Or I can't— ? I mean, am I not supposed to take this?" I ask, placing my hand over the key when the spider pulls back.

The spider doesn't make another move, its unblinking eyes watching. Somewhere nearby, I hear a whimper, like I had earlier. When I turn around, a Salamander enters from behind me, slinking down the stairs with speed and ease. I catch its movements with the corner of my eye as it loops around the outer circle of stairs, racing along the walls instead of the stone steps. When I look back, the spider is no longer there.

My hand immediately plunges into my pocket expecting the worst, but the key is still there.

"What am I supposed to know? Why am I shown this key and then given the impression I'm not meant to take it? I wish you could communicate with me," I say, frustrated at the lack of information I've been dealt.

~Who said we can't communicate?

The voice is soft and almost slurred, but definitely audible somewhere in my mind. Instantly, I know it's coming from the Salamander.

"The eLink—Adrian said returning would damage the—"

~This has nothing to do with the eLink. Your communication with us is all your own, Daughter of Five.

I blink, watching the Salamander getting closer and closer.

Then why do I have to speak out loud to get an answer?

37

The question pops into my mind and I grunt. Seems a bit ridiculous they can invade my mind with their thoughts and answers, but I can't do the same.

~You make many assumptions, Daughter of Five.

I slump to the floor and rest on one of the steps, waiting for the Salamander to come to me. This is a bit much to handle.

When the large black face and deep blue pools for eyes finally stand before me, I sigh.

"Are you the same Salamander as before?" I ask.

~Would there be another?

"Stop doing that. Yes or no. It's an easy question."

Now that I've found my voice, I feel no need to do everything mentally anymore. It's actually nice to be firmly grounded in my vocal chords rather than bound by the constraints of my mind.

~Yes.

"Good, now we're getting somewhere. How about some answers?" I ask, standing up and brushing off my trousers.

I need to know what my mission is. Why I'm here...The Salamander is my best chance at figuring all this out and untangling this mess.

~You're here because your mission requires it to be so. You already have your mission parameters.

"Don't do that. Don't read my mind and answer me before I ask the question," I say, lowering my eyebrows.

~As you dictate.

The Salamander bows, as if taking my command is important to her.

"I'm not dictating any—" I say, but cut myself off. Yes, I really am dictating terms, and I guess that's fine. I need answers, and I need them on my terms.

"Why didn't you speak to me before now?"

~Because you were required to pass the first trial.

"Trial? What trial?" I ask, pacing back and forth.

~Their predetermination does not require your understanding before implementation.

"Talk in English, please."

~You will be made aware of the trials when the time is ready.

"Aren't I technically aware now?" I snort.

~No.

"What do you mean *no*? You just told me —"

~I told you of a trial you were required to pass. You have no information on what the trial is, nor what the others will be. Therefore, the answer is no. You have no awareness.

"I see."

~Do you? I was not made aware your vision has returned.

"Returned? What are you talking about? I didn't know it had gone." I say, frowning at the Salamander.

~I have said too much. It is up to you to find, understand, extrapolate what is necessary.

"You're speaking in riddles again," I warn.

~Your time of understanding will come. For now, you must trust your path will make more sense in the near future.

"But not now," I say matter-of-factly.

The Salamander says nothing, but instead circles around to the other side of me, effectively blocking the stairwell going back down.

"Alright, I get the hint," I say, making a face and turning to head up the stairs.

~Know this, Daughter of Five. Upon completion, you will be capable of facing anything which comes your way. Believe me, there will be much to ward off and you must be ready.

"Gee, thanks," my eyebrows pull in as I shake my head at all the cryptic talk.

The Salamander guards the steps as I work my way

upward. The stairs have a completely different feel with the fire torches versus the natural plume of light from the center. For some reason, it's both more cozy and more ominous.

As I enter the circular cavern room, I hear the whimper again, louder this time. I look down the staircase, expecting the Salamander to be directly behind me. However the lights have extinguished themselves, one by one, as I ascend. If she's still there, she's chosen to blend into the darkness.

I strain my ears, listening for the whimper again. For the longest time, I wait, holding my breath. When nothing happens, I let out a soft laugh.

I've gotta be hearing things. Or perhaps the cavern has its own moans as it settles in the heat outside. Following the fires back the way I came, I stop by one and turn the key over again in my hand. Despite my vision originally cluing me in on its importance, it feels utterly ordinary. Not at all like the crystal hanging from my neck.

A sniffle nearby makes me freeze. This time knowing without a doubt I'm not hearing things.

"Who's in here? Answer me," my voice quivers and I take a few, uneasy steps forward.

The sniffle erupts into a full-out sob and I rush forward, searching the space all around. I pull up short when on the floor behind a large rock outcropping is a tiny body. Hands and feet are shackled to the wall with strange chains that extend out of the rock. Extremely frail, with boney ribs and shoulder blades protruding is a young boy clothed only with a ripped up modesty cloth. His hair is as black as the cavern when the lights went out.

I rush over, dropping to my knees.

"Are you alright? Wh—who did this to you?" I ask, gently rolling the boy over.

His face is black and blue; his eyes black mounds and

swollen shut. He lets out a final sob and promptly loses consciousness.

"Hang tight, hang on," I mutter, repeating myself over and over as I scan the shackles and try to find a way to free him. There is no lock, no keyhole—nothing at all to help me determine a way to get him out. I wrench at the wall, trying to pull them out of the rocky formation, but it's useless.

"Who did this to you? How long have you been here?" I ask as I continue to assess the situation, and in a feeble attempt to keep him here with me. The little boy doesn't move or regain consciousness. His frail body suggests he's been here a while and needs immediate help.

Who would have done such a thing?

4

RUNA

*H*OW CAN THIS LITTLE BOY be shackled to a wall with no discernible way to unlock the restraints? I have to be missing something.

I take off my NanoTech jacket and place it over his frail body.

"I'll be right back," I promise in a whisper, "I'm going to bring you some water. Don't worry."

He mumbles something inaudible as I run my hand over his dark hair, hoping in some way to comfort him. Black and blue streaks cross his forehead and continue into his hairline. How did this happen to him? He must be in so much pain, but he sighs softly as I stand up.

I hate leaving him, but if I can't figure out how to get him out, I can at least get him some water so he doesn't die of dehydration. I take off running toward where I began my trek deeper into the cave. One good thing about spending time in the Haven and Lateral, I feel like I have a better sense of direction underground than I ever thought possible. I run the corridor, hoping I can bring the water back to him quickly without wasting too much time. His swollen eyes and bruised face are burned into my mind as I race back to the small alcove.

Who—or what—could do something like this to him? How could the little boy be in here, of all places... Perhaps more worrisome, will whoever did this be back? And if so, when?

Shivering away the thought, I push myself to run faster. When I reach the water, I scan around for something to bring it back with. I kick over rocks and stones, hoping to find one with a bit of an indent, but there's nothing even close. All of the rocks are smooth and round —not a single one offers the help I need.

"Ugh—there has to be something," I cry out, throwing my hands down in disgust.

When I was first found by Trae and the others, I couldn't drink water straight. I vaguely remember a swab or something, they didn't pour it in straight away. When they did, it felt like they were pouring sand down my throat and not water.

With my limited supplies of only the clothing on my back or the Caudex at my feet, I decide to go with the book.

"They're all blank anyway," I say justifying myself as I scramble to get the Caudex from its hiding place. I pull at my necklace to reveal the aquamarine stone, which lights up brightly.

The Caudex lock releases and I flip open the tome. Skipping to the last pages of the Caudex, I tear out a worn looking piece of parchment. Rushing to the water, I crumple the paper in my hand to make a ball and thrust my hands into the water. I allow the liquid to soak into the page so I can bring back as much water as possible. When I'm satisfied there's enough, I cup my hands and race back to his small, crumbled body.

"I'm back," I say, kneeling down beside him.

He whimpers softly as I pull his head into my lap. I hold the soaked piece of paper like a sponge above his mouth and let a few drops fall, wetting his parched, cracked lips. At first, he gurgles and sputters, trying to adjust. After a moment, he regains his bearings and allows the water to flow into his mouth. With my free hand, I stroke his cheek gently with my thumb.

"Everything is going to be okay," I whisper.

Once the water is gone, I adjust my NanoTech jacket over his body for optimal warmth. Though it's hot outside, the cavern's temp is far cooler. I look around for clues, or possibilities on how to release him. The chains and shackles look like they've grown directly out of the stone wall and have no discernible way to remove them from the rocky encasement. I have no tools, or weapons to help in any way.

I fold the damp page and cram it into my trouser pocket, in case I need it—after all, it could still be important. Perhaps when the little boy's rested, I'll be able to get some information from him. I rest my back against the stone wall and stroke the boy's face gently until my eyes feel droopy.

"I'll close my eyes with you…just for a minute," I whisper.

Tilting my head back, I settle in, allowing sleep to take me over. As odd as it may be, it's nice to have someone else with me. Someone else to focus on. My hand stills beside the boy's face and something about his presence eases me into a relaxation I haven't felt since I left Traeton.

"You're very beautiful," a voice whispers in the darkness.

"Thank you," I say, accepting the compliment without a fight.

"You should have been told before now. I wish I could have reached you sooner."

"I'm not sure I—" I say, trying to understand where I am and who's speaking.

"I've been trying to reach you, but it's been so hard. I keep forgetting how."

"Who are you? Why have you been trying to reach me?" I ask, still listening only to the sound of the voice.

"I...I don't know," the voice says, "I've been in this dark for so long. Then there was you."

"Me?" I ask. It seems such an odd thing to say, because I've always been right here. Or have I?

"Yes, as though you've been here all along, but I just couldn't find you," the voice reasons.

"Well, I'm here now. Is there more you need from me? Was there a reason you're here?" I say. There's something about the voice. It makes me feel as though I've heard it before. Or as though I should know the person on the other end.

"Yes, there is," the voice says, "At least, I think there was. I—I can't remember."

"You can't remember?"

This is the strangest conversation I've had in a long time. I'm not sure what to make of anything. It's almost like when you know there's something important you want to remember, or perhaps tell someone—but you can't hold onto the information long enough to relay it.

"Hello?" Silence meets my question and I ask again, "You can't remember?"

"Don't wait too long..." the voice finally echoes. Then, it's gone.

I WAKE UP WITH A JOLT.

My neck aches from the odd angle I must have slept in and the boy's head still rests in my lap. I watch his body rise and fall with his shallow, but labored breaths. He doesn't have much time. Reaching out, I pick up one of his small hands, turning it over so I can get a better look at the underside of his restraints.

"How on Pendomus did they get these on you?" I whisper to myself.

I run my thumb over the underside and though there's nothing to see, I distinctly feel an indentation.

Shifting to get a closer look, I run my fingertip across the indent again as I lean in.

The Salamander made a remark about my vision—about it not being returned. At the time, I didn't think anything of it because I could see just fine. I even saw the key's importance in the well-like area. But now...I wonder if she's right. What if there's something here and I simply can't see it?

The boy stirs, sighing, and reaching out to me.

"Are you okay?" I ask, setting his arm down and focusing on him.

"Mmmm...yeah," he nods.

"You can speak," I say. It's not a question, but a statement. In my experience, it means something. Mostly, that he's unique. Or he's lived away from the Helix.

"Do you know who did this to you?" I ask, stroking the top of his head.

"No, woke up like this... Dunno how long ago. Feels like ages. Everything hurts," he croaks.

"I'm so sorry. I wish I could do more to help," I say, "My name's Runa, by the way."

The boy tilts his head, as he tries to peer at me through his swollen eyes.

"Ammon," he finally says, "that's me."

"Nice to meet you Ammon."

His stomach growls loudly and mine joins in for good measure.

"Do you have any food?" Ammon's voice is soft, but clear.

"No, I'm sorry, I don't. I was hoping to find something—or figure out— "

"How can you not have food?" Ammon interrupts.

"I…I just don't," I stammer, realizing I don't have a great answer for him without making it sound like I'm insane.

"How'd you end up here?" he asks.

"I was sorta…uhm… ed here, I guess. I was out in the heat and needed shelter."

"Heat?" Ammon says indignantly.

"Yeah. We're on the desert side of the planet, Ammon. Didn't you know?"

He shakes his head softly, "No."

"Where are you from?"

He purses his lips, "I don't think I should tell you. It's supposed to be a secret."

I laugh, because in a sense, where I come from now is too.

"Okay, then I'll start. I used to live in the Helix, but I left because things weren't working out so well for me there. I've got friends in a hidden place deep in a cavern—much like this one, actually."

"I never lived inside the Helix, but know about it. We live in a cavern like this, too. I thought it was the same one. Thought maybe one of my friends did this to be funny. But… it wasn't them."

My lips tug downward. "I'm sorry, Ammon. Who does this sort of thing to another person? Not to mention, if you're from the Helix side of the planet, we've traveled a good distance."

"How far are we from the Helix, do you think?"

"I honestly couldn't even say," I admit. I've traveled for days and seen nothing but sand and rocks.

"Did you end up here like I did? Could it have been the same way? The same person?"

"Maybe? But I doubt that, too. I was somewhere else, then I was here. However, I was in a place I trusted. And I kinda— well, I kinda expected to be somewhere new when I left."

He nods, as if what I say makes complete sense and isn't as crazy as it sounds out loud.

"Look, regardless of how we got here, we have each other now," I say, "I'm not going to leave you. We'll find a way to get you out and find food. Okay?" I say, trying to give him more hope than I actually have at this particular moment.

"Okay."

Ammon pulls back on his restraints and the chains dangle from the cavern face. He swallows hard and frowns.

"Can I ask you something?" I say, reaching for his wrist again.

He nods, but doesn't say anything.

"Do you feel anything when you run your hand over this spot on your cuff?" I ask, flipping his wrist over and guiding his other hand to the spot I noticed earlier.

Ammon struggles to sit up and I place a hand on his back to help him. With a shaky finger, he runs his pointer against the shackle.

"Yeah. Feels like there's a hole or something here," he says, nodding.

"That's what I thought, too. Do you remember anything about being chained here? Did you see how they were locked?"

"Wish I did," he says, "I don't remember nothin'."

"It's okay. We'll figure this out," I say, determination

48

seeping in, "Maybe there's something in plain sight? Something we're missing."

Ammon props himself against the cavern wall while I stand up, walking around the space in front of us. Surely, if a key was hidden, it wouldn't be within reach, but perhaps it's somewhere nearby?

In the back of my mind, a voice tells me to try the golden key in my pocket. Who knows, right?

But it can't be that easy, surely.

After a few minutes of searching, I sigh and return to his small frame.

"Let me try something," I say, putting my hand in my pocket. I pull out the large skeleton key and turn it over in front of me.

Ammon's tilts his head, "What are you doing? You're not gonna cut my hands off, are ya?"

"No, of course not. I found this key in another part of the cavern. I just want to see if… " I pick up Ammon's wrist and bring the key to the invisible indent. When the two come in contact with each other, large sparks fly and screeching fills the air, like some sort of alarm.

Ammon immediately brings his bound hands up to his ears and covers them.

"Not good," he hollers.

I stand up, turning circles and covering my own ears.

Guess it wasn't the right key. How do we shut it off?

The obnoxious screech echoes off the walls, getting louder and louder. My foot kicks the now dry ripped piece of paper from the Caudex. It must have fallen out of my pocket when I stood up. There are markings on the page, so I drop to my knees and pick it up, quickly flattening it open.

There's a pictograph of some circles. It's a simple thing, but for the life of me, I can't figure out what it means. There are three circles beside each other. The first circle is surrounded by two larger circles, like ripples of water. The second circle is alone, and the third has four rings around it.

I know enough about the Caudex to realize whatever it's showing me is significant. This has meaning, I just need to figure out what.

"This is the key, I can feel it," I say to myself, tapping my forehead. The squeal of the alarm makes it impossible to think properly.

"What did you say?" Ammon says, trying to talk over the alarm.

"Nothing, just give me a moment," I say. Three circles, one circle, five circles…

Do I need to draw them somewhere? I look around and see nothing evident to draw with.

Maybe it's a reference to the sundog? Do we need to view it a certain way? Or wait a number of days?

"Gah—that can't be it. What am I thinking? We're not going to sit here for days listening to this," I say, frustrated with myself. "Come on Runa, think."

Ammon hunches forward, bobbing his head up and down, trying to ignore the sound. I watch him for a minute before I have a brilliant idea.

Rushing back to him, I drop to my knees and pull his hands in front of his body.

"Hey—" he says, startled. His swollen eyes widen into partial slits, and his mouth drops open.

"Please, let me try something," I say.

His eyes lock with mine, and he nods in agreement, "Go on, then."

I find the groove on the cuff and place my pointer finger over the top. I tap on the groove first three times, then once, then five times.

Nothing happens.

"Damn," I curse, sounding more like Trae than myself. "Maybe I should try laying my fingers in order?"

"What are you doing?" Ammon says, pulling his hands to his lap.

The squeal of the alarm has reached a deafening level—which means someone will be here soon to check on things.

"Gimme another try," I say, reaching for his wrist again.

I place my fingertips in order, my middle finger sitting in the indent. Then I tap three times with my pointer finger, once with my middle finger, then five times with my ring finger. Instantly, the alarm cuts off and the cuffs vanish into thin air.

Ammon grins broadly and rubs his wrists.

"Nice work," he says.

"Thanks. Now let's see if we can get out of here before we're spotted. Besides, we still need to find some food for both of us."

I don't want to worry him, but I'm on high alert. The alarm wasn't there for the fun of it. His captors will be back.

Ammon licks his dry lips and says, "Best idea yet."

I grin. Even sitting here, black and blue and emaciated, this little boy rolls with the punches so easily. It's like we've been doing this for years, not hours.

"Even better than figuring out how to get you out of your restraints?" I ask, chuckling, wanting to keep the mood light. Ammon's been through so much.

"Well, they're equal, I s'pose."

"Okay," I laugh.

"How did you figure out what needed to be done?" Ammon asks, trying to stand up.

"I got the idea from a page I tore out of a book."

Ammon's face scrunches in like he's eaten something sour, "You *tore* a page from a book? Are you insane?"

"What? You needed water and I improvised to bring it to you," I say, sheepishly. "Besides, how do you even know what a book is?"

"None of your business," he says, a little color flooding to his cheeks. It does him some good, and almost makes him look normal.

"Hey, kiddo, I just saved your life," I remind him.

"I just like books," he mumbles.

"Me too," I concede.

"So how come you don't have food on you?"

"I just don't..." I say.

Ammon huffs.

"Okay, look, I was sorta teleported here. I have no idea why or even specifically *where* we are," I admit, sounding utterly idiotic.

"No way—" Ammon says, his eyebrows high up into his hairline.

"Yeah, strange, right?"

"Are you kidding? That's the most amazing thing I've ever heard. I was reading a book about that sorta stuff not long ago. How'd you do it?"

"Well, uh... You know, I'm not a hundred percent on the logistics of it. It sorta just happened."

"C'mon. There's gotta be a device or something? What's the story behind it? My friend and I were talking about the physics behind..."

"Whoa, wait. Did you just say 'the physics'?" I say, cutting him off.

"Yeah," Ammon says, shrugging. His eyebrows pull in like it's completely normal for a kid his age to be talking physics.

Even in the Helix, that program doesn't start until they're fourteen.

"How old are you?"

"Ten," he answers, standing up as straight as he can.

The thought of this frail, scantily clad ten-year-old talking physics with his friends blows my mind and I can't keep my jaw from slacking open.

"What?" he asks defensively, tilting his head again trying to see me through his swollen eyes.

"N-nothing. I'm just kinda...*wow*. Impressive," I whisper.

"Anyway, as I was saying..."

"So where did you learn about physics? I mean, how did that first start coming about?" I ask, again over the top of him, "Sorry."

I grin sheepishly.

"I learned from my dad. My gran tells me all the time that I'm just like him."

"Must be nice," I say, trying to squelch the blossom of jealously bubbling up unexpectedly. What I wouldn't give to have a life with both of my parents together.

"Sure," Ammon says, making a face. "Anyway, as I was saying, we were talking about the physics behind teleporting and the energy output necessary to make it happen. It'd need to be astronomical."

"That's amazing," I whisper. In all honesty, it's never occurred to me to think about the energy output, or how it's been done. I've been too consumed with figuring out where in the world I was.

"So c'mon. How'd you do it?"

"Well, I was sorta...there was a..."

I don't even know what to call her. Is Adrian human? Or something else entirely? I have no idea.

"You know, I'd rather not discuss this right now," I say, my face growing hot.

"Awwww," Ammon says, frowning. He sways slightly and leans against the wall for support.

"Easy there," I say, reaching for him. "You need to get your strength back before you go bounding down the cavern."

Ammon doesn't say anything, but the color has faded from his face.

"Are you alright?" I ask, placing a hand on his forehead.

He whimpers again and backs up further down the rocky wall, "I hear something, movement."

Hot breath from behind my left side makes the hairs on the back of my neck prickle. My back stiffens and I swallow hard.

"There's something behind me, isn't there?" I whisper to him.

A grunt behind me is the reply.

5

TRAETON

*W*HERE IN THE HELL would Kani go?

"Kani?" I call out again, listening to my voice reverberate off the tunnel walls.

Scrambling to my knees, I feel around for the lamp we brought with us—anything to illuminate the space so I don't feel so disoriented.

My fingers brush against a sleep sack and one of our packs. Listening to the sound of my ragged breath, I dig into the small pocket in front and pull out the microLight I packed for each of us.

I press the on button and ambient light floods the cavern tunnel.

Kani's pack rests on the floor beside mine, along with both sleep sacks.

None of this makes any sense.

Where would she go?

I get up and walk further down the tunnel, toward the way out. I meander through a few twists and turns, but there doesn't seem to be any fresh prints in the dirt floor, so I turn around and head back the way I came. As I make my way around the final corner to where I began, I run smack into Kani.

"Thank god. You're awake," she says, pushing me off her and taking a step back.

"Yeah, no thanks to you. Where'd you go?" I ask, relief flooding through my veins.

"While you were being sleeping beauty over here, I realized my necklace was missing, so I went back to look for it," she says, fiddling with the chain at her neck.

I take a step forward, pointing at the bronze gear dangling from the chain.

"Fenton made this for you," I say.

She nods slowly, her fingertip circling the round inner circle of the gear. I remember when Fenton gave it to her. He was trying to find a way to connect with her and he thought somehow an old gear found in the Archives would be the way to go. Of course, she laughed at him at first, telling him that was the dumbest thing she'd ever seen. Still, she accepted the gift and since Fenton's death, she hasn't taken it off.

I don't know if he ever told her the reason he chose it. When he'd picked it out, he had to point out to me the way the gears interlock—working together as a unit. He felt somehow, that symbology would make its way back to her.

"So anyway, now that you're back up and running, are you ready to get our asses to the Archives?" she asks, changing the subject. She kneels down to pick up her things and her black and green ponytail drops over her cream colored jacket shoulder.

"Yeah, I'm ready. But can you not wander off like that? Nearly went out of my mind when you weren't here. With Videus and his cronies capable of being just about anywhere, we can't be too careful," I say, grabbing my supplies.

Kani sighs, "Sorry. I didn't think you'd notice. I was only gone a couple of minutes. Turned out it wasn't far."

"I wish I could trust the ComLinks. We coulda stayed in contact that way. But it doesn't feel safe anymore," I say, grabbing my pack and sliding it over my shoulders.

"I know what you mean," Kani says, "I promise, I won't run off again without letting you know."

"Good," I say, putting my sleep sack under my left arm.

With our ambient lighting, Kani collects the rest of her things and we walk the tunnel for a few minutes in silence. Both of us have walked this cavern enough to do it sleep-walking. Anytime we had questions, or just wanted to dig around for cool new stuff, the Archives was the place to go. It's like our own secret world, since very few people are even aware of it. Hell, I'm not sure many people even want to make the trip if they did know. Even Landry's like that. More engaged with what's new, than to look back at what once was. It's about the only difference between him and Fenton. Fenton at least could look both directions and be amazed.

"Did you remember to bring the handheld to open the wall when we get there?" I ask, breaking the silence.

"Yep," Kani says, nodding.

"Good," I say.

"Well, it woulda kinda sucked if we went this whole way only to find out we had to go all the way back. Don't you think?" she says, making a knowing face.

Fenton was always the one who handled grabbing the device. It was sorta an unspoken rule. I'm not sure when it started—maybe always.

"Very true," I say, my memory jabbing at my gut.

I hate that he's gone. I hate how much I miss him. I hate how it comes and goes at such odd moments. Fine one minute, hurting the next. I hate how remembering him leads me to worry about Runa; which brings me back to feeling guilty that I'm worried about Runa after thinking about him. It's a horrible, vicious cycle.

"How's that headache of yours? Feeling any better?"

The medic in Kani has surfaced.

"Yeah, it's okay. Still hanging out in the background, but otherwise alright," I lie.

It's technically still there thumping just as bad, but I hadn't given it a second thought. It's sorta becoming the norm. Plus, I don't overly want her to worry. She'll start getting all involved and fussy. There's nothing she can do anyway.

"Keep an eye on it and let me know if it gets worse again. I can do some more research at the Archives to see what I can do."

"Sure," I say, shrugging.

A blast of fresh, arctic air permeates the tunnel, announcing the eventual end of the cavern. We turn the last corner and I kneel down so Kani can use my leg as a platform to pull herself up to the ledge that leads out. Once she's made it, her head pokes inside and she holds out an arm.

"Hand me your stuff," she says.

I remove the sleep sack and toss it up to her. Then, I take off my backpack and lift it to where she can grab it.

"Thanks," I say, grabbing the rough edges of stone, and pulling myself up and out.

"Don't mention it," she says, handing it back.

We've got less than a hundred yards to go and we're outside the safety of the cavern walls. The freshness of the breeze sends shivers down my spine. The last time I was out in the open was…

The first time is always the hardest, I remind myself.

The first time I had to face my mother and my sister

Cecilina after turning Ava in…that was hard. In fact, so hard I've been too scared to go back. They didn't say I was the reason Dad was gone, they didn't have to. Their eyes did all the talking.

Yay, more guilt.

I breathe deep, trying to ignore my inner struggles. As I do, I see Kani is dealing with her own. Her back is rigid and she stands with one hand resting on the knife clinging to her hip. The same knife she used on Fenton.

"You okay?" I ask, resting a hand on her shoulder.

"Nope."

We stand in silence for a moment, letting the situation rest with us as we both work to move past our memories.

"C'mon, Kani. We'll get through this," I whisper. "We need to get moving. Standing here freezing to death won't change the past."

I grab hold of her elbow, dragging her down the remainder of the tunnel and out into the blinding white light. The snow glistens and sparkles. Fresh snow has fallen since we were last out here, decorating the ground and tree branches with its paint of renewal. The low sun shoots rays of colorful light through the branches, offering in a weird way, some kinda hope. The halo is brilliant in the crisp air, and I stand in awe for a moment. You don't realize how depressing being in the darkness of the caverns can be until the darkness is all you have.

We trudge our way through knee deep snow, watching for any signs of movement. Everything is our enemy, even the birds in the trees. We know that now.

The breeze blows softly and the trip is relatively silent, with only the crunch of our feet in unison. When we reach the entrance to the Archive's hidden tunnel, I take a final glance through the trees. Their branches look inviting and cheerful, but I know better. I always knew there was something not right with those damn birds, though.

Too freakin' happy.

Kani dusts off the hidden doorway, pushing the new snow aside with her foot, and together we lift up the large lid. It groans loudly, clearly not impressed to be moved. I know the feeling.

"You go ahead first. I'll be right behind you," I say, nodding to the black hole at our feet.

With a tip of her head, Kani drops into the darkness, climbing downward rung after rung.

I take one more glance through the trees and drop inside. With my left hand on the ladder, I use my right to slam the door shut behind me. Instantly, we're plunged into darkness until Kani's feet hit the bottom, triggering the motion sensor lighting system leading to the Archives door.

"Weird being back here," I mutter, more for myself than anything.

"Yeah," Kani whispers.

The last time we were here, I was making an idiot of myself. Because of that, Runa was upset and ended up racing to the Helix alone. Not my best move ever, but it worked out in the long run. Sorta.

My mind tiptoes to the area of my memory I've been trying to keep locked up, just in case. The kiss was something more powerful than anything I've ever experienced...but if she's gone—if we can never be...

I close the doorway to that train of thought.

I need to focus on what I can affect right now. And that's finding out more details on the Tree of Burden. If I can help Runa return, I need to be ready.

Plus, we need to know as much as possible about Videus and his vassalage. If this madman has Runa's brother Baxten kept hostage there, or anyone else for that matter, we need to find a way in. But we need to be real damn cautious. Either way, I need to be effective—helpful. Not sit around dwelling on what was. I guess I'm taking my own advice.

We reach the end of the tunnel and Kani waves the small, circular device in front of the wall. There are no words, no goofy comments like Fenton would have done. Just silence until the wall shudders aside, the gears in the wall grinding loudly.

"Where do you want to start?" Kani asks, as we enter the main area we typically go to.

My eyes flit to the holographic screens of the mainframe we'd been at just a little over a week ago. Maybe more? I've begun to lose track of days. Seems like they all blend together.

"I'll…" I wet my lips, "I'll take the mainframe. You take the books. There has to be something here. Maybe look for anything that has to do with the colonization? Or the history of the Helix? Or why we chose Pendomus. I'll see if I can crack in to search for information on the history of the Tree of Burden, whether or not there was any chatter about it being a portal and whatnot. Then I'll do some recon on the vassalage. Maybe we can figure out where its located and hell, figure out a way to get in."

Kani's eyebrows raise, "Do you even remember how to use the mainframe?"

My lips press into a thin line. She knows me too well. Any other time, I'd be the first one to head to the books. But if I can save her from any painful memories, I'm gonna do it. It's really the least I can do.

"Nope, not a clue, but how hard can it be?" I say.

Shaking her head, Kani walks away mumbling something about Landry.

Taking a deep breath, I make my way to the screens and take a seat. A hand written note scribbled in Fenton's handwriting sits on the table:

Who's Runa's real father?

I'd forgotten all about that, what with all the death and missing persons. Once the pang of seeing a memento from Fenton's own hand subsides, I tuck the piece of paper in my chest pocket. I flick on the mainframe the way I'd seen Fenton do a thousand times. How hard can it be to log in without being detected? My insides twist. There's a good reason it was always Fenton's job.

I rifle though some of the things nearby, cursing my lack of technical know-how. I've always relied on those more adept in that area.

"Why couldn't he leave instructions or something, dammit?" I mutter to myself.

"He did," Kani states, matter-of-factly a few yards away, "They aren't in written form."

"Well, that's just great," I say, halting my digging. "Don't suppose you know what form they *are* in?"

"Fenton kept a holographic backup of how to log in hidden in plain sight. He said that you'd know it when we saw it, so he never felt the need to elaborate. I'm guessing he gave you more credit than you deserve," she says, continuing to walk down the aisles of the large bookcases.

I blow out a burst of breath, "Well, that's...*swell.*"

I kneel down, looking under the table, feeling around for something he would have hidden.

"In plain sight," Kani calls out, making me jump.

"Plain sight? How the hell would I find anything in this mess? It could be anywhere," I call back.

I pick up a few books stacked on the table near the holographic screens and shift them aside, hoping there's a hidden compartment or something on the top of the desk. There's nothing.

Taking a seat in front of the holographic screens, I flick through some of the commands and folders he's set up.

It can't be completely obvious.

If it was, anyone could activate his instructions and figure out what to do. I'm sure as hell Fenton would be more careful than that. He of all people knew we needed to tread lightly around the Helix. And around other people, too, I suppose.

"Dammit," I curse to myself.

I push back, kicking my feet up on the table and shrouding my eyes with my hands. The pounding in my temples worsens, but I know I can't let it get to me.

If I were Fenton, what would I do?

Dammit, this sucks. Why couldn't he've just told me to begin with where the hell he was going to leave instructions? It's just so like him to do something important and forget to follow through—

My foot sends a stack of books flying to the floor.

"Great. Just great," I mutter through gritted teeth as I kneel down to pick the five books up off the floor.

This is not helping my head.

I fling them, one at a time back up on the table, my mind more entrenched with Fenton than anything else. On top of it, I'm irritated at myself for being irritated at him. Such a stellar combination.

Standing up, I lean against the table, staring at the mess in front of me. All the books were ones on the Helix, or Earth. All of them except one: *Across the Multiverse.* My favorite book of all time. The one title I could not be without, even when I was considering leaving Fenton and Kani and going with Ash for an indefinite amount of time. He knew how much it meant to me.

My eyebrows furrow and I pick up the book. Oddly enough, it looks almost brand new. The blue hardcover binding isn't tattered and frayed like mine is. I've carried the book with me, felt it in my hand so many times, I've unintentionally memorized its weight. This, however, feels far too light.

I flip open the cover of the book, to see it's been hollowed out inside. My first reaction is horror—why would anyone vandalize the book this way. But my eyes are drawn to scribbled writing. Drawn on the inside cover is an inscription:

Traeton, just read me.

Confused, I stare at the words. What in the hell is that supposed to mean?

Of course I've read the damn book. Everyone knows I've read it. Hell, even Runa probably knows.

I close the book, flipping it over in my hands. With the exception of the inside being carved out, the book looks perfectly normal. There's no buttons or wires. Nothing.

"C'mon, Fenton. What in the hell am I supposed to do?" I say, flipping the cover open again, "I didn't *just* read this. It's been...*months* at least."

I stare at the words with absolutely no clue what I'm supposed to be doing. How's this supposed to be obvious?

I stare at those words, parsing their various meanings.

"Wait a minute. Read me?" I say, sitting up straighter, "Read what? Read the book? The title?"

I scratch my head.

Nah...can't be that simple.

"Across the Multiverse," I say.

I stare at the book, half expecting it to grow horns or something. But nothing happens.

"Traeton just read me." I mutter out loud, rolling my eyes, "Why can't it be— "

A holographic image of Fenton pops out of the book.

"If yer able ta see me, tha' means yer Trae and ya figured ou' me masterful beauty of a password," holographic Fenton says.

My jaw drops and I blink at the large replica face of my deceased friend. The surreality is not lost on me. Not one little bit.

"I uh…"

"Before ya start tryin' ta talk an' all tha' bus'ness, stop. Yes, I know ya were trying' ta talk ta my hologram," Fenton rolls his eyes and pushes up his yellow glasses, "Don't bother. Until I fully integrate, I can't understand you - a' least no' in tha conversational way. It'll take a few minutes ta be fully operational. Now, then. Let's get busy. Yer tryin' ta ge' inta tha mainframe fer tha Helix witout me. Am I righ'?"

I open my mouth to respond.

A large holographic palm materializes in front of his torso, "Don' answer tha'."

"Ugh. Here we go. Can't even give normal holographic instructions, can you Fenton?" I laugh. He never was one for the straight basics. Always had to throw in a bit of himself.

"Now then, I've se' up parameters ta allow ya easier access than anyone else, Trae. Even easier than Kani, but don'tcha tell 'er I said so. Tha firs' thin' ya gotta do is plug the voice recognition software inta tha system."

"Ah…?" I look around, trying to figure out what he means by voice recognition software.

"Before ya ge' all busy wonderin' wha' tha 'ell I'm talkin'

about, le' me make it simple. I'm it. Or shall I say, tha book is it."

I scrunch up my face and roll my hand in the air, "C'mon, Fenton. Get on with it."

"Okay, okay... Now ya gotta bring tha book within a short distance of tha holographic mainframe. Then you—and only you—need ta say tha connection password. Yer gonna love this," holographic Fenton wiggles his eyebrows up and down, "Tha voice recognition password is 'Gettin' it on wit' Runa'. Just changed it from 'Gonna be a virgin ferever', so stop makin' tha face and be grateful."

Fenton's smile is large and toothy and he bobs and weaves his head in a weird dance, his shoulders shimmying.

"Oh, for the love..." I groan.

"I just though' of it while ya ran off ta chase her down at tha Helix. Hmmm...wonder if you'd do it there?"

He shakes his head dismissively, as if trying to get rid of visuals he just conjured.

"Anyway, password time."

"I am not saying that," I tell the hologram and crossing my arms over my chest.

As if reading my mind, Fenton says, "There's no other way around it, either, tough guy. Ya want inta tha Helix's mainframe, ya gotta say the password. Then, in my humble opinion, ya should also go an' *do* it."

You have got to be kidding me.

What if Runa had been here when I needed to do all this?

Knowing Fenton, he'd love the thought of me having to explain what all this means to her. My cheeks burn. Talk about horrifying.

I shudder, more grateful Runa's not here than I've been in days.

"Fine. Whatever," I say, picking up the book and dropping

it beside the holographic screens with a little less care than I should.

"Eh-eh. Don't forget ta say tha password," Fenton tick-tocks a finger back and forth.

I scratch the top of my head and lean in close to the hologram.

"Getting it on with Runa," I whisper through clenched teeth.

"Wha' was tha'? I can't hear ya," Fenton says, placing a hand to his ear, "Tha voice recognition needs ta recognize yer voice. It's no' a damn breathalyzer."

Geezus, this guy thought of everything. I don't know if I like the level of knowledge he had with the inner workings of my mind. It's almost scary. He knows me better than I know myself.

"Fine," I say through gritted teeth, "Getting it on with Runa."

"What did you just say?" Kani calls out from a few aisles away.

"None of your damn business," I say back, feeling the burn in my face scorching.

"Really? Because I thought you just said—"

"Do not finish that sentence if you know what's good for you," I warn, holding a hand up toward her direction.

As if this wasn't humiliating enough.

"Ta-da! Magic password 'Gettin' it *on* wit Runa' accepted," holographic Fenton says, winking.

I run my fingertips over my eyebrows and take a deep breath. If he wasn't already dead, I'd kill him myself.

Dammit, even in death, he loves to embarrass the hell outta me.

Staring at the holographic screen, it automates itself,

running through some parameters and eventually entering the main database screen.

The ethereal Fenton hovers, watching me in a creepy, voyeuristic way as I try to ignore his presence. Instead, I hunt for the search function, but nothing is evident.

Grumbling, I lean back and run a hand through my hair.

"Okay, Fenton, why couldn't you leave instructions on searching through this thing?" I say.

"Took ya long enough. One thousand, three hundred an' twenty-four seconds, ta be exact. Though' ya'd figure ou' sooner I'm yer interface, now. Seriously, Trae. Ge' wit tha program. It's why ya needed the voice recognition password," he says, "Wha'cha searchin' for?"

I stare at my friend. Fenton clearly didn't mean to create this thinking he'd be dead when I need it, because frankly, I can't shake the creeps over seeing him talking as if he's really here.

Clearing my throat, I say, "Anything we can find on Videus."

"Videus. Two secs," he says, then grins, "No, not sex. *Seconds*. Ge' yer mind outta tha gutter, Trae. Yeesh."

I roll my eyes at his dumb joke. I heard him correctly the first time around. Only he thinks about sex that much. I swear it.

There's a long pause as Fenton's face blanks out momentarily.

"Okay, tha data is really obscure. I'm finding details with a 9.7% relevancy which describe Videus as tha original innovator behind tha Pendomus colonization. But fer some reason, it's no' overly reliant."

I nod, "We know that already. Well, sorta. What I'm really looking for is any relevance behind Videus and the Tree of

Burden. Or anything that might give me a better idea of where Runa could be. Or if she's even safe."

Fenton's eyes go distant, but he starts to squint one as if he's deep in concentration. I chuckle under my breath.

Leave it to Fenton to include facial expressions with this interface. Too bad he probably didn't consider how he just looks constipated.

"M'kay. There're zilch relevant results listing tha two search queries in correlation wit one another. However, there're fourteen distinct results on the Tree of Burden."

I sit up straighter.

"Okay. How about the Tree of Burden and Runa?" I say.

"Negative. Zero matches."

I think for a moment, then it dawns on me. I don't think Videus had any idea who Runa technically was. If he had, he would have taken her from her family much sooner. Hell, probably disposed of her before she could ever fully develop.

"Scratch Runa. What about...*Daughter of Five?*"

"Ding, ding, ding," Fenton chimes, "Twelve of tha fourteen results cross reference this search parameter."

Gotcha.

6

TRAETON

ALL KINDS OF HORRORS cross my mind. This is one of those times when I could really use Kani and her skillful, albeit creepy knife wielding. Or at the very least, the ability to do it myself. In the space of microseconds, I make a mental note to have Kani show me how she does it if I get back—*when* I get back.

Turning around slowly, I come face to face with the enormous spider from before. The creature's white tusks are inches from my face and I slink back against the wall, pushing Ammon further away so I stand between the two of them. The spider didn't harm me last time, but I'm not taking any chances with the young boy. For all I know, it's the spider who brought him here.

"What do you want?" I ask, unsure if anything I say will matter.

The silent spider's large leg taps my pocket where the key is held again. The same, slow mannerism from before is unnerving.

"I—I know. You want me to give it back, but I can't. At least, not yet."

The large black eyes feel like they peer past the surface of me, going deep inside of my mind. A sudden flash of insight hits me, almost as if the creature is trying to share thoughts in images. The impressions are so similar to the way Tethys communicates, but lacks the depth of feelings, colors, or sensation. In the vision, I see a large open field full of lush green grasses. Large fruits hang from vines and trees. Animals I've never seen before munch lazily at the green grass and birds chirp happily. In the middle of a grove of swaying trees sits an enormous table brimming full of food.

My mouth begins to water at the thought of tasting one of the large, ripe fruits my body has already become accustomed to. It's certainly not something I would have experienced inside the helix where we only had RationCaps. I'm filled with a sudden urgency to get there. Wherever *there* is.

A basic understanding of proximity is translated, but nothing definitive. The creature doesn't completely know herself. This is going to be a task of hunt and find.

I blink back from the images and impressions to find the spider has vanished. Again.

"What the heck was that? I heard clicking, but couldn't fully make out what it was," Ammon says, tilting his head to listen.

"It's okay, I don't think the creature wants to hurt us," I say. "I think she was giving me information about where to find food."

"Creature?" Ammon's voice peels up an octave. "Wait a minute...food? What kind of food? And why are you calling it a she?"

A strange part of me is actually sad to see the spider go. There's something quietly serene about her and she's obviously trying to help.

"You gonna explain the food or tell me why this thing is a *she* instead of an *it?*"

"I...I don't know," I shrug, "I don't like calling things *it*, I guess. I always sorta give them a gender, even if I'm not sure. She gave me images, sorta like the eLink—you know what that is, right?"

Ammon nods.

"I think they were directions of sort."

"So, you don't know if it's a she?" he says, going back to the gender issue. He attempts to quirk his eyebrow, despite his puffy eyes.

"No, I guess not."

"Good," he says, in a relieved sigh, "because if the thing started telling you it was a girl or boy...well, that would be weird. Then again, it's kinda weird it told you there was food. Are you sure you didn't just imagine it because that's what we want?"

I scrunch my face and say, "On that note, we should get you to water and come up with a plan from there. Might be best to have you rest while I hunt for the food. You know, just in case."

I'm tempted to call the water area the Oasis, like we did back at the Haven, but I resist the urge. Too many references to the Haven makes my heart constrict to the point of breathlessness and I can't bear to deal with those emotions right now. The sooner I figure out what I'm meant to know —the sooner I'll be back with my friends. At least, I hope.

"Wait—you're not gonna leave me alone, are ya?" Ammon's voice raises an octave.

"Well, I really think I—"

"Absolutely not. Nah uh," Ammon shakes his head frantically. "Wherever you're going, I'm going too."

He weaves his tiny fingers through mine and squeezes.

His vulnerability reminds me just how young he really is, regardless of his intelligence. I wasn't even allowed to go outdoors at ten, so a part of me can relate to his neediness.

"Okay, it's a deal," I say, breathing out, "But it will mean getting some rest first and coming up with an escape plan as quickly as possible. Your body has been through a lot. We need to make sure you have strength to mend."

"Right now, the only thing my body is worried about is the grumble going on in my belly," he says.

"Well, with a little luck, we'll be able to remedy that soon. I got the distinct impression there's food nearby," I say. Though, what makes me think that, I'm not sure. It's not as though large fields of grass grow inside caves.

"I hope you're right. I'm starving. Who knows how long I've been here, seems like forever. I miss the food from back at the Lat—" Ammon cuts himself off.

"Me too," I say, nodding, "Wait a sec, were you going to say back at the...*Lateral*?"

Ammon's bites his lip, wincing.

"That's it, isn't it? You're from the Lateral, too. How on Pendomus did you get all the way out here?" I say.

"How do ya know about the Lateral?" Ammon asks, his voice suddenly full of suspicion.

"I've been there. I have friends who live there and now I sorta do, too," I say, "What about you?"

"Who are your friends?" he asks.

"Landry and Fenton Tabet, Kani Ling...Trae Revasco." I say, swallowing my heart with the final name.

Ammon considers for a moment, the hard lines of his pinched lips softening.

"Whatever ya say, Runa," Ammon says, finally shrugging again. "So far your hunches have been pretty good. I guess I can trust ya one last time."

"Thanks, kid," I laugh, messing up his hair slightly. "Now come on, let's get outta here. This place gives me the creeps."

"Makes two of us," he nods in agreement.

I put an arm under his shoulder and let him rest his weight against me as we hobble toward the water area the Salamander had brought me to. The trek takes much longer than when I was on my own, but Ammon does remarkably well, all things considered. His body is light, but awkward as we make our way. When we reach the water, I help him drop to his knees and he leans forward, cupping his hands much in the same manner I did earlier. He drinks the water in until his little belly has expanded outward. Then he crawls back, leaning his back against the cavern wall. Even with my NanoTech jacket over his shoulders, it has to be freezing.

"Isn't that cold?" I ask, pointing to the rocky face behind him.

Ammon shakes his head.

"Can't tell anymore. Been in here like this too long. It all feels the same to me," he says, rocking his head from side to side.

The Caudex rests in the small nook I placed it in, a meter or so away from Ammon. Abruptly, its pages begin to burn brightly. The aquamarine stone around my neck tingles against my skin, a silent plea to push forward and have a look.

"Ah, what's that sound?" Ammon asks, wiggling his pointer finger in the direction of the Caudex. "It's like electricity or something?"

"It's okay, just give me a second," I say.

I walk over to the Caudex, then sit down cross legged in front of the large book. Placing the heavy tome across my lap, I wave the crystal in front of the lock. The ornate clasp disengages and the pages whirl open as light bursts from within.

I glance at Ammon's worried face.

"Don't worry, it's nothing bad," I say, peering at him to see how much he's able to take in.

"If you say so," he shrugs. "Did you find a light or something?"

"Sort of," I say.

Quickly, I hunt the pages, searching for whatever I'm meant to read—meant to know. Finally, I find what I'm looking for.

"My book, the one that I took a page out of," I say, "it sometimes informs me of things. And by that I mean, almost like we're having two-way communication. I know it sounds strange, but bear with me, okay?"

"Wish I had a book like that. Sounds cool."

I smile. Kids can be so accepting.

I look at the page and read out loud.

THE FIVE TRIALS

When the time of renewal dawns, the Daughter of Five's purpose shall be revealed in all its glory. She has been imbued with gifts that even she cannot fathom. In order for her to master her innate abilities and eventually take on the Creator, she must first be set to face her hopes and fears and overcome each of the Five Trials. Within these trials, she will find pieces to uncover her purpose, her gifts, and learn how to master them. As each is revealed, all will become clear. Upon completion of each trial, the symbol of accomplishment will be given.

Each will bring about its own unique challenges and will present themselves in whatever manner and order is deemed best by the state of her being at presented time. Within each trial, lies the lessons of the original inhabitants, imbued with love and trust that she will wield her power for the good of all.

One thing the Daughter of Five must remember: she is not alone in the control of this process. She must never lose sight or faith, or be lost to the world until she is ready.

"What does that even mean? Be lost to the world?" I say, looking up at Ammon.

His face is somewhat quizzical, "Are you kidding? Who's this Daughter of Five? Oh wait, are ya saying—*oh.*"

"Yeah," I say, sighing, "that would be me."

"That's so wicked," he proclaims, a big grin spreading across his face. "It's like you're on a magical quest."

"I don't know how *wicked* it is, because I'm definitely confused. How will I know when I'm facing one of these trials? There's absolutely nothing in here about what I'm going to be up against."

"Yeah, not much other than to be *prepared to be scared,*" Ammon says, wiggling his fingers and pursing his lips like a fish. "How do you even know this stuff is about you?"

"Trust me, I know," I say, returning my gaze to the Caudex.

"Well, how friggin' awesome is it that you're a part of some 'big trial.' I mean, I bet there's even a prophecy that goes along with it," he says, laughing. "Wait until I tell the guys back home that I got saved by some girl who's like, infamous, or something."

My eyes widen, but I can't bring myself to say anything. Though I have no idea what the prophecy says, I know there is one, and I somehow play a key role. You can't imagine what the weight of that feels like.

"Why are you so quiet?" he asks, turning his face my

direction, "Don't you think it's great to be a part of something big like this?"

"Yeah, it's wonderful," I say, frowning. "Couldn't I be tested on something nice? Silly things like learning how to finger weave?"

"Who knows, maybe you will be," Ammon says, sitting up straighter and taking on a sage-like stance, with his legs crossed. He tries to raise a prophetic eyebrow, "Tell me, young Runa, are you afraid of finger-weaving, my dear?"

I roll my eyes in response, but a smile cracks my lips. It's good to have him here. If I'd been alone, I don't think I'd take this news quite so lightly.

"What does the finger weaving symbolize for you? Look deep, my dear," he says, trying to make his voice deeper than its ability to go. It cracks as he says my name, making us both laugh.

"Why do they always feel the need to be so cryptic?" I ask, rereading the passages, "And what's this mean, 'the symbol of accomplishment will be given?'"

"Maybe they hand ya an award," Ammon grins.

"Somehow, I doubt it. Maybe a crystal, or an object will be passed on? A door opens?" I say, fiddling with the aquamarine crystal at my neck. "Wouldn't be completely unheard of. I have a crystal I wear with me at all times because of this."

"Really?" he says, his mouth agape.

"I never completed something to get it, though. At least, I don't think I did."

It never occurred to me I might have completed some hidden initiation to find the stone. How far back could these trials go? Could I have been challenged by one already and just didn't know? What if this stone was a symbol of accomplishment? Either way, the little blue crystal holds a special role in the path I've ended up on.

"So, what do ya want to do about this? I mean, can I help?"

"Ammon, I don't have any idea what this means. Or how to—"

Light spills from the pages again, and scrolled across the brittle paper, as if written by an invisible pen, words appear.

It has been decided. Each of the five trials will take form in the basic elements as brought to life by the Daughter of Five.

The first is hunger. In order to truly know the essence of life, the Daughter of Five must face the deepest levels of the human body's needs.

No sooner do I speak the words out loud, the cavern begins to shudder and Ammon whimpers.

"Uh, this isn't good. We need to get outta here," he says, trying to scramble to a vertical position.

I look down at the Caudex wanting to read on.

"Ammon, it's just a tremor. Probably due to the volatility of this side of the planet," I offer, trying not to overreact, "Even the Lateral was experiencing them not long ago."

"No, this is not that. *Trust me*," Ammon urges.

I sit up straighter, taking note of the edge in his voice.

"What do you mean? How do you know?" I demand, slamming the book shut.

"Because this happens every time *he* arrives."

The hairs on the back of my neck prickle at the way he says the word *he*.

"You told me you never saw who brought you here," I say, scrambling to my feet.

He smiles sheepishly, pointing at his swollen eyes, "Well, could ya see like this?"

"You lied to me," I cry, grabbing his arm and tugging him closer.

"No, not *lied*. Not technically. I didn't see him, but I didn't have to," he says.

"Ammon, it was an important question. Whoever brought you here could be someone extremely dangerous."

My mind instantly goes to worst-case scenario.

Videus.

Who else would capture people on Pendomus for the intent of torture or deprivation? Humanity isn't so sprawling here that there'd be more than one maniacal megalomaniac.

"C'mon," I grab Ammon's hand, and help him move forward. I'm not entirely sure where to go, but hope my instincts will guide us in the right direction. "Who is he? Do you know his name?"

"N—no," Ammon says, trembling.

"What is he like?"

I pull Ammon behind me, trying to see in the darkness for a tunnel branch to take that isn't easily visible off the main path. The further we get from the lit fires, the darker everything becomes until we are finally plunged into absolute, disorienting darkness.

"He's strange, always breathing on me, getting close into my personal space," Ammon says when I pull him into a small crevasse in the stone wall and force him to crouch, "He always wears a mask. I can tell because of the way his breath sounds when he's close."

"Ugh. Okay. Sit here and stay quiet. Not a peep, do you hear me?" I say, getting ready to go out and do some recon.

"Where are ya going?" Ammon squeals.

"I'm going to check to see if I can spot anything. I won't be far. Trust me."

Something in the sheer terror of the little boy's stature tells me even if this isn't Videus, whoever he is, he's just as dangerous.

The rumbling of the tunnel gets louder and angrier before finally halting altogether.

"Not a word," I breathe.

Ammon shudders beside me as we wait in utter silence. I haven't even left his side when we hear it—*footsteps.*

They echo and reverberate off the walls of the cavern.

"He could not have vanished into thin air. Find him. In his condition, there's no way he could have gotten far."

The voice is distant, and muffled, just like Ammon said— but still eerily familiar and I listen more intently, trying to decide if it's because it reminds me of Videus. It's hard to tell, considering he used Fenton to speak to me before.

There's no answer in reply, only a grunt and the continuing shuffle of footsteps.

Ammon clutches my arm tightly, cutting off the blood supply to my right hand. I place my left palm over his fingers, trying to reassure him.

"Check every side chute, every pathway out. The fire lights are lit for a reason. He's here somewhere and I want him alive, for now," the voice says.

A slithering sound shuffles past the small shaft leading to where we wait and my back stiffens.

Please go by. Please go by.

I repeat the mantra in my head, willing to find some way to hide us; keep us safe. For a moment, it works.

Then the Caudex bursts open, orange light spilling into the tunnel around us. I drop Ammon's arm to hide the book and find a way to dampen the light as best I can.

"There—do you see the light? Check it out and report back immediately," the voice says, commanding the silent partner.

The light of the Caudex goes out as I try to find a way to extinguish its light, but it's too late. A new light outside our tunnel grows brighter.

All too quickly, the slithering sound grows louder, until we're face to face with the largest Salamander I've seen yet. Flames glow at the bottom of his feet and his body is as black as the deepest recesses of the cavern, but a large blue marking consumes half of his face and descends over his right shoulder and down his leg. For the briefest of moments, the Salamander tilts his head to the side, watching. Almost as if he's as surprised to find us as we are to be found.

Ammon squeals, groping at my shoulder and trying to hide behind me. My heart races as I look for a way around the Salamander.

Orbs of light begin to dance around the Salamander, emerging from inside the stone walls, though he takes no notice at all. For a brief moment, I shake my head. Has my sight returned? Then an ear-piercing screech escapes the Salamander, an alarm sounding to call his master. He doesn't move toward us, or try to capture us—he just simply screeches.

"Ammon, back up. Go back as far as you can," I command, pushing him even further behind me.

The orbs of light move from the creature in front of us, spreading to both sides of the cavern, dancing a cold blue light against the warmth of the fire produced by the Salamander's feet.

"Ahhh—" Ammon cries out behind me.

I whirl around to find we're surrounded. Behind us, the

enormous spider has returned, blocking us from retreating further—while the Salamander stands vigil in front of us.

A low, agitated growl escapes the spider, who stomps forward angrily towards us.

Trapped between the two, I clutch at Ammon and the Caudex, which is still shining dimly between the clamped covers.

"What do we do?" Ammon squeals.

"I don't know," I say.

One way is most certainly death—the Salamander and the one controlling him. While the spider hasn't yet attacked us, her angry stature is one I'm not about to challenge, either.

The spider growls again, stomping forward and pushing us even closer to the Salamander—flushing us out of the tunnel.

"What is it? What did you find?" the voice asks, coming up from behind the Salamander.

Ammon whimpers and I grip his small hand tightly. The man in front of us is dressed in some sort of black armor from head to toe, not at all dissimilar from the skin of the Salamander. Along the front breast plate is the only flash of color on his outfit—a snaking spiral of blue fire, which appears to be truly alight. I don't have time to question the how's or why's however, because I can't take my eyes off his face—or lack thereof.

He's not wearing a mask. Not as such, anyway. Much like the Labots, this man's face is completely missing—wiped clean of all features. Only, instead of a blank slate of skin, as they have, this man's face is a running pool of blood. Atop his head is a large, extravagant headdress in the shape of the vulture-like birds that attacked us at the Tree of Burden. Blood flows from the mouth of the great bird, feeding the undulating surface where his face should be.

Though with no perceivable mouth, the man without a face says, "This trap could not have worked more perfectly. Do you know who you've just stumbled upon? You've just captured the infamous Daughter of Five. Most excellent work, Frunam."

The man with the vulture atop his head walks forward, petting the Salamander in a strange, lovingly way, but never moving his face from our direction. His absence of gaze makes it beyond uncomfortable to look at him.

"I believe you have something of mine, my little *Everblossom*," Videus says, "And I want him back."

7

RUNA

T HE SPIDER'S LOW GROWLS suddenly switch to a soft, steady hum. The orbs of light I saw earlier are back, and begin to grow increasingly brighter on either side of Videus, but he takes no notice whatsoever.

"Here, I was coming to check on my little...*project*. Imagine my surprise to find the elusive Daughter of Five available for the taking. I figured it would be more difficult than this. Especially after all that's happened," Videus says. "I mean, I knew ultimately, you'd be lured here, but I never dreamed it would be so soon."

I jut my chin out, standing straighter, and stepping forward, "You can't have Ammon."

As expected, Videus laughs. A hearty, deep, and jolly laugh.

"Oh, child. I assure you, I can and I will. He certainly can't go with you. That would be disastrous," Videus says.

His cockiness irritates me and it feeds my growing decision to overcome not only this situation—but him. He has to be stopped, by whatever means necessary.

"Runa, stop moving toward him," Ammon says, tugging my arm, trying to pull me back to him.

I hadn't even noticed I was walking closer to Videus and taking Ammon with me. It was as if an invisible string was pulling me to Videus and I was unconscious to stop. But why hasn't Videus come towards us further? Why hasn't he attacked yet?

Behind me, the spider stomps heavily, shaking the ground beneath our feet and forcing us all to lose balance. I glance over my shoulder to see her barreling down on us, large furry legs penetrating into the dirt and rock as she nears. The air fills with static electricity and the orbs of light burst into bright, tiny stars on either side of the cavern between Videus, Ammon, and I. All at once, the orbs react to each other and start spitting out strings of light that weave together into a blue, luminescent web separating us from Videus. The spider's song cuts off and once again she roars behind us, then charges.

My eyes widen in horror as she slams into Ammon, forcing him into me and shoving us toward Videus and the blue web. My feet dig into the ground and I throw my arms out, trying to grab hold of the rocks along the wall. It's no use, though. The spider has too much mass and too much force behind her.

We're going to be trapped in the web and there's nothing we can do about it.

I close my eyes in utter disbelief, waiting for contact with the strings of light. The moment we hit, it's like being forced through a warm waterfall. Rather than being stuck, the silky strands of the web brush my cheeks and tug at my hair. After a moment, I open my eyes.

"Uh, why's it so bright?" Ammon says, releasing my arm and tipping his head up slightly, trying to see through his swollen cracks for eyes. "And so nice and warm? Ah, man, I haven't felt this kinda warmth in ages."

We're surrounded by white light and I shield my eyes with my arm trying to get my vision to adjust.

After a few moments, sand dunes take form. Then the horizon and the blazing sun.

We've been transported elsewhere on the planet. By the looks of things, not terribly far, though.

"How?" I ask aloud.

"No clue over here. One second I figured we were spider food. Next thing I know I was getting pushed straight toward certain death—well, then we were here. How did that happen?"

My mind is reeling as I try to make sense of things. The spider wasn't pushing us to a trap. She was helping us to escape? I should have realized.

"I think—I think we were just helped out of a sticky situation," I say.

"You're not kidding," Ammon says, shuddering, "I thought *he* was using some sorta force to pull us to him."

"Didn't you see the blue web of light? Or any light at all as we were being pushed?" I ask.

Ammon shakes his head, "I could almost make out glowing orange, but that's it. Everything's so blurry."

Of course—the orbs, the blue web, it was something only I could see. My gift from Tethys. The spider was opening some sort of portal and getting us to safety. All right in front of Videus' nose, too.

I turn to Ammon and say, "I think we were just sent here by a *TerraDweller*."

"A TerraWhater?" Ammon says, scrunching his face.

"I read about them in my book here, remember? They're creatures of Pendomus who lived here before humans took over. No one has really seen them before. I guess I kinda understand why. They're hiding in the darkness," I say.

"If they have the kinda power to send us other places, why send us here and not somewhere with food and shelter?" Ammon mutters, shifting from side to side on the hot sand.

That's actually a really good point.

Using my hand as a shield, I survey the landscape, trying to get a clue to explain why we're here. In the horizon, the sunlight dances across the golden white sand, but there's nothing immediately evident.

"We can't just stand here. We should get outta the sun. Ouch..." Ammon says walking forward on his toes. Then he vanishes in front of me, as though he walked through a curtain.

"Ammon—" I call out, holding my hand out in front of me in disbelief.

"Uhm...Runa, what just happened?" Ammon asks.

I blink back, surprised to hear his voice, "Where are you?"

"Right in front of you, I think? Keep walking."

With an arm outstretched, I walk forward. One second I'm in the desert, the next I'm standing in the lush, green field from my vision with the spider—*TerraDweller*.

Ammon walks forward, running smack dab into a fruit dangling from a low branch. He reaches up, and plucks it off the tree.

"Is this—fruit?" he says, bringing it to his nose and inhaling deep.

"Yes, Ammon, it is," I say in amazement.

Ammon doesn't hesitate. He takes a big bite and juices squirt out in all directions, rolling down his hands and fore-arms. It smatters his face and he smiles broadly.

"Runa..." he says, food dripping from his mouth, "you have gotta try this."

My belly rumbles as he reaches out, handing me the fruit. As it passes from his hand, it drops straight through mine and onto the ground.

"Way to go, butterfingers. You're supposed to eat it, not drop it in the dirt," he says, waving his arms above his head to find another one.

"Ammon, I didn't drop it," I say, peering closely at my hand.

Am I not really here?

"What do you mean?" he says, plucking another one off a branch.

"I mean..." I take a step toward him and hold out my hand, "I didn't drop it. Try again. Place it in the middle of my palm."

Ammon's eyebrows flicker, trying to tug in, and he flips the fruit over to pass it to me. Once again, it drops straight through to the ground.

"Oh, this is just wonderful," I mutter, my stomach growling louder.

I walk over to the tree and reach for one of the fruits myself and as suspected, my hand goes straight through it. Beside me, Ammon juts out a scrawny finger and jabs it into my arm—hard.

"Ouch. Do you mind?" I say, rubbing the spot where he poked me.

"How can you feel that?" he asks.

"Ah," I say, realization dawning, "It's obvious, isn't it?"

Ammon quirks his face, "It is?"

I walk to the large table from my vision filled with lush, wonderful looking foods displayed across its top. Setting down the Caudex, I dangle the aquamarine stone in front of it and splay the pages open.

The first page I see holds a warning that would have been convenient to know:

Trust in Kantella; her web will be your salvation.

Ammon maneuvers to stand nearby and I help him take a seat at the table.

"Are you looking at your book again?" he asks.

"Yeah—it says to trust the TerraDweller, go figure," I laugh.

"Nice," he says. "Woulda been better to get the memo sooner."

This must have been what the book was trying to warn us of when Videus was getting close. Or perhaps when Ammon was warning us to leave and I was trying to read more. Sighing, I flip back to the last page I was reading before the cavern started to shake and Videus showed up.

Again, I read the passage aloud, "It has been decided. Each of the five trials will take form in the basic elements as brought to life by the Daughter of Five. The first is hunger. In order to truly know the essence of life, the Daughter of Five must face the deepest levels of the human body's needs."

I look at Ammon, who's mouth is gaping wide in recognition.

"Oh, right," he says. "Well, that kinda stinks."

"It truly does. Especially since there's a table here with the most delicious looking food," I tell him.

"There is?" his hands fly out as he spins around and feels across the top of the table. He tilts his "Does this mean we finally find food and you can't have any? Kind of a cruel joke, if you ask me."

"Yeah, it kinda seems that way. But you don't have to wait," I say, guiding Ammon's hands to some of the foods for him to grab. "Well, the sooner I overcome the trial, the sooner I can eat."

I pace away from Ammon and his voice and muffled chewing drifts off as I get caught up in my own thoughts. Despite the interaction, my body is surging with a strange tingly sensation and every nerve in my body feels alive— ready for whatever comes next.

My stomach rumbles and I keep my back turned to the array of delectable foods a few feet away. How does simply facing the fear of hunger help one overcome it? There has to be more to it than that... How long will I really have to go without food before the test is over? What if I have to learn something specific before the trial ends—and what happens if I don't learn it...

I shudder at the thought.

Surely they wouldn't push a trial to the point of death?

I shake away the ludicrous thought. No way would they jeopardize the Daughter of Five.

Two bright blue eyes blink at me from behind a tree in full pink bloom and I stand still, watching the creature hiding in the shadows. After a moment, a medium sized mammal with the appearance of an earth wolf steps forward, holding my gaze. Then he turns deliberately, walking alone through the pathway of trees.

Instinctively, I start to follow after him.

"Hey Runa, are you still here?" Ammon calls out through full cheeks.

"I'll be right back, Ammon. Stay at the table," I say, holding my hand outright.

"Suit yourself," he says, shrugging, "Just don't go too far, mkay? I still can't see all that well, and I sure as heck don't want to come looking for you."

"I won't," I mutter, slowly following after the wolf.

He stays a few feet in front of me, his energy always aware of the distance I follow him at—just as my energy is aware of his. In a way, he reminds me of Tethys' with her all-knowing aura and protectiveness.

We reach a small cliff and the wolf takes a seat precariously at the edge. Slowly, I sit down beside him, letting my feet dangle over the edge as I peer out into the vast abyss in front of me. A soft haze blankets the far away reaches of the planet where my eyes can see. The sun, oddly enough, no longer carries the same halo as it had in the frozen side of the planet I'm from. But it's still beautiful in its own way as it bleeds orange and reds across the canopy of the sky.

The wolf's tail twitches from time to time, but he sits majestically patient.

Birds flock against the blue sky, twirling in a spectacle dance off in the distance. A shudder runs down my spine and a hint of fear creeps its way into my soul.

"Why am I here?" I ask, turning to the wolf, half-expecting him to answer. Stranger things have happened on Pendomus. "How do I overcome a trial of hunger? How long will this last? What am I missing?"

The wolf meets my gaze, his blue eyes the color of cold ice, and very similar to the color of the Salamander who helped me. Suddenly, he tips his head back and a howl bursts from his throat. The resonance is so loud, I cover my ears to keep them safe.

The birds in the distance switch directions, their flock practically coming to a halt in mid-flight before they come streaming toward us. I scramble upward, away from the ledge and back to the safety of solid ground.

There was once a time when I loved the sight of birds on the breeze—but no longer. Their presence has become ominous and synonymous with suffering, death, and betrayal.

I glance around, looking for a place to run to and hide. But beyond leading them straight back to Ammon, there's no where to go.

"Please, tell them to stay away," I cry out.

As if confused, the wolf's head tips to the side and he perks one ear to the sky.

Turning around, I race back to the cover of the tree line. When I reach it, I duck behind the closest tree, waiting for the convergence with the birds. However, the sky is devoid of their presence; as if they never existed at all.

The wolf saunters to me, a single gray bird in its mouth and he drops the corpse at my feet. Horrified, I cover my mouth.

"Why would you bring this to me?" I ask, "Why on Pendomus would you do this?"

The wolf and bird merge, transforming before my eyes into a naked man, lying on his side on the warm ground. His brown hair flutters in the breeze revealing hints of red hues. His back is turned to me, but I can't take my eyes off his body and the familiarity in its lines. My eyes resting on the small of his back, traveling downward.

"Hello?" I whisper, refusing to move from my location.

The man rolls over, and I shield my eyes before taking in the entirety of his naked body. Something odd stirs in the depths of me—curiosity, I suppose. But it's more than that. Almost an odd sense of hunger—one I can't begin to describe.

As he stands up, my heart threatens to burst from its cage. How—how can he be here? Was he transported too?

God, I've missed him so much.

"Traeton, you—you have no clothes on," I blurt out,

wanting more than anything to run to him and wrap my arms around him. Instead, an awkward restraint keeps me from him.

He chuckles, "It's *Trae*, Runa."

"I—I know that. It's just—you've caught me off guard. Where are your clothes? Can I help you find some?" I ask, turning around and calling over my shoulder. "And what—what happened to your hair? Are you okay?"

My thrumming heartbeat pulses in my ears, and I'm acutely aware of the rigidity of my stance.

I hear Trae shift, walking over to where I stand, and I freeze. How can he be here? Finally, now? After all this time, and all my wishing.

"Clothes are unnecessary, don't you think?" he says, standing directly behind me. The heat of his body radiates along my entire backside, making me shiver.

"I don't—I think—" I begin.

Trae grabs hold of my wrist, gently pulling my hand back behind me, and slowly dragging it along his hip. My insides clench, and a heady wanting threatens to consume me.

"You feel that, don't you?" he says. "The way I want you. Do you want me too?"

"I—of course I want you, Trae. I've missed you so—"

I shiver.

Every nerve in my hand burns intensely as he uses it to gently stroke the skin on his thigh. I'm acutely aware of his body, of the fact I've never seen anyone naked in my life— and the fact every fiber in my being wants to turn around. Yet, the overwhelming programming from the Helix taunts me from the back of my mind. It says I shouldn't. It's dangerous.

"Do you, really? Do you understand what I mean?" he whispers in my ear.

His words curve around me, lulling me into wanting something more.

My heart races, my breath is shallow and ragged, but I wait as still as I possibly can.

"I—what is this, Trae? What are you trying to— " I breathe, closing my eyes.

I don't know what this feeling is, but it's consuming. I should be able to control myself better, but the urges are overwhelming. I want to step out of my own clothes and feel his skin against mine. I don't even know why—I just do.

Trae closes the last remaining gap between us, his body pressing against the back of mine. I feel every aspect of him as our bodies touch.

"Runa, men and women—we're meant to connect. We're meant to *physically* connect. And that's how I want you. How I've always wanted you, but was too afraid to say. I knew you wouldn't know what that meant before. But now—I can't help myself. I need— " he says, his voice low and husky.

A shiver runs down my spine. Then what does he mean?

"Traeton, I don't understand, but I think you know that already," I say, sighing heavily. A part of me wants desperately to turn and face him, to understand, to kiss him and allow whatever happens to unfold.

As if reading my mind, he takes my shoulder in his hand and slowly spins me around so I face him. Refusing to look down, I consume myself with the way his hair is its natural brown, rather than the blue I've come to love.

He grins, his dimples emerging, "There you are."

He stands, unfettered, unembarrassed; simply himself while I stare into his deep brown eyes. Taking my hands into his, he places each on either side of his hips, then rests his own on mine.

Something in the way he's leading me—or perhaps the

look in his eyes—his natural hair—it awakens my awareness. There's more to this than meets the eye. There's something just slightly off—

"Where are your clothes, Trae?" I repeat, blinking. Right now, it's all I can think to say. It's so hard to stay focused, to not take all of him in. The hairs on his chest are in my periphery, taunting me to take my gaze further.

It occurs to me—had this been Trae, *my* Trae, he would have been startled by his lack of clothes. He would have wanted to know where they were—and at the very least, attempted to be modest.

I remove one hand and gently place it on his chest, just above his heart, needing to know if he's real or just a mirage. I maintain eye contact with him as he lets it rest there, allowing me to feel his heart beating through my fingertips. His heartbeat is as fast as mine feels, and just as real. Slowly, he reaches up and pulls my hand downward...

"Trae—what are you—?" I whisper, unsure what to do, but wanting desperately to follow wherever he's leading.

"I'm showing you," he says, "the way we are meant to be."

He lets go of my hand, allowing me to decide what I do with it. Placing his hands on the sides of my face, he draws me closer, pressing his lips to mine. Gentle at first, then more hungrily. His lips tug at my own, his tongue working some kind of magic as I sigh into him. Every part of my body is humming and radiating an intense heat—a vibration all its own.

Desire.

The word comes to my mind, and I realize that's what this is. A desire for Trae, but one unlike anything I've ever experienced. It's a desire to have him. *All of him.*

I allow the desire consume me, my fingertips tracing the hairline further down his torso, not wanting to let this moment pass. Not wanting to go back to the horrors, the trials—

Suddenly, I remember myself; my mission. What am I doing? I'm not here for Traeton. I'm here to pass the trial of hunger. How could I be distracted with this?

Traeton grabs hold of my hand, pressing it to his lower abdomen. The warmth from his hand burns mine, and I pull back, staring into the desire mirrored back to me.

However, those pretenses drop—and a more reserved Trae emerges.

"Hunger comes in more ways than one, Runa. When it comes to humanity, there's much to learn—and desire—the hunger for another is one you'd never experience in the Helix. Videus removed it intentionally through his own anger and frustration. But it's also the way you were brought into being. Without the knowledge of desire—love, *lust*—you cannot possibly understand the humanity burning inside you. You'd lose your connection to where you came from and why," he says. "Don't lose sight of your humanity. Allow yourself to feel it, to embody it without shame or denial."

Placing a gentle kiss on my lips, he evaporates like steam dispersing.

Confused, I take a step back.

My heart is still racing, still thrumming loudly in my ears, all over my whole body. Every ounce of me wants something only Trae can give me.

Suddenly, intense pain sears in my left wrist and I claw at my NanoTech jacket, pulling it back. As if someone were drawing on my skin with pure light from inside my body, I watch as a single petal takes shape on my wrist. I don't have to even question the shape it will eventually take the shape of; the everblossom.

It would appear, I've just overcome my first trial.

8

RUNA

HE LANDSCAPE SHIFTS and I'm suddenly alone beside a small fire. I blink away my surprise, trying to regain my composure. I stand up, trying to ground myself in these new surroundings.

Oddly enough, it's dark outside. In all my life, I've never seen the night. Not once. I've heard stories about it, but I've only seen the same beautiful sun, with halo locked in its designated spot. Well, that or high in the sky and demandingly hot, like it is on the desert side. With a tidally locked planet, warm nights like this one are not something any of us are accustomed to.

I look up, searching the black sky for a sign. A sign of anything—that I'm still on Pendomus. Still in my trials. Still technically alive.

The longer I look up, an astounding thing happens. The sky fills with the twinkling of lights as the stars I've heard about in my eLink downloads emerge. Truthfully, they're not all that unlike the orbs I've seen, guiding me since I acquired my new sight. At first, I thought it was just the fire's ashes flickering into the sky, but its become evident I was mistaken.

I step away from the fire, straying further than I probably should, but an imaginary force tugs at the middle of my body, propelling me forward. The further I get, the brighter the stars become. Some are dazzlingly bright. Others are dimmed, but still there. One section appears like a puddle of light; dense, but full of colors and intensity. I can't take my eyes off of it.

~Beautiful, isn't it?

Holding my breath, my shoulders stiffen. The sensation is one I've grown accustomed to, since it has always been a part of my life. But it's out of place here.

The eLink was supposed to be damaged upon my return to the present time.

I shake my head. Maybe I just thought I heard—I mean, no way someone just—

~Of course someone just tried to talk to you. It's me. Why is that so hard to believe?

Instantly, I turn circles, trying to locate the source of voice. How does it know where I am? I swear, it's so familiar.

~You won't find me, Runa. I'm not there. Hell, I'm not even sure I know where I am.

"Who is this?" I ask, scared to accept someone has meandered into my mind without permission.

~You know, I honestly don't remember. How weird is that?

"Is this some kind of sick joke? A game?" I sputter.

~No, I don't think so. It's weird though, I guess. I know your name, but not my own. Kinda messed up, actually.

I squint into the distance, weighing my options. How does one escape their own mind?

~You look pretty tonight.

"How would you know? You said you weren't here," I say, looking for something I could use as a weapon if needed.

~I'm not, but I can still see you. In my mind, somehow. You don't need to be scared. I won't hurt you. You're all I've got.

"What does that mean?" I say.

~Just that. Here I am, talking to you and I don't even know who I am. Or where I am. But I know you, so—you're all I've got.

Making my way back to the fire, I sit down and stare into the glowing depths.

Of course, this is the next phase; the next test. It has to be.

Why I always let these things catch me off guard, I'll never know. You'd think after all I've been through already, I'd be used to it—not so naive.

"Okay, if you're not really here and you're not going to hurt me...what do you want? And what should I call you?" I ask to the ether.

~Call me anything you want. I don't care.

"I have to call you something, otherwise this is just creepy," I say, lowering my eyebrows and frowning.

~Then call me 'Something'.

"Very funny."

~I wasn't kidding. It honestly doesn't matter. Just as good as anything.

"Alright, if you know me, but don't know yourself or where you are... Do you know where you were? Where you started before you were here?" I ask, trying to draw out the information I need to pass the trial.

~I—I remember white before this. And searing pain. Could I be dead?

"I don't think that's how things work. I've never had a conversation with a dead person before," I say.

~Then how do you know you can't?

"Well, I guess I don't, but it also doesn't mean I am," I say, laying back and looking up. My eyes return to the sparkling blackness above me.

~The stars, they're beautiful tonight, aren't they?

I hold my breath for a moment.

"They really are," I finally say.

~I wish we saw them more often.

"I've never seen them. No one has. It never gets dark where I am," I whisper. "Well, until now."

~You know, I don't think I've ever seen them, either.

"Then how did you know what they are?"

~I just—do. I think I read about them in a book. Maybe a lot of books?

"Hmmmm…" I mutter, lost in thought. "Am I still on Pendomus?"

~Where else would you be?

"I thought you didn't know where you were," I say.

~I don't. I said where else would you *be. Not me.*

"Convenient," I laugh. The simple, but passive sentence reminds me so much of…

~Who was he?

"Who was who?" I ask, startled.

~The man you were just thinking about. He—feels familiar. Like I should know him.

"How can he feel familiar when he was just in my thoughts? I didn't even fully imagine him," I blush. My mind is instantly drawn to the most recent memory of the last trial. Technically, I'm not even sure it was Trae, but simply an echo of him. But the likeness was profound and I know he was meant to invoke the feelings and sensations he did.

~Oh, now that's different, but—whew. Does he know how you feel?

"Oh my—get out of my head!" I say, covering my face. I'd let my guard down and my mind wander a little too much.

This is so inconvenient. Of all the ways a trial could test me, a stranger digging into my most private thoughts and memories really sucks. It's not fair.

~Why? I just want to understand. The memory—it was, well hot, to put it bluntly.

"For the love of all that's holy. Those are my memories. Mine. Not yours. And he knows— at least, I hope he knows. Ugh. I don't know. I don't even know what I feel for certain. It's all so new."

I scratch at the newly acquired symbol of achievement at my wrist. The light sparkles like the stars from the outline of the petal.

~You know, I think maybe he does.

"Oh, you're in his head now, too?" I say, laughing.

~I'm just saying I'd be surprised if he didn't. With the kind of energy you both share—even the memory has power behind it. That means something.

"Well, I'm glad to know it was special, but Trae's off limits to you, okay?" I say, shifting in my seat.

~Trae?

"Yes, his name."

~Why is he off limits?

Gosh, it's like talking to a child. I wonder if I was this bad when Trae first found me?

"Because, he just is," I sigh.

~Do you love him?

"Wow, you have an utter lack of understanding what the term 'off limits' means, don't you," I say, rolling my eyes.

For a moment, there's silence in my head and an insane urge to giggle bubbles to the surface. If anyone were to see me, I'd look stark raving mad to them. Granted, you think I'd be used to that by now.

~If it's any consolation, I think he loves you, too.

"You cannot possibly know that," I snort.

~I know I shouldn't, but I do. Energy like that—it can't happen one-sided.

"Well, that's great, but I'm not even sure the memory is really of him. And right now, there's nothing I can do about it."

~Why not?

"Because, we're apart," I sigh, "And don't ask why."

~Then how am I meant to know?

I take a deep breath. Why not...

"We're apart because I had things I needed to take care of."

~Because you're the Daughter of Five?

"Yes, precisely," I say, returning my gaze to the fire.

~I see.

I suddenly feel mentally exhausted from this exchange. This person, entity—whatever he is, knows more than most, but his own confusion is difficult to handle.

"Can we just let this go for now? Why don't you tell me why you're here instead?" I say, mentally counting the stars. Who knows how long I'll get to actually see them, after all.

~I don't think there's a specific reason. I just remember things going wrong. Then, I was wishing I was home and for some reason, there was you.

"Well, that's odd. You know, since I'm not a home. And I'm about as far away from anything resembling a home as I could possibly be," I say, chuckling.

~Don't ask me, I didn't control it.

I smile. I can actually relate to that.

"Then I guess we're both here for reasons unknown."

~Guess so.

"Well, *Something*... what else should we talk about?" I ask.

A moment passes. I search the stars, waiting.

"Something?" I repeat.

The silence is deafening.

As fast as he arrived, he's gone. But that's not the weirdest part. For a brief moment, I felt safe. Like I was talking to an old friend, not a strange new mental acquaintance.

"There you are. I've been looking everywhere for you—"

I blink, and I'm laying near the edge of the cliff where I last saw Traeton's echo. The nighttime evaporated the moment I looked away and took in the sound of Ammon's voice.

Standing a few yards away, his chin is tipped upward as he tries to see me.

"When you didn't come back, I started looking for you. Do you know how hard that is when your eyes are swollen shut like mine?" he says.

"Ammon, I—" I begin, but stop.

What just happened? I didn't complete a trial—but I felt like I was meant to have that exchange.

"You okay?" he asks.

"Yeah, I think so," I nod. "Was it just nighttime for you?"

Ammon makes a face, "Uh—no. We're tidally locked, Runa. Unless you want to go into the frozen depths on the other side of the planet, we don't see nighttime. Pendomus don't revolve."

"Right," I say, shaking my head and walking toward him. "Your face is starting to look better. Not so swollen. And your cheeks have some color. The food must have done you some good."

Ammon's face lights up, and he takes a seat next to me. He flops on his back, resting the same way I am, staring at the sky.

"Runa, it's delicious. I've never had such amazing foods in all my life. There's this one dish that's fluffy in the center with a creamy, sweet layer on top—mmmmm," his lips stretch out broadly and he sighs in content. "It reminds me of the birthday cakes my Dad tried to make for me once, but this is waaaaay better. I wish you could try it. Have you figured out how to pass—"

I jut out my wrist to show him the glowing petal.

"Whoa, what happened there?" Ammon asks, sitting up and pulling my arm closer to get a look.

"It happened after I passed the trial," I say.

"It looks kinda like a tattoo, only glowy," he says.

I nod in agreement.

"You passed? Already? Yeesh, that was fast," he says, then shrugs to himself.

"Was it?" I ask, turning to him.

"Sure seems like it. Then again, I've been trying just about every food I could get my hands on. Felt sick a couple of times, but it passed," he laughs. "C'mon, you gotta try some of this."

He takes my hand and together we make our way back to the table of food. We push through the trees and low lying bushes. As we approach the laid out table, I clearly see where Ammon has been. The foods in front of the seat where I left him have bites and pieces removed from them in a wide berth from his location.

I smile, "Ammon, you hardly made a dent. You had me thinking you barely left me a bite."

"Did I?" he asks, serious.

I laugh, "Yes, there's still plenty."

"Well, go on then, try something. See if you can eat something now," he urges.

I reach out, grabbing one of the lush fruits that had been dangling from the tree earlier. They rest in a heap inside a large bowl with other fruits of various colors and textures.

Ammon's eyes are on me as I grab the nearest one and pull it to my nose. I take in the fragrant aroma and sigh. My stomach grumbles in response.

"Well, go on," he says, nudging my shoulder.

Slowly, I take a big bite. It's the first real food I've had in days and my stomach groans loudly at the prospect. The juicy, soft texture coats my mouth and entices my tongue.

"Oh my—it's delicious," I say. "I've never had this fruit before, but it's the best thing I've ever tasted."

"Oh, it gets better. You haven't tried the cake-thing I was talking about," he says, pointing to a large cylindrical object in the middle of the table. It has a large chunk removed from the side where Ammon has clearly made his mark.

"Well alright, with a recommendation like that, who could resist?" I laugh, getting up to try a bite. I dip my fingers into the cake and pull out a gooey chunk. The white creamy stuff surrounds the inner fluffy bit Ammon was talking about. There are tiny red fruits placed along the edge of the cake and I pluck one off to try, too.

"C'mon, c'mon. Try it already," Ammon says anxiously.

I put the entire bite, fruit and all, into my mouth and close my eyes. Ammon was absolutely right—it's beyond delicious. The gooey outside mixes with the fluffy pastry part and the fruit adds one last burst of flavor.

"Oh my—this is fantastic, Ammon," I say, reaching for another bite.

"Told ya," he grins.

"What else should I try?" I ask.

"Anything. Everything," he offers.

Grinning I take his suggestion and start trying a little piece of everything, deciding what I like best. We spend the next few hours, eating and drinking the waters and juices; getting our fill for the first time in so long.

"RUNA, do you think he'll find us again?" Ammon asks, his tone suddenly serious.

I sigh, knowing exactly who he means. I wish I could tell him no.

"Ammon, I'll keep you safe. Regardless of what happens, you have me, okay?" I say, turning to look at him.

"Yeah, I know," he says, reaching for me and wrapping his arms around my waist.

For a moment, I'm taken aback. The contact of affection, any affection, is still so new to me. However, I lean into his embrace and stroke his dark hair. He sighs with content, and relaxes into me. We sit on the bench at the table like that for a few minutes, just watching the breeze through the trees— the insects as they float from flower to flower—the sun's rays as it filters through the branches.

"You never told me how you passed the first test thingy," Ammon says.

Warmth creeps into my cheeks, and I take a deep breath.

"There—um—wasn't much to tell. I followed a wolf, or an animal who looked like a wolf. He brought me to the edge of the cliff and basically we... talked about the meaning of hunger," I cough.

"Talked about hunger? That's boring," he says. "You'd think there'd have to be more to it than that. Not much of a test. The wolf didn't quiz you afterward, did he?" Ammon giggles.

I laugh, too, realizing my lie does sound pretty ridiculous, but I can't figure out a way to tell him the truth. I have trouble enough wrapping my own head around it.

I glance down, noticing as I stroke Ammon's hair that my fingertips have been stained an inky black.

Ammon tilts his head up and tries to look at me, "Hey, why'd you stop?"

"Ammon, what color is your hair supposed to be?" I ask.

"What a stupid question. Are you the one with swollen eyes?" he says.

"Hey—it's not a stupid question. My hand's turned black from running my fingers through your hair. Has it always been this color, or did you alter it?"

He sits up, running his own hand through his hair.

"It's black?" he says.

Pulling up a few strands, he makes them stand on end.

"Yeah, it is," I say. "It's been that way since I found you. I take it, it's not supposed to be."

"Er… I always wanted black hair, but no—" Ammon says, shaking his head.

"Why did you always want black hair? And who did this, if it wasn't you? Did Videus?"

"Who?"

"The man who kept you hostage. He—his name is Videus."

"What a weird name," he snickers. "Anyway, I've always had light hair. Sometimes it would just be nice to have a change. I've seen so many people at the Lateral with dark hair—sometimes I wish I was more like them. I suppose blonde is no big deal, though. You have blonde hair, right?"

He tilts his head, trying to get a better look.

"Yeah, I suppose it is," I say, glancing at my near white locks.

"Weird about my hair, though. Wish I could see what it looks like black," he mutters. "Bet I look awesome."

"You look great," I laugh. "But I wish I could wash my hand."

Before our eyes, the tree behind us, the lush forest in

front of us all melts away and my back is resting against a sink in an allayroom. Ammon scrambles to his feet.

"Whoa, how wicked was that?" he says. "You wanted to wash your hands, and I wanted to see my hair. And POOF, we're in an allayroom."

He stands in front of the mirror, trying to prop his eyes open with his fingertips.

Laughing, I stand up and look into the mirror as well. He's a full head shorter than I am, but he's right, the black hair suits him. Though, I can't help but wonder how the blonde hair looks on him, too. It would be weird to see him with lighter colored hair now.

I reach forward, turning on the facet and washing my hands in the warmth.

"So, is that how this system works?" Ammon asks.

"How does what system work?"

"You ask for something and it shows up," Ammon says.

"I'm beginning to think so," I reply. "At least, sometimes."

"Ask for something really awesome—" he exclaims. "Like a mountain of books, or games, or—or—"

"Well, why not," I say, wiping my hands on the towel.

"I wish my friends were here with me," I say. It's the only thing I really actually want in all of Pendomus.

We both wait, expectantly, searching the room. Waiting for something to change.

Nothing happens.

"Hmmm…maybe you did it wrong," he offers.

"Or maybe I only get one wish?" I say.

"Or maybe, you have to say thank you for this wish before you get another wish," he giggles.

"There are a lot of 'what ifs' happening here. Maybe the way we thought it worked isn't how it really works," I laugh.

"Or maybe, eh—" he waves his hand dismissively, "maybe we should just look around and see where we are now."

I laugh, "Yeah, okay. Probably wise."

We walk out of the allayroom and into a large, open floor plan. It's a main room with high ceilings and beams that look like they're made from trees. Sunlight streams into the room and we both tentatively walk toward the windows, trying to put a location to where we are. Outside, beyond the immediate vicinity, is still a sea of sand dunes and rock outcroppings.

"Well, doesn't look like we've gone far," I say, disappointment settling in. I had hoped that we would have been transported closer to Trae and the others, since my wish didn't bring them here. "We're still on the desert side of Pendomus."

"And we're not near the awesome food anymore either," Ammon points out with a frown. "Sucks, too. I was going to go back for fifths on the cake stuff."

"That does kinda stink," I say. In all honesty, though, I can't see myself eating anything any time soon. We gorged on so much, the thought of food right now isn't even appealing.

"Well, should we have a look at the—" I spin around, facing the interior of the house, "—the Caudex."

I take in the enormity of the large open room, the kitchen off to the left hand side, the hallway leading back the way we came. I left the Caudex on the food table before we were transported here. I should have had it on me, or nearer to me. I'm supposed to guard it with my life, and now—

I don't even know where it is.

9

TRAETON

ONE THING'S FOR CERTAIN, Videus and the Helix don't know squat about the Tree of Burden and what its significance really is. Honestly, I don't get it either, but I sure as hell know more than they have in these documents. If Videus has more details, the Helix mainframe isn't showing them, that's for damn sure.

After scouring through all fourteen of the relevant searches, the only real piece of intel I glean off the data is they were certain the Tree was some kinda portal. It's not as if we didn't know that, but confirming it is the best damn news I've gotten in a long time. If the tree really was a portal, then Runa's alive despite it being burned to the ground. The bad news is none of us have any damn clue where the portal leads, or hell—if she'll be able to return.

For a while, I was able to forget the gentle throbbing in my temple, but the intense pounding has returned. I try to ignore it, but it's getting more persistent. I push off from the table and walk down the long length of shelves in search of Kani. My footsteps echo on the stone floor in a strange, haunting kinda way.

"Kani, where'd you end up?" I call out into the vast array of ancient books and artifacts.

"Over here," she says, waving a hand from beside a shelf, but not fully coming into view.

"Find anything?" I ask.

"Depends on your definition of *anything*," she calls back.

"Anything *useful?*" I reiterate.

"Nope. Not a damn thing," she says, dusting off her trousers and leaving the book she was engaged with sprawled open on the ground at her feet. "You?"

I shrug, "Possibly."

She waits expectantly for my answer, her eyebrows slowly quirking into a high arch.

"Well, if the intel from the Helix is right, there's a slight possibility Runa will come back. They think the Tree was a portal of some kind."

"A portal to where?"

"It doesn't say exactly," I say, biting my lip, thinking. It has to be some place important, or safe for her. Otherwise, why else would Runa be called to it?

"Well, it's a start. Anything more on the vassalage? Do we have any clue where its location is?"

"No. Haven't gotten that far," I say.

"Well, let's do some more digging on that, then," she says, ushering me back down the corridor toward the mainframe system. "I could use a break from dusty old things anyway."

I nod in agreement and turn back toward the way I came.

Fenton's ghostly lookalike must have gone into sleep mode because when we return he's gone. Gotta admit, I'm relieved because the last thing Kani needs is to come face-to-face with a holographic version of him right now. It would surely send her into a tailspin and we both need to stay focused and motivated.

Kani paces back and forth in front of the table, considering the details we've uncovered.

"Does it say anything about the Tree itself? Like, does she need to use the Tree to make it back? Because if she does…" she says, her voice tapping into the same worry I have.

"I don't think Videus or the Helix have that much information," I say.

"Well, I suppose it wouldn't be real convenient if he did," Kani nods.

"I'm hoping whoever created the portals were smart enough to create a fail-safe. Or at least, a back door in case of emergencies. If that's the case, Runa should still be able to make it back. Hell, maybe she's not even far and could just walk—"

"I doubt she'd be that close. Otherwise, why is there a need for a portal in the first place? But a failsafe would make a certain amount of sense," Kani says in agreement. "Then again, when did any of this make sense?"

"True," I say, rubbing at my temple.

The pounding in the side of my head has worsened, and I fumble for the NeuroWand, despite Kani being nearby.

"I wonder if there's any details in here that could explain who woulda had the ability to create portals on the planet," I muse out loud, waving the NeuroWand near my temple.

"Trae," Kani warns, "you really shouldn't be using this so much. You could overdose and then where would we be?"

"It's been a while, Kani. I can't even remember the last time," I mutter, blinking away the dark blots creeping into my periphery.

"You better not be lying," she say, with a sideways glance.

"I'm not, honest."

"Hmmm," she says, raising and eyebrow and crossing her arms. "If there are any details about who created the portals,

I'm guessing they pre-date the mainframe, Trae. We'd be looking at books or scrolls or something and that could take ages to go though. Hell, maybe it wasn't even humans who made the portals. Maybe they've always been here. This could mean ancient stuff. Who even knows if it's here. Trust me, I was just knee deep in old histories. If you're hoping for intel on finding Runa that way, it's next to impossible. We don't have that kind of time. We need to come up with a faster solution," she pauses her pacing and stares at me. "Hasn't that thing gone yet?"

I stop rubbing my temple and shake my head, "Not really. They go for a bit and come right back. It's no big deal."

Kani shakes her head, concern written across her wrinkled forehead. "It's not like you to get so many headaches."

"I'm not worried. They'll go. It's probably all the stress," I offer. "Not like this is the most peaceful of times, you know?"

"Maybe you're not worried, but I am," Kani says.

"Well, stop. We have bigger issues to contend with," I mutter, slapping her hand away from my forehead.

Kani strolls over to my pack and pulls out the Neuro-Wand. I flinch knowing what's coming next.

"Traeton Revasco—You're down to thirty-eight percent efficiency. Were you aware of that? How many times have you been taking this?" she says, pacing back and forth.

I stand up, walking to where she stands and snatch the medical device from her hand.

"Only a few times here and there. It was already low in percentage when I got it. Like I said, no big deal," I say, shoving it back inside the pack and wishing I could already try it again. No way in hell am I stupid enough to try with Kani hovering, though.

"Look, I'm not about to lose anyone else close to me,

Traeton. Especially by their own negligent doing. If I'm worried, you should be, too."

"And I appreciate your concern. I just think it's misplaced," I say.

"And what if it's not?" she says, raising an eyebrow.

"Then you can say, 'I told you so' later," I say, grinning.

"If there is a later," she mutters.

"I'm sure there will be. You're not losing anyone. In fact, the plan is to get one of us back."

I flinch at my words, hoping they don't set something off in Kani. Feigning nonchalance, I walk back to the mainframe to scroll through the last entry again. As I do, Fenton's hologram reappears. Instantly, I wish I hadn't even touched the damn thing.

Kani gasps and breathes out, "Whoa."

Her face goes tremendously white, which is saying something given her naturally olive complexion.

"It's just the holographic backup Fenton left," I say, fiddling with it to try to shut it down.

"Oh, right," she breathes, her lips pressing together in a tight line.

"He—ah—he's the actual interface," I say. "So if you don't want to help with the vassalage stuff, I totally—"

"Yeah, not so much," Kani says, unable to take her eyes off the hologram. After a few awkward moments, she says, "He looks so...normal."

"Yeah," I agree. "Sounds like him, too. It's kinda, well—at first creepy, but I suppose in the end, it's kinda nice."

"No, it could never be nice. Nice would be him still here. Nice would be never having to— *Nice* would be not living in such a messed up world," she says, turning on her heel. Her black and green hair spin around with her movements, as she rushes to get away.

"Kani—" I call after her, but I know it's pointless. It'll be a while before I see her again.

I look up at holographic Fenton, who shrugs. "Whatcha waitin' fer? Do ya go' a burning question? How ta ge' Runa alone, perhaps?"

I roll my eyes, "I need help finding the vassalage thing Videus is hiding."

"Wan' me ta pull up all tha results fer vassalage?" holographic Fenton suggests.

I rub my temple, trying to think through the pounding.

"Nah, we went over those a number of times. I don't think that's how we'll find it," I say.

Sighing, I looking into the ghostly eyes of my best friend. He looks exactly the same as he did just days ago—of course he would, he recorded the basis for this days ago. I hate that Videus was able to do this to him. Take over his mind, take him away from us. It should have been me he took over—I have the eLink embedded, after all. Why Fenton? *How* Fenton?

"Search for anything related to the Helix and mind control," I say, sitting up straighter.

"Tha results are kinda obscure, bu' there's three results wit similar search parameters," Fenton says. The three results show up on the holographic screen in front of me, and I lean in.

The first one is gibberish. Talking about dreams, access points, and dating back into the times when we were on Earth. Shaking my head, I move on.

The second one is closer...

...The experiments have been inconclusive. So far, all of the subjects exhibiting schizophrenic symptoms continue with them well after the cognitive restructuring and neuronetwork has been

replaced. Others continue with mild-to-extreme aggression. So far, the most exciting, albeit unnerving result has been the brain-personality alterations. A number of subjects appear to be having a personality shift as part of the process. Sometimes the results are for the better, softening the subject and making them more compliant. Others, however, have the opposite reaction. They become more agitated, harder to control. When the dosage is increased, the agitation increases. To what effect, we have yet to determine...

...We're finding there is a percentage of the population that is unable to let go of the people close to them, even when they know their own person is in harms way. We need to find a way to scare them into submission. All for their own good, of course...

...We've found broadcasting a holographic illusion when a rehabilitated subject is taken over to be most effective. By wiping the facial features clean, we're able to scare the relatives into submission. It appears the lack of what makes a person recognizable is the most effective...

...We've managed to maintain control of Subject A for more than fifteen minutes. Her original defiant and risk-taking qualities have been effectively subdued, as to not harm herself, her son, or her infant daughter. Unfortunately, her husband was not as fortunate. Subject D was not able to handle the Neuroshift process, and it appears his heart is failing from the voltage used. I suspect he doesn't have more than a couple of years left, maximum...

...Subject D has slipped into a coma. We're monitoring closely the effect it has on the rest of the subjects in the Living Quarters. Subject A has exhibited exemplary behavior, completely responding as she should. She's no longer seeking to run away or demanding to

be allowed to live her life the way she wants. Her daughter, on the other hand, is exhibiting familiar defiant tendencies, as we suspected may happen through her genetics. She's of particular interest as we watch her interaction to the depletion of her father figure...

I run my tongue across my lower lip. How could they do experiments like this and be so nonchalant? Watching the interactions and the imminent death of someone with such aloofness? It doesn't even seem human. It's as if people have never been anything more than a tool, or experimental material. Not living beings with lives of their own.

It's pretty clear to me, Videus does this sort of thing just because he has some sort of God complex. He has no problem messing with other people's minds because they're not his own.

In a way, Ava was like this... Hell, for all I know, we were monitored. Probably my entire family, too. When I was living it, I thought it was strange to watch her tendencies, but what if the whole family was the experiment? Maybe that's why it always felt off to me. Hell, for all I know, they were applying pressure to see how much she could handle before she cracked. Before any of us cracked.

Disgusted, I push back from the desk and walk in circles around it. I reach my hands up and clasp them behind my head, stretching. My back groans, telling me I should really lie down and get some rest soon.

All of this is so ludicrous. I mean, I knew the Helix was bad news—always did—but this? Why would they do all of this? Why would this Videus guy go to such lengths? To what purpose? Just to make Labots?

The pulsing in my head begins to creep into my right eye, and I take my seat again. I need to rest soon; try to get rid of the damned thing. I really wish all this stress would just give me a break. I don't have time for this.

"Show me the last entry," I tell the holographic Fenton, pinching the bridge of my nose and willing the throbbing to go.

"Ya go' it," he says, the last entry flashing up on the screen.

...Subject A-2 has begun exhibiting signs of delusions. She sees things that are clearly not there. Often, she'll talk in nonsense. The standard Neuorshift process doesn't seem to have any effect on her, and we're beginning to believe she may need more drastic measures. If A-2 does not respond to those, we may need to dispose of her before she becomes a threat to the safety of the Helix...

...The Faceless Project has been working better than expected. Subject A-2 has been able to be assimilated in the underground facility. It appears the heat does these types of subjects some good...

The *underground facility?* Heat? Hmmm... I sit up a little more. Now we're getting somewhere. Where could this underground facility be hidden?

"Fenton, can you find me any more references to this underground facility?" I ask.

"Sure thang," he says, his holographic face going blank for a moment. "There are twelve entries."

They each pop up on the screen and I bend in. Sifting through the details will take some time, because each entry is pages long. Craning my neck, I stretch it, trying to get it to crack. I wiggle my jaw, hoping to alleviate some of the pressure. Nothing helps.

Blinking hard, I lean in to read the first entry.

...We already know the best way to deal with the difficult subjects

is to incarcerate them in the underground facility until they've had the rehabilitation course. But there are some who seem to be beyond help, and need to be disposed of in the appropriate manner...

Disposed of? What does this even mean? Why do they talk like they're just taking out the garbage?

I shake my head. Maybe to them, they are.

I flip to the next one, then the next, and the next. All of the entries have similar details, and all blend into each other as I try to concentrate through the pounding in my head.

"One more," I whisper to myself, "Then, I *need* to rest."

...The people of the Helix seem to have given their own mythological name to the Faceless—Labots. The name has spread like wildfire to those who were aware of their presence. Seems an almost fitting name. We plan to take it on as our own. We've been wondering what to call them, and there's no better way to tap into their innate fear than to use the name they have already given...

...There are a number of faceless Labots who are not functioning as they should. We can't get them to disengage the holographic image that erases their faces. We've had to store them in the underground facility for safe-keeping until they can be sorted out...

...We have had a number of people who are in question for causing problems in the Helix. Two have been know to actively search for information they have no business digging into. They've all been given the standard professional appointment for disposal...

The standard professional appointment for disposal? So there were people who received professional appointments to get rid of them? The Helix did a good enough job making sure the people who stayed in the Helix as part of the society were given the correct appointments. I suppose so no one would question the validity. But if there's a standard appointment for disposal, what the hell would it be?

I wish I would have asked more questions of Runa about her professional appointment, about why she left. I could kick myself now.

Biting my lip, I keep reading.

...So far, we've had three people refuse their professional appointment. Unfortunately, we were able to activate the eLink to initiate the Labot program on only one of them. For some reason, the other two seem to have malfunctioned, and they have escaped to the nearby woods. There's no point in hunting for them, they will likely be dead by morning. None of them can survive out in the wild...

...The heat from the facility has taken Subject F. It appears he was unable to fully compensate for being in charge of dispersing the ashes of his wife and infant. He threw himself into the incinerator, alive. This is the second time a subject has behaved in such a manner. We may need to keep them locked in their cells when they're not taken over; or find a way to keep access to their minds indefinitely. This would be unfortunate, since there aren't many cells for relocation. Perhaps a new project for our Labots, as we expand beneath the city...

Expand beneath the city.

The words jump off the screen. They're beneath the Helix —and now I know where.

"Kani, Kani— I think I figured out where the vassalage is," I call out.

The pounding in my head increases, pulsing behind my

right eye to the point I have to close my eyes. I sit back down and set my head on the table in front of me, trying to breathe through it. The room feels like it's spinning and there's nowhere I can go to escape.

In a weird way, it feels like my skull has been split apart and someone has their fingers wiggling around inside my brain.

"Trae? Trae?" Kani's voice is so distant.

Though I know she's calling my name, I don't have the strength to answer her. I have to keep the room from spinning or I'm going to lurch. Besides, my head is so heavy...

Consciousness departs to the high-pitch squeal of someone screaming.

RUNA

*I*T HAS TO BE HERE. I race back to the allayroom, seeing as it was the place we entered this new location.

"Where are you going?" Ammon says, calling after me.

"The Caudex. I didn't have it on me—I don't know if it made the trip with us to this place," I say, pulling back the shower curtain.

"Why would it be in the allayroom?" he asks.

"I don't know, I just thought maybe—" I sigh, "ugh. How could I have been so careless?"

I rake my hands through my hair.

"Did you expect to be transported like that?" he asks.

"Well, not exactly," I mutter.

"Then stop being hard on yourself. It's gotta turn up at some point," he says, sitting down on a plush looking couch. "This is a nice place. I wonder if anyone lives here."

"Who knows," I say, opening cupboard doors in the kitchen area, hoping the book was brought with us and just stored somewhere for safe keeping.

"Well, if it was me transporting you around the planet, I'd

make sure that your book went with you," Ammon says, matter-of-factly.

"Me, too. Especially since I think those wanting it to stay safe are the same ones moving us around," I say.

"Hey now, that's a good point," Ammon says, sitting up straighter.

"What is?"

"They transported *us*," he says.

"Yeah?" I say, turning to face him.

"Well, I coulda been left behind, right? Someone somewhere knew I should go with you. So, maybe the book did, too. I wish I could help you look, it's just so hard to see where I'm going," he says, rubbing at his puffy eyes.

I walk over and take a seat next to him. The black and blue markings across his face aren't as angry as they were when I first met him, but his eyes can still only open in small slits. In a way, they almost remind me of the shape of Kani's eyes at the moment. Reaching out, I run my hand across his cheek, rubbing his cheekbone with my thumb.

"Don't worry about it, Ammon. You need to rest and heal more. I can look around. The Caudex is my responsibility anyway," I say, smiling, "but let's hope you're right."

"It would be kinda dumb if they left it there. Don't you think?"

"I would think so, but then again, I don't always have all the information. Sometimes I wonder if they like it better that way," I say, standing up again and looking around the room.

Along the main wall is a fireplace that extends all the way up to the apex of the vaulted ceiling. On either side are two massive windows that cover most of the expansive wall. I walk over to the window to the left of the fireplace, holding onto the sill.

For as far as I can see, there is nothing but sand dunes and rock outcroppings. It looks exactly the same for all of those initial days I was out in the world alone. At least we've got a roof over our head for the time being.

"See anything out there?" Ammon asks, craning to see around me.

"Nope. Nothing but more and more sand," I say.

"Isn't it kinda pretty, though? I only saw the inside of a cave—well, at home…and when that lunatic kidnapped me."

"Yeah, I guess," I say, shrugging, "Not very hospitable, though. Are you able to see better now?"

"Yeah, a little. The puffiness is going down, anyway. So why do you think we—"

I wait for Ammon to finish, but when he doesn't I turn around, confused.

"Why do you think we, what? Did you forget what you were going to say?" I ask.

Ammon's mouth begins to move, but absolutely no sound comes out.

Bewildered, I shake my hands out in front of me, "Ammon, stop. I can see you're talking, but no sound is coming out. Are you okay?"

One of his puffy eyes twitches, as he gives me a funny look. His mouth begins moving again, more rapidly than before, but still nothing comes out.

"No, stop—stop. You're not making any—"

Ammon pulls both of his hands apart, and brings them together right in front of my face.

Nothing. Not a sound.

It's not Ammon, it's me.

As if a switch was just flipped, I no longer have the ability to hear.

"Ammon, something's happened to me. I can't hear

anything," I say, cupping my ears as if they need to somehow be protected.

He smirks, then mouths slowly, "Told you."

"Well, you stopped in mid-sentence. How I was I supposed to know?" I say, looking around again for the Caudex. There has to be answers there somewhere—if I can just find it.

This has to be the next trial—but what does it mean? How do I overcome this? How do I make sense of anything without being able to hear?

I go from door to door, cupboard to cupboard hunting for the book that's been my guide. I look under tables, the couch, the beds, inside closets, everywhere I can think of. But the Caudex isn't with us.

Sitting down next to Ammon on the couch, I bury my face in my hands. This can't be happening. Not only am I in the midst of my next trial—at least, I hope that's what this is —but I've lost the one thing I'm supposed to guard with my life because it's been guiding me through everything. How on Pendomus can I be trusted to be the Daughter of Five, if I can't even keep track of one object? It's huge, for crying out loud.

"Ugh—" I cry in disgust, thumping the cushions beside me with my closed fists.

Ammon's eyes widen as far as they can, but he doesn't try to say anything. He simply rests a hand on my shoulder, trying to console me.

"This stinks. I feel—I feel like a failure and I've barely begun. How could I be so reckless, Ammon?"

He shrugs, his lips turning downward.

I close my eyes and pull my legs up close to my body. Resting my head in my knees, I close my eyes.

This isn't helping. Getting upset, berating myself over this

—it's not going to solve anything.

I look up at Ammon, who yawns in response. Glancing around the room, I look for some way to measure the time. It must be close to when we should be sleeping, surely?

Standing up, I hold out my hand.

"I think we should get some rest. Maybe we'll think more clearly when we wake up." I say, thankful at least I can communicate, even if I can't hear Ammon's response.

He nods, taking my hand and yawning again.

I lead us both down the main hallway to the bedroom area. One bedroom has a large, massive bed in the center of the room, the other has two slightly smaller ones separated by a table of sorts.

Ammon lifts his finger, pointing to the one with two beds and mouths, "Please?"

Nodding, I follow him inside. He takes the inner bed, nearer the wall and I take the one closest to the door. Should anyone come back, I can protect us from this position. Well, if I can hear anything.

Crawling into the bed, Ammon seems to instantly fall asleep. But my mind rolls over and over all of the events. The people I'm missing. Wondering where the Caudex is.

I wish there was a way to make this trial go faster. I need to get back home, get back to—

Yawning myself, I decide to get up for a sip of water. I scavenge through the cupboards again, finding a small cup and getting a sip of water from the sink, grateful for the running water.

The windows in the house have begun to autodim, slowly filtering out the light from the sun, and I notice for the first time the light still shining in the allayroom. I walk back to shut it off. My hand hovers over the switch as it shuts off, but my eye catches a glint of metal near the sink. Turning the light back on I step into the allayroom. A pair of old-fashioned scissors lie across the countertop right beside the sink.

Reaching out, I pick them up, turning them over in my hands.

"Were these here before?" I say to myself. For the life of me I can't remember, but then, I was pretty focused on finding the Caudex.

I remember once being told via my eLink lessons what scissors were meant for, but I've never seen a pair in real life. In the Helix, we don't overly have a need for such a primitive device. In a weird way, they remind me of my friends, as if the scissors are something I'd find on another expedition to the Archives, or something.

Setting them back on the counter, I consider taking a shower to help me relax. Unfortunately, I have nothing to change into and the idea of putting the same outfit back on doesn't incite any joy. Instead, I lean on the counter, looking in the mirror.

I certainly look tired, and a bit worn down. There are dark circles under my eyes and my once white hair lays limp and disheveled and almost a burnt sienna color thanks to the sand particles clinging to it.

Maybe I *should* shower.

"What could it hurt?" I mutter, flipping on the dial and instantly feeling the warm water rush over my arm.

I lock the door and undress before stepping into the warm mist and water droplets. I feel like I haven't bathed in years. The water feels so good as I relax into the pounding on my back as I pull my hair to the side, letting it fall over my right shoulder. It's the oddest sensation to feel the water, but not to hear it.

When I've finally had enough, and my body feels ready to rest, I step out, grabbing the towel hanging from a hook on the wall nearby. To my surprise, resting on the side where the scissors had been lies a freshly laundered NanoTech outfit, folded and waiting. One set for me, and a much smaller set—the perfect size for a little boy.

"Hello?" I call out, suddenly alert. "Who's here?"

I glance at the outfit briefly, clutching the towel close to my body as I unlock the door and step out into the hallway.

Walking through the entire home, not a single thing looks out of place—except for the outfits. And of course the scissors.

Maybe this is part of the trial. Ammon had mentioned I got whatever I asked for before. What if this is like that?

I check in on Ammon, who's sound asleep, and turned to face the door so I can see his restful face. I'm so glad he's sleeping, he certainly needs it.

Sighing to myself, I walk back to the allayroom and close the door. I pick up the outfit, unfolding the trousers, top, and the undergarments. Nothing seems out of the ordinary about them. In fact, they look utterly ordinary.

"Oh, why not?" I say, grabbing the new outfit.

As I step into the trousers, a small vial drops from the pocket, skidding across the floor. Pulling the trousers all the way on, I lean down and pick the vial up. Inside is a blue liquid, no label or instructions of any kind to give away what the contents actually are.

I set the vial on the counter, only to find the scissors have reappeared, except on the opposite side of the sink.

"This is so strange," I mutter, "What am I meant to do with these?"

I scratch my head, completely lost. It's pretty clear by now, they're meant for me. But why? What could I use them on? I look around, trying to figure out if there's something to cut—but there's absolutely nothing in the room.

Shrugging, I look in the mirror again. My hair is no longer the reddish color, but instead a wet, tangled mess. It's not like in the Helix where the water automatically smooths away the snarls. And I don't see a brush anywhere in sight.

Okay, maybe a shower wasn't the brightest idea.

I comb my fingers through my hair, trying to get it to lay flat, but nothing seems to work. Forget trying to rebraid the sections the way I've done my whole life.

My eyes flit back to the scissors.

My hair has been this way for so long, maybe it's time for change? I lift the scissors to my hair, half expecting them to not work. To be a mirage, or something the way the food was. However, I bring out a section to the front and close the blades around it. The white strands fall to the ground in slow motion, almost dancing as they drop. I continue around the rest of my head, pulling the hair forward, and swiping it with the scissors. Eventually, there's no more hair to cut and I've managed to make it look pretty. No longer down to the middle of my back, my hair stops just above my shoulders. It reminds me of some of the hair styles I've seen in the Lateral.

Smiling to myself, I clean up the remainder of my long hair and place it in the garbage chute. In an instant, my childhood appearance is taken away from sight.

It's interesting how something so simple can make such a drastic change. For some reason, my hair makes me look older, wiser. I can't say I always feel that way, but I suppose I am in many ways.

Happier with my accomplishments, I set the scissors down beside the little blue vial and walk out of the allayroom and back to bed. I hope my hearing will be back in the morning. I want to know what Ammon thinks of what I've done.

Crawling back into bed, I pull the blankets up close. As if sensing I'm in bed, the lights dim and eventually go out. The house falls into complete darkness, and I let it consume me as I drift off to a deep, dreamless sleep.

I OPEN my eyes to find Ammon standing over me, watching me like a hawk.

"Ammon, what are you doing?" I ask, bolting upright and clutching my chest.

I watch his lips mouth the words, "Can you hear me?"

Unfortunately, silence is all I hear, so I shake my head. He frowns, and then jabs a finger at my head.

"What?" I ask, then reach instinctively for my hair. It takes a moment, but I remember what I'd done the night before.

"Oh," I mutter, "yeah, I sorta …"

He leans to one side, cocking his head.

Then he mouths, "You did this?"

I nod. "Yeah, I couldn't sleep. Kinda just … happened."

He pushes up a thumb, nodding.

"Thanks," I smile.

"What happened to your eye?" he mouths slowly.

Instinctively, I draw my fingertips to my face, tracing the scar left by Tethys. I almost forgot it was even there.

"The blue eye, or the scar?" I laugh. "They were both gifts from Tethys."

Ammon quirks his eyebrow a bit, then shakes his head.

It's nice to know he's able to see more—hopefully, his eyes will be fully healed soon.

We spend the next few days searching the house, the area nearby and all of the rock outcroppings for signs of what I'm supposed to be learning. Ammon is thankful to finally have real clothes to wear—even the strange ones from the Helix.

By the third day of not being able to hear a single word, or a single sound, I'm about ready to go insane.

We've tried a number of different ways to communicate. Drawing in the sand with sticks, hunting for paper and an old fashioned writing utensil, you name it. But nothing has gotten rid of my lack of hearing.

"I'm going to bed, Ammon. I need to—I don't know. Relax. Rest. Clear my head. Whatever."

He opens his mouth, but I swat at the air in front of me, not wanting him to try to give me another muted response.

It's gotta be near bedtime again, anyway.

I climb in the bed and pull the covers up and over my head.

I don't know how much more of this I can take.

~Hello? Are you there?

~Who is this?

I instinctively ask, surprised.

~It's me again. You know, Something.

I take a moment, remembering the last exchange we had. He'd left before without so much as a goodbye.

~Where have you been? You sound different.

~I sound like something? That's weird. I can't hear myself.

~Well, okay, not exactly. But you make sense to me.

~That's sorta the point, right?

~Yeah, I guess. But I shouldn't—I don't think I'm supposed to be able to hear anything. So how can I hear you?

~Maybe you're not hearing me. Not exactly.

There's truth in his words, because in an odd sort of way, it's more like I see them, in my mind. But they still come fast, and my brain translates them for me.

~Are you going to answer where you've been?

~I had to go. For a while I was somewhere else, but I'm back now.

~Where was somewhere else?

~I'm not sure, but it was familiar.

~Why do you keep coming to me, I ask.

~I already told you, whenever I think about being home, I find you. You must be home.

~I'm not a location, Something. I'm a person.

~Well, then you are an important person to me.

~I don't even know you. Not really.

~That's true, but maybe we've met before. It would make sense, right?

~I doubt it. There aren't many people I know, and even less who know me.

~Why couldn't I be one of them, then?

~Because they're them. They can't be you and them at the same time.

~Oh.

~Is there something you need to say? Why are you here again?

~I didn't know where else to go. Sometimes it gets hard to be in the other place. So I come here.

~I see. Well, I'm having a hard time here, too.

~What do you mean?

~I'm supposed to overcome this trial, but I don't know how. It's been three days and nothing.

~What's so hard about it?

~For starters, I can't hear anything. And when I mean anything, I mean zero. I don't even hear the wind or the sound of a door creaking, or my NanoTech clothing rustling as I walk anymore. I'm frustrating Ammon—

~Who's Ammon?

~He's my friend.

I wait for a response, but silence expands between myself and the written voice that is Something.

~*Something? Are you still here?*

~*Do you like him? Ammon.*

~*Yes, he's sweet.*

~*Oh.*

~*He's also only eleven years old.*

I laugh. What a weird conversation, justifying my friendship with Ammon with a voice in my head.

~*Well, good. Good then.*

~*Yes, it's been good. He would have died had I not found him.*

~*I wish I could find my friends. They're all so far away.*

~*Why is that?*

~*I'm not sure. They were taken from me, and I don't know how to get them back. It's a strange feeling.*

~*I'm sure you'll find them.*

~*I've got—there's no—it's here—got to—*

A MOMENT PASSES, and there's no more exchanges from Something. I sit up on the bed, trying to focus to see if his presence is still with me. Instead, I can tell it's just me in my mind again.

Disappointment washes over me. It was the first communicative exchange I've had for days and it wasn't even a real conversation. Just fragments, and strangest of all, it was all done in an old fashioned text exchange.

I wonder how that was even done. How could it be translated in my mind that way?

Wait a second—

I look over at Ammon, now resting peacefully in the other bed. Could I do the same thing with him? If I can do this with someone who isn't even in the same location, is it possible I could figure out a way to tap into it to communicate with Ammon? But does he have the necessary implants to even receive the exchange?

Then again, I've never been the one to initiate the exchange. It's always been... Something. What makes him so different? How can he access my mind in a way that I have absolutely no idea how to tap into?

My eLink was supposed to be destroyed when I left Adrian, but—what if it wasn't? What if in some way, it still works?

Snickering to myself, I shake my head. If I was using the eLink, Videus would have found us ages ago. The eLink was his system, his tool for monitoring everyone in the Helix. There'd be nothing to stop him from pinpointing our location. It can't be that. But what?

I push aside the blanket, feeling my feet hit the cold ground. The coolness radiates up from the soles of my feet, making me feel more alert. Stepping out of the bedroom, I walk down the hall and open the door leading to outside. Light streams into the hallway, bold and bright and no longer inhibited by the daylight dimming windows.

Taking a seat on the stairs just beyond the house's overhang, I dig my feet into the warm sand. The sensation extinguishes the chill from the floor inside, warming the rest of my body.

Who is this Something, anyway? Why does he keep finding me, of all people? Is he someone attached to Adrian? Is he confused because he's having a hard time connecting? Or is it something else? Someone else?

I've never got the impression that I should be afraid of him. Instead, he always feels sorta—safe. Maybe I'm just too trusting.

I close my eyes, feeling the heat of the sun though my closed lids. I can sense it, too—even though I can't see it directly.

What if that's what this is? A test in understanding or sensing something, even when its hard to get the full picture. Goodness knows, I've only been getting bits and pieces of what needs to be done, but I also know to trust the process. To trust that at some point, my path is going to be revealed here. It has to be.

It doesn't take hearing something to get information. I have a number of other senses I can rely on and I can't sit around ignoring them all. That's for sure.

With more ambition and enthusiasm than I've had recently, I stand up, looking at the house with brand new eyes. Maybe this could be like the scissors. Maybe there's more I'm missing, more I need to dig into. To understand.

Why is this house here? Who's would it have been? Is it really here, or is it an illusion?

I run my hand along the stone face, letting the rough edges cut into the palm of my hand. It feels real enough. I walk around the outer edge in a clockwise fashion, taking in every inch of the structure, seeking something—anything—that could give me a clue to what I've been missing.

Suddenly, something taps on my shoulder, making me jump. Spinning around, I come face to face with Ammon. He scratches his head, yawning. Then, with a shrug, he points back inside. It's a question.

"I'll be there in just a minute," I say, turning back to the stone facade. "Then we can start breakfast."

He nods, sleepily rubbing the top of his head.

There has to be some reason for being deaf. Some reason to be tested in this way. How could it help me in the long run? It doesn't seem to make any sense.

I continue walking around the outside of the house, looking for any sort of clue that could help me, but nothing is evident. Nothing I see screams *this is it*.

A shadow comes up behind me and I smile.

"You just can't wait, can you Ammon," I say, smiling as I turn around. "I said I'll be in in a minute."

I squelch a scream. This is definitely not Ammon.

11

RUNA

*T*HE MAN BEARS AN UNCANNY resemblance to Traeton, but much older; more worn. Words appear to be flying out of his mouth, but I can't make out a single one because he's also talking with his hands. My eyes don't know where to focus. Bewilderment is painted clearly across the man's face.

"I'm sorry, I can't hear you," I say, backing up a bit and pointing at my ears.

The man stops short, cocking his head to the side and narrowing his eyes. I don't know whether to run, or to wait to see what he does.

After a brief moment, he jabs a finger toward the house, then back toward himself.

Slowly and deliberately he points at me and then he mouths the words, "Should not be here."

Nodding, I back up a bit more, "I'm sorry, we didn't know. We found it vacant."

"We?" the man mouths, his forehead wrinkled with concern.

Coming up behind him, I catch a glimpse of Ammon. He's

only clad in the boys trousers he found in the bedroom closet and he sneaks up behind the man with a large wooden stick. I raise my hands to tell him to wait, but it's too late. With arms raised above his head, he swiftly brings the stick down on the back of the man's head.

I feel the reverberation of the sickening sort of pop as it makes contact. The man's eyes roll backward and he drops to his knees.

"You didn't have to do that," I tell Ammon, catching the man as he falls forward. "I think he was just surprised to find us in his house."

Ammon scrunched his face.

"Help me get him inside. Then I'll explain," I say groping for the man's arms.

Ammon's shoulders rise and fall, clearly disappointed that I didn't say thank you—or congratulate him on a job well done. But he could have seriously hurt the man, and he may have the answers I need to figure out how to get my hearing back. Despite being clearly irritated, Ammon helps me get hold of the man and drag him inside. We place him on the couch in the living room area and wait for him to regain consciousness.

Pacing back and forth, I can't help but notice how much he looks like Traeton. The resemblance is truly uncanny. The only difference is age and his hair is dark brown with hints of gray running through it. Could this be Trae's father?

I shake the idea off, knowing his father and sister never made it out of the Helix. At least, I think that's what happened. I drift back to the story Trae told me about when he left the Helix and ended up finding Fenton's group at the Lateral. His father and sister Ava never made it to the rest of the group and he thought they were dead.

But what if they aren't? What if—

I shake my head. It's only speculation at this point. And besides, it could be I'm so desperate to see Trae again, that I'm making up correlations to make myself feel better about leaving him behind.

Ammon sits on the arm of couch, his arms crossed over his chest, and his eyes following me as I walk back and forth.

"Does this guy look familiar to you, Ammon?" I finally ask.

I stop pacing long enough to see Ammon's answer. He takes a minute to look at the man, but shakes his head no.

He mouths, "Why?"

Sighing, I take a seat in the middle of the room, "Probably sounds dumb, but this man looks like someone I know. I think it could be his dad."

The bruises on Ammon's face have diminished a bit, and he purses his lips.

"Oh, don't make that face," I say.

Anytime I bring up my friends, particularly Traeton, Ammon gets a bit jealous. It's cute, but he needs to understand he's far too young to have a fixation with me.

Suddenly, the man starts to stir. His hands immediately raise to his head, as he rubs his temples with his palms. Then his eyes fly open, and he bolts upright. His eyes roll a bit, and he grips the cushions of the couch for support.

"Are you okay?" I ask, watching closely for his answer.

The man stares at his boots, taking slow deliberate breaths. Finally, he lifts his head, his eyes meeting mine. He rests them with me for a moment, taking me in before turning to look at Ammon.

He starts speaking with Ammon, but I can't understand a word. I stand up, trying to catch what's being said, but his head is turned to the side as he and the little boy discuss something very fast and heated. Ammon's hands fly up and down, the way I've seen apes do in my eLink history downloads. Every once in a while, Ammon will look my direction, but he turns back to the conversation.

"What's going on here?" I demand.

Neither of them stop talking or take time to try to fill me in.

"Stop!" I yell.

Both of them pause in mid-sentence, turning to look at me with quizzical expressions.

"Please, will someone fill me in on what's happening?" I ask.

The man throws a significant look to Ammon, then stands up and walks to the kitchen area. He opens a drawer and pulls out a piece of paper and a writing instrument from his chest pocket.

His hand flies across the paper, scribbling something down. Then he walks back to me, holding it out for me to take.

I grab the piece of paper, and try to read the scribblings. Reading isn't something that comes easy, particularly with his messy handwriting.

You can't stay here. Your friends are in danger the longer you're here. You need to get back to them. Now!

I look up from the paper. How does this man know anything about me or my friends?

He snatches the paper back and scribbles more.

You need to trust me. I don't know why you're here now, but you need to go back.

"If you know who I am, or my friends, then you know

being here is part of my trials. I'm supposed to be here. I don't have a choice."

The man shakes his head.

I snort. The audacity of this guy, thinking he knows more than I do. Worst of all, his words give rise to a panic twisting through my insides that wasn't there before.

"Are my friends—are they okay?" I ask.

I watch his response closely. He fidgets a bit, licking his lip in the same manner I've seen Trae do. After a moment, he nods.

"Then you need to be more specific," I announce. "I can't just leave this place without a good reason. "I need to know why they're in danger."

The man pulls the paper back again, scribbling furiously. He thrusts the paper back as soon as he's finished.

I can't tell you everything. It would affect too much. You have to trust I wouldn't lead you wrong.

I look up from the paper. He watches me closely, his eyes following my every movement.

I fiddle with the neckline on my NanoTech jacket and say, "How do I know you wouldn't lead me wrong. I don't even know you."

I crush up the paper into his hand and close it.

The man pulls his eyebrows in, biting down on his lip again.

What is it he's not saying? I can tell there's more, but he's just not willing to come out with it. Why?

Shaking his head, he stalks out of the room, making his way to the other bedroom with the large bed. He closes the door without even turning back. In a weird way, it reminds me of the way my mother would shut me out when I was in the Helix.

Anger bubbles up inside at the thought, and I walk down the hall and bang on the door until he opens it.

"You're Traeton's father, aren't you?" I blurt out.

The man's eyes widen, his eyebrows tugging in. A deep frown surfaces and he eventually shrugs.

"How do you know about me? Or about them? Have you been watching us?" I say. "Your son thinks you're dead."

The man starts speaking, but I still can't hear a word, frustrating me even further. This is absolutely absurd. I should be able to have this conversation. I should be able to understand what needs to be said, what needs to be heard. Instead, we're fumbling around with paper and hand gestures.

"Ugh—" I cry, raising my hands and walking away. "I can't hear a word you're saying. This is so ridiculous."

The man grabs my hand, spinning me around to face him. He pulls my face into his hands, making me stare directly into his eyes. For a moment, I consider kneeing him in the groin, but the longer I look, the more I see hidden in the depths of those brown eyes.

Those *familiar* brown eyes.

My mouth drops open, and he places my hand over his heart—a final confirmation.

This isn't Traeton's father. I don't know how or why, but this is *Trae*.

As soon as the realization hits, more information starts to rise in my mind. If this is Trae, how did he age? Was he captured?

"How?" I whisper.

Trae's eyes are sorrowful, but he leans in and kisses me briefly on the lips. Then, the cheek.

"You're not supposed to be here," he whispers in my ear, "you're out of time."

Blinking at him, I pull back.

"What did you say?"

He stiffens, then says, "Can you hear me now?"

"She can hear?" Ammon calls from down the hall. "Thank the stars. It's about time."

Lifting my hands to my ears, I shake my head as if it can't possibly be true. My wrist suddenly burns and I reach down to pull back my sleeve. Sure enough, the second petal lights up my wrist. I clutch at the spot, the mystical ink burning my skin.

"Yeah, I can hear you," I say. "You have to tell me—how did this happen? Who did this to you?"

I take Trae's hand and pull him back into the bedroom.

"Runa, you shouldn't be here. I don't know what's going on, but—you need to go back."

"Then you're coming with me. Look, we can go right now if you want—but we need—"

Trae shakes his head, "I can't go with you."

"Why not?" I ask, confused.

"Because I'm meant to be here. I have to stay here now," he says, his eyes glazing over as if he's gone elsewhere.

"Don't be ridiculous. We need to be together," I say, reaching for his hand.

"No, not anymore. Not like this," he says. "You'll understand."

"Help me understand now, because you're not making any sense," I say, tears welling up in my eyes.

Reaching up, he pulls a strand of my shorter hair forward, then lets it fall back into place.

"You cut your hair," he says, smiling.

I nod, "I thought it was something I was meant to do. A

part of my trials to get my hearing back. Turns out, I just wasted my time."

"It looks good on you," he says, "but it won't last."

"What do you mean?"

Traeton rubs the spot just under his lip, smiling, "I've said too much. If I say anything else, I could damage things further. You've never—"

"I've never?" I repeat.

"Nothing," he says shaking his head. "Look, you know me. You know I wouldn't lead you wrong, Runa. I was surprised to see you here, to say the least. But you need to go back. Things have to be set right."

Trae's eyes darken, and sadness emerges in their depths.

"That's what I'm trying to do. That's *all* I've been trying to do. These trials—I have to pass them before I'll be able to go back."

Traeton shakes his head.

"That's not true. If you don't leave—if you don't go back now, I think you'll be trapped."

"No, that can't be. You're not making any sense."

"The Tree is gone, Runa. Videus burned it to the ground," Trae says, sighing.

"Well, that's just—it shouldn't matter. The others, we've been—it's hard to explain, but I have help here. I think I'll be able to get back to the Haven. They can transport me—"

Again, Trae shakes his head.

"Runa, no one is helping you. They're all gone. You're the only one now who can—" he sighs, "it's just you."

I may have my hearing back, but things are no more clear than they were before. I feel like we're talking in circles and I have no idea what we're even discussing.

"Trae, can you please just tell me what you have to say. Why are you being so cryptic?" I say, taking his hand.

"Because if I say more, it may alter things beyond repair. I shouldn't even be talking to you now. You're not supposed to *be here.*"

"You've said that before. But I was transported here. I know I'm meant to be here. But come to think about it, maybe you're not?" I say, standing up and pacing in front of him.

"What's that supposed to mean?" he asks.

"Well, Ammon and I were brought here and for a week or more, you weren't here. Where have you been? Why are you in this place? Are you being held captive?"

"I'm not being held," he says, looking down at his feet.

"Then what is this place?"

"I live here, Runa," Trae says. "It's my home. I built it."

"What are you talking about? You live in the Haven with me, Kani, and Fenton," I make a face, and roll my eyes. "You can't possibly live here and there at the same time."

"You're right."

"I know I am," I say, glancing at him. His eyes have softened, but he looks at me expectantly.

"What?" I say, biting my lip.

He shakes his head, but continues to look at me with the same expression.

"Runa, I've been out hunting. When I do that, I'm gone for a week or more at a time. There isn't much to eat out this way anymore," he says, "I have to go further and further out.

"What's that supposed to mean?"

"Look, I can see you're the same stubborn woman as always. Come with me for a moment. It might help make more sense of things," he offers. Standing up, he takes my hand, dragging me toward the front door.

"Hey, where are you guys going?" Ammon asks.

145

"Wait here," I call back to him, "we won't be gone long. Right?" I say, turning to Trae.

He nods, but doesn't say anything.

"Suit yourself, but if the new guy kills ya, I'm outta here," Ammon snorts.

I roll my eyes, and close the door behind me.

Sunlight beats down on me, and I'm reminded of what it was like being left out on this side of the planet not long ago without food or water. I thought I was going to die.

We walk for a bit in silence, but I appreciate the sounds of our footsteps; the crunching of our boots. I listen intently to the sound of the wind as it whips the sand around our bodies. I pay attention to every minute detail I've missed for days.

"Where are you taking me, Traeton?" I ask.

"Not far. Just a couple of more minutes," he says, his eyes trained ahead of him.

"Why didn't you tell us who you were right away? Ammon wouldn't have—"

"Is that his name?" Trae says.

"Yes, Ammon," I say, giving him a sideways glance.

"Tell me about him," he says.

"Well, he's sorta been my companion these past few days. I found him in a cavern not long ago, shackled to the wall."

"Days?" he says. "Is that all it's been?"

"Yes, days. I know it must seem longer to you, considering…" I glance at him again. It's odd, but I've already gotten used to his older appearance.

"Why was he shackled?"

"Videus," I say, as if no more explanation is needed.

Traeton nods, "You know he's important, then."

"Yeah, I suppose he is," I say, biting down on my lip.

The fact of the matter is, I hadn't even given a second

thought to Ammon, or why he was being kept by Videus. I'd just been so grateful we'd escaped when we did.

"Trae, do you have any idea why Ammon was kept there? When you were researching on the mainframe the other day, did you—"

Trae snickers, but shakes his head.

"What's so funny?" I ask.

"Nothing, just that word again," he says.

"What word?"

"It's better if you just see for yourself," he says, continuing to walk.

"How far are we—"

We come around a large rock outcropping and I stand just meters away from what used to be the entrance to the Haven. Instead, it looks like a sunken crater with the Helix still weaving in and out in the background. The side of the Helix has a gaping hole in one section, as if something attacked it. Everything about the location is different. There's no snow, no dead trees, only sand and piles of rocks where my friends should be.

"How—how did this happen? How could I not have known?"

"Runa, you've been gone for thirty years. You walked into the Tree and we never saw you again," he says, turning to me.

Despair wells in his eyes, but he looks away.

"Traeton, I—I don't know what to say. I'm so confused. I've only been gone a few days, weeks at most. How could I possibly have been gone thirty years? I mean, look at me," I say, throwing my hands down.

"Believe me, I know how you look. It's what caught me so off guard when I first saw you. I thought I was hallucinating again," Trae says, shaking his head and rubbing a hand across the back of his neck.

"Again?"

"Runa, we don't have time to go over all that's happened throughout three decades. What we need to do is find a way for you to go back where you belong."

My eyes shift from him, to the mounds of rock, stone, earth, and sand.

I wave my hand out in front of me, "This *was* where I belonged."

"Which is why we need to find a way to get you back to *your* friends. *Your* time. You don't belong here," his eyes narrow, and he blinks rapidly. "We need you, back then. We need what the Daughter of Five was meant to be."

"And what's that, Trae? I don't even know what that moniker means yet."

"Runa, you're meant to heal the world," he breathes.

12

TRAETON

IRDS CHIRP OVERHEAD and I wake up with a start. My eyelids flip open and I sit up far too quickly. The moment I do, my insides roll and I lean over to empty the contents from my stomach onto the snow beside me.

My brain is fuzzy in texture and my thoughts are muddled.

How in the hell did I get here?

Where is here?

I wipe my mouth, and squint at my surroundings.

I'm outside, but for the life of me, I can't remember how I got here.

Pushing myself away from the mess beside me, I come up to my knees and take a deep breath. Something isn't right here... I don't feel well at all.

My brain is an empty slate as I try to access any recent memories, hunting for a reason I'd be lying flat in the snow. No matter how hard I try, it's as if the recent events have all been wiped from my mind.

Slowly, I stand up, taking my time to catch my balance.

My body is slow and sluggish, like it's been asleep for far too long, or I've taken some sleeping agent. Actually, this feels like being hungover from one of the Langcaster twin's special brews, but it's been years since the last time I escaped that way. Besides, Kani wouldn't let Fenton or I—

Familiarity of Kani's warnings tickles at the edges of my mind, but I can't quite place what it was about. It isn't about the perils of drinking, but something else. I tap my temple, hunting for the reason.

Think, think.

The repetitive tapping to my temple shifts something loose and the faintest glimmer of recognition slips in.

Headaches. I remember headaches…

I nod to myself, realizing what must have caused this. The NeuroWand.

Kani had been warning me of using it too much, and what the effects could be. The last time must have been one too many uses and now here I am without a clue. I hate when she's right.

Taking a few steps, I trudge though the snow, trying to regain my bearings on where I am. It doesn't take long, since I'm one of the few who've studied the topography of Pendomus. I know this particular place like the back of my hand.

"Why on Pendomus would I be stumbling all the way out here?" I muse. "There's nothing out here."

The fogginess starts to lift ever so slightly, but I still can't come up with a reason for being outside.

"I thought—I thought we were trying to get help," I mutter. "Or information?"

Blinking furiously, I hold my forehead trying to pull out the information I need.

"I'm done with that damn NeuroWand," I say. "This sucks."

A quick glimpse of putting it back into my pack at the Archives flashes through my mind and I realize I'm far from where I started.

"What the hell?"

I stumble a few more steps, looking around.

"I'm nowhere near the Archives."

How could I blank out this badly? Why would Kani let me go in such a poor state?

It's going to take me a good hour to walk back to the entrance of the Archives.

How long was I exposed out here?

I hate that there's never a definitive way to tell because of the sun's locked position.

Trudging along slowly, it takes me longer than expected to return to the entrance of the Archives. I need far more breaks than I would normally, but I know if I push it, I'll be sick again.

Lifting the heavy lid, I crawl down the ladder. My feet hit the ground with a muffled thud and I'm consumed by darkness as I walk into the chasm that has become the last few hours of my life. Most of the lights in the tunnel, for some reason, don't seem to want to light up.

When I reach the other end, I pull out the disk that opens the door and signal the wall to shift aside. A moment later, it shudders, sliding back and leaving a plume of dust in its wake.

Still raking my memories for a reason I was outside, I walk out into the open area of the Archives, but come up short. Everything is in complete disarray—the tables where I had been sitting are flipped on end. Artifacts are strewn about and toppled over. Broken shards and papers are scattered everywhere.

My eyes fly around the room, searching for any sign of

Kani. The only sound is my own labored breath and foot-steps. I squeeze my eyelids tight. I can't wrap my mind around what I'm seeing. There's a stillness to this space that makes my skin crawl.

"Kani— " I cry out, listening as the echo of my voice travels down the expansive series of rooms. "Where are you? Are you in here?"

Please tell me she's here, that she's okay.

I rake my hands through my hair, trying to think…to concentrate. But my mind is a whirling cyclone. I can't slow it down.

What can I do? Where should I—

Somewhere nearby, a muffled whimper permeates the stillness. Though barely audible, my head snaps up.

"Kani?" I repeat, stepping around the remains of a heavy book on Egypt, smattered across the floor. "Is that you? Are you okay?"

A contained sob erupts, but stops as quickly as it began. Fortunately, it's just enough to give me a direction, and I follow the sound with my eyes. Buried between a statue of a cat and an archaic light fixture, a large wooden crate is tipped on end—but it's big enough for a person to hide inside.

Racing forward, I stumble over some of the debris and land hard against the box. A scream erupts from inside, and I straighten myself, struggling to dislodge my elbow. I pull the light fixture away easily, but unfortunately the cat statue is way heavier than it looks and jammed up against the crate's lid. I pull with all my strength, trying unsuccessfully to remove it.

"Kani—is that you? I'm here. Hang tight, I'll get you outta there," I grope at the crate lid, but I have no chance of opening it without removing the cat.

Another whimper bubbles up, clearly from inside, and I take a firm hold around the cat statue's neck. Using my legs as leverage, I push off the box and manage to rock the statue. I try again, this time with as much effort as I can muster and it begins to topple. Following the momentum, I narrowly miss the statue landing on top of me as it crashes loudly against the stone floor.

The reverberation makes my ears ring and I lie motionless on the ground, unable to breathe. I roll onto my side, taking a few jagged breaths, and remove a smaller Egyptian artifact from my side.

I need to get to Kani.

Coughing, I push up to a stand and fling back the crate's lid. Inside, Kani is huddled at an awkward angle—face down —as if she'd been in the box and it had been thrown. Her hands are firmly planted over her ears, and she shakes uncontrollably.

"Kani—what *happened?* Are you okay? What happened here?" I say.

My eyes leave her, searching frantically around the room for any signs the intruder is still here.

She slinks away from me, but I help her to right herself anyway. Blood streams from a gash across her forehead and when she looks up at me, her eyes are hollow.

"Gone...Gone...Gone..." she mutters.

I reach in, pulling her out by the front of her jacket and forcing her to look at me, "Who's gone? Gone *where?*"

I look around the room again, hoping she means whatever did this.

"Gone...Gone...Gone..."

Her face is as pale as the snow outside and she presses her hands to her body in an attempt to get them to stop shaking.

Releasing her jacket, I pace in front of the wooden crate

where she stands. Without my support, she slowly sinks back down, resting inside. Muttering to herself, she pulls her knees in and begins to rock back and forth.

How could any of this happen? I had the damn disc in my pocket. How could anyone get in here and do something like this?

The blood drains from my face and I take a step back.

This is how I ended up outside.

Whatever did this must have attacked me first so I lost consciousness. I remember… I remember needing to rest. Damn, I would have been an easy target.

This is all my fault for not being on guard.

Had I been alert, working on finding the information we need, Kani would be fine. No, more than fine. *None* of this would have taken place. I would have been able to stop it.

We have all been warned about Videus and what he's capable of. I should have been more prepared than this. I should have—

"We need to go, Kani. Get up. Get *up*," I command, "Now—"

She cries at my insistence, covering her ears again and rocking harder. It's so out of character for her.

"We need to get back to the Lateral," I tell her, holding out my hand. "We need to find help."

Kani stares blankly at me, watching my every move. Eventually, she pushes up slowly to a stand and accepts my extended hand. I help her step out of the box and onto the floor. Her legs are wobbly and the lack of control she has is alarming.

This is not the Kani I know. She's always been a rock under pressure. Whatever caused this kind of reaction from her had to have been beyond frightening.

I shove my right shoulder under her left and wrap my

arm around her waist. Half walking, half dragging her along, we make our way to the exit. The debris on the floor makes our trek cumbersome and we each take turns slipping and sliding.

"Gone…Gone…" she continues to mumble over and over.

"I know, Kani. I know. We'll find help," I repeat, trying to reassure her.

At the entrance to the tunnel, Kani freezes, refusing to go any further. Her feet lock in place and she starts to skid backward.

"Kani, we're not safe here—" I look deeply into her eyes, pleading with her. "We need to go, we need to get to safety."

I'm not technically sure how safe we'll be heading back, but I do know we've gotta try. Waiting here to see if whatever did this wants to finish the job—not such a good idea.

Kani shakes her head, backing away and trying to get out of my arms.

"Kani, we need to get to *Landry*," I command.

At the sound of Landry's name, Kani's face twitches and she grabs my hand. Her jaw is resolute, but her eyes search my face filled with terror. Slowly, she takes a shaky step forward, allowing me to lead her down to the other end. Behind us, the sound of the stone wall closing echoes, making us both jump.

I turn back to Kani, but in the darkness, her expression is lost.

"Come on," I wrench on her arm and resume our walk. "It must have just sensed that we walked through. I have the disc in my pocket."

With each step further from the chaos, I start to feel agitated. How could all of this have happened and I had no idea. Why would they attack the Archives and Kani, but drag me outside in the middle of nowhere? Was it so I could die of exposure? To separate us? What would be the reason?

How do I reconcile any of this?

Will I be putting Landry in danger by involving him now? Guilt crashes over me, chipping away at my resolve. I have no one else to turn to for answers. Kani needs to be somewhere safe right now. Whatever happened to her, she needs to get back to being herself so she can help make sense out of what happened.

The further along we manage down the tunnel, the more control Kani regains over her legs, giving me much-needed relief. My stomach is still not well, and nausea continues to bubble to the surface. Most of the lights still aren't working properly, but luckily they still give enough light to see where we're going and how far we have left. Finally, we reach the end of the tunnel.

"Go first. I'm right behind you," I say to Kani.

Her eyes are wide, but she doesn't budge.

"It'll be okay. There's help up there. Trust me," I urge.

At this point, I need to make sure she doesn't fall down the ladder. She's not as aware of herself as she should be. Besides, if there's anything still down here, it will give her a fighting chance to get the hell outta here.

Kani swallows hard, but takes a trembling step upward. I climb right behind her, watching her movements closely. When she lifts the door open, the clean, fresh air wafts down to us, stirring my senses and helping to clear my mind.

She hesitates for a moment, but climbs out and disappears into the light above us. I lift myself out behind Kani, and flip the door closed. Kani promptly sits down in the snow, continuing her movements of rocking back and forth. Her arms clasp around her knees as she buries her face in between them.

Holy hell. I've never, not in all my life, seen Kani lose it like this. It's completely unnerving. Without her stability, well, if you can call it that—how in the hell am I going to make it through all this? I don't have Fenton's dumb humor, or Runa's gentle strength—

Coaxing Kani by the hand, I get her to finally stand back up and move onward. Our progress to the Lateral is excruciatingly slow. I have to half-walk her, half-drag her with me to get anywhere. I'm inches away from just picking up her scrawny little ass and carrying her—but this damn thumping in my head is threatening to come back and I better follow her advice to lay off the NeuroWand business. At least for a while.

Permanently, if possible.

A remnant of blood lingers in my mouth. I musta bit my tongue or something in my NeuroWand blackout.

"Kani, work with me, here. Dammit, woman," I curse. Kani's vacant eyes haunt me as she sits down plainly on her butt, staring at me. We're almost to the cavern system, but for now we're still exposed out here.

What in the hell happened in the Archives? What could have been so bad to do this to her? As far as I was aware, not many people even know about the Archives. It's a select few of us on Delaney's team. So the fact someone got in there at all—now, that's something.

If it was *someone*.

Because, there's that. I've seen some crazy stuff in the past few weeks. Stuff I couldn't have even dreamed up before meeting Runa. This could have been caused by any number of things.

Looking into Kani's vacant expression, I ask, "Kani, what did this to you? Was it Videus? Did you see him? The others—?"

My questions don't even faze her. She doesn't bat an eye or quirk an eyebrow. Instead, her face remains the same pale shade of green. Her eyes, vacant.

Sighing, I grab one of her arms to help her stand and then pick her up. We're getting nowhere fast and we need answers.

"WHAT DID YOU DO TO HER?" A small kid asks as I walk by, dragging Kani behind me. I've got no more strength after the hours of carrying her in some shape or form, and my head is ready to explode.

I practically growl, making the kid jump and scamper off. *Good.*

Finally standing at our destination—Alina's doorway—I pound on it and slump onto the steps with Kani. I hear beeps and weird mechanical noises, a loud scrape and stomping footsteps until the door flies open.

"I thought I said I was fine, Lane," Landry growls as he steps out, nearly tripping over my hand as he tries to miss stepping on it. "What are you doing down there, Trae? What's—what's wrong with Kani?"

Kani's expression hasn't changed. She looks like some little girl's doll; eyes unblinking, but wide open.

"I dunno. She—*we*—were attacked," I sputter through the thumping in my temple.

"Attacked? Again? Attacked by what? By who?" he asks, rushing forward snapping his fingers in front of Kani's face. "Kani, can you hear me? Kani?"

"Don't bother. She won't answer you. I've been trying for hours."

"She's in shock. We need to get her back to my house so I

can diagnose her properly," Landry says, heading back into Alina's for a moment.

"Oh, so *now* it's worth seeing us," I whisper under my breath, nodding to myself. "Just took some traumatization to make it happen."

"—Yes, I'll be fine. Come with if you want, but please, don't be on my case about this," Landry steps out, closing the door behind him.

No sooner does the door close, but reopens.

"I'm coming with you guys," Alina says, eyeing Landry. Her eyes widen when she looks around to see both myself and Kani on the steps. "Are you guys alright?"

"Been better," I say.

"Come here, Kani. Let's go to Landry's house," Alina says, helping Kani to stand.

Kani seems to relax into Alina's soft demeanor, allowing her to take her by the hand and walking her down the street.

Landry turns to me and says, "What the hell happened, Trae?"

I shake my head, "I honestly don't know."

"What do you mean?"

"Whatever happened, it happened while I was blacked out —or maybe drugged—I dunno. I woke up outside the Archives, flat on my back in the snow. I got back to an absolute disaster in the Archives and Kani trapped inside a crate. It was—mental. I've never seen anything like it."

"Did anyone else know you were heading to the Archives?" Landry asks, his eyebrows pulled in.

"Nah. Just you guys," I say.

"You blacked out you said. How did that happened?"

"Dunno, maybe the NeuroWand. Been having headaches lately—hell, I have one now— and Kani thought I was using

159

it too much. It's the only thing I can think of. Well, unless someone snuck in and did it somehow," I offer.

"Do you remember anyone coming in?" he asks.

"Not even a little bit. I've tried to get details out of Kani, but it's pretty useless right now," I say, "She's just too out of it."

"You can say that again," Landry concedes. "I know how she feels."

I turn to look at Landry, whose face has gone ashen.

"How are you handling things? You know we've been worried about you."

"Eh—" Landry shrugs, "been better."

Walking up the steps to Landry's place, he reaches for the handle, but pauses a little longer than expected. After a moment, he turns back and stares at me.

"Everything okay?" I ask, watching him closely.

"Look, I'll do what I can to help Kani. I owe you and her that much. But when she's better, I'm leaving. I can't stay here, not anymore. It's just not the same. I know you, of all people will understand that. But Alina—she can't know."

"Why? Why can't you just take her wherever—"

"—Because I can't. She deserves better than me. She deserves someone who's here for her," he says, scratching at the back of his bald head.

"Anything else?"

"Yeah, let's keep things low key. For everyone involved, but especially Kani. If I'm gonna help her, I need her to relax, not relive whatever went on."

"Yeah, okay," I say, shrugging.

"Excellent," Landry says, nodding to himself and opening the door.

I take a last quick glance up and down the street before heading inside.

13

RUNA

*H*EAL THE WORLD. Yes, because that doesn't sound daunting. I can't even figure out where I put the Caudex, how on Pendomus am I supposed to heal the *whole world?*

"Trae, I don't—" I begin, but he lifts a finger, hushing me.

"You don't need to understand the healing the world part, but after everything—after this—" he sweeps his hands out in front of the devastation, "I know without prophecies, or messages from higher than we are, or whatever, we needed you. You were the one that would have stopped this from happening. And now—" he shrugs, "now, after all these years —I believe you still can."

Sighing, I look down at my feet. I see now why it was necessary to bring me here. I wouldn't have believed I wasn't in my own time. I thought for sure it was him—somehow brought here by Videus, or changed by one of his minions, *something.* Not this.

How could I have? Everything has seemed too ordinary. Well, with the exception of being on the desert side—or where I thought was the desert side, I guess.

"This is all so…" I begin, and finally sigh, "strange. I had no idea we were out of our timeline. Or that it was even possible to be out of it for that matter."

"I wouldn't have believed it either, Runa. Not until—well, seeing you look—you're just as I remember you. With the exception of your hair," he says, reaching forward to tuck a strand behind my ear.

I smile, taking his hand in mine and pressing it to my cheek. Leaning into it, I close my eyes. How must he have felt all this time, thinking I was—

I open my eyes to watch his.

"Did you give up hope on me?" I ask, unable to help myself.

"It's been thirty years, Runa. I came to terms with never seeing you again long ago. It was—difficult. For the longest time, I thought I'd be able to save you. Find a way to bring you back without the Tree. I even hunted for your brother, oh what was his name? Baxter?"

"Baxten," I correct.

"Right, *Baxten*," he nods, "I found the Vassalage."

"You did? How? Where was—" I start.

He opens his mouth, but closes it again, narrowing his eyes.

"What? What is it?" I ask.

"I'm just not sure how much I should tell you. What difference it could make with the timelines. With your destiny," he says, blinking rapidly as he thinks.

"Traeton, from what you're telling me, my destiny has me locked here while Videus destroys everything I hold dear. I'm lucky you made it out alive—I don't even—" my voice cracks as I realize he's alone and I haven't even asked about anyone else. "I don't even know if anyone else made it. Kani? Fenton?"

Trae flinches at the sound of their names, and I know the worst has happened.

Dropping his hand I walk away.

How could this happen? How could *any* of this happen?

"Forget the timelines, the continuum, whatever destiny you think I have, or might have. I need to know where the heart of Videus resides. If I make it back to my timeline, I'm hitting him—hard. I'm not letting any of this happen. I promise you."

"It's not that simple, Runa. Not all of it—not everything happened at the same time. Or for the same reason."

I walk back to him, looking deeply into his sad, worn eyes. He looks tired; defeated even.

"What are you not telling me?" I ask, watching him closely.

"Let's focus on the one thing you may have control over," he says, sighing.

"No, let's start there. Then continue on with the rest," I say, raising an eyebrow.

After a moment, he narrows his eyes, but nods.

"So spill it, where do we find the Vassalage?"

Trae tilts his head nodding in the direction we came from, "Let's walk."

We continue in silence for a couple of minutes, getting outside of visual sight of the Helix and the devastation at the cavern before he finally speaks again.

"Do you remember your professional appointment?"

I pull in my eyebrows, and turn to him, "Of course I do. It was only a couple of months ago."

"Right, I keep forgetting," he says, running his fingertips over his wrinkled forehead, "Anyway, turns out your placement there held significance."

"How do you mean?"

"In my research, I found the Crematorium was actually the Vassalage, hidden in plain sight."

"The—what?"

My mouth drops open, my head spinning with the revelation.

Trae nods and continues, "The Cremators were the ones who were turned into Labots—at least, initially. The Crematorium was where they sent the "problematic" people who they deemed a security threat to the Helix. Then, those who couldn't be turned, would end up in the Vassalage. It started out only a couple of cells, meant to house those they were trying to rehabilitate and turn. But as the process grew, more and more people were kept there for—other reasons," he says, turning to me.

"What kind of other reasons?"

"Mostly to torture for information. To find out what they knew. Then, it was as a way to study those with different *abilities*, for lack of a better word," he says, his eyes falling to the ground.

"Are you saying there are people on Pendomus who can do things? Things that aren't normal?" I ask, holding my breath.

If that's the case, what does it mean? How do I play into it all? Am I not as special as I thought? Or does it mean something entirely different?

"There are lots of people on Pendomus who have low grade psychic ability. Like my sister Ava. She was one of them, turns out. They tortured her, trying to find out how she could do it. From a very young age—and under our noses. I had no idea," he says. "Videus wanted to learn how to control it. Master it with science, I suppose."

"Wow," I mutter, more to myself than Trae, "this is unreal."

"Exactly," he says, his eyebrows raised.

"What about my brother? Did you find Baxten?" I ask.

Trae's lips purse. "Yeah, I found him."

There's an odd silence that falls, as I wait for him to continue.

"Runa, pulling Baxten out was the beginning of the end for us. It set off a chain reaction that led Videus straight to us. It's the reason why he and his creatures attacked. The reason there's a crater where our home should be and why everyone—"

"I need to get back. I need to find the Caudex," I say, my footsteps picking up speed.

"What is this Caudex, anyway?" Trae asks, keeping up along side of me.

"It's all I have left of the Tree of Burden and it's my key to finding out what comes next; what I need to do. If I can just find it, or go back to where it was—maybe I can find something in there that will help me get back to my time-line," I say. "This can't be the way of things. I have to find a way to stop it."

"That's my girl. How can I help?" he asks.

"I have no idea. When Ammon and I were transported here, the book didn't make it with us. I'm not sure why."

"How did you get here? Was there a phrase or something you needed to say? Did you walk through another portal like the Tree?" he asks.

"Honestly, I'm not sure what caused the transportation. One moment we were sitting beside a tree, the next minute we were in your allayroom," I say, trying to think and run at the same time.

"Well, that's vague," Trae says, scratching his head.

I stop short, looking at him for a second. "What happened to your hair? Why didn't you keep the blue hair color?"

Trae's dark brown eyes widen, pain surfacing again in their depths.

"It just didn't—it wasn't me anymore," he offers with a shrug.

Nodding, I lean in, taking his face in my hands and staring directly into those sorrowful eyes.

"Trae, I promise you, I will do whatever it takes to make this right. There's nothing I won't do to make it happen. Whatever changed you, whatever made you lose yourself—I won't let it come to pass."

Stepping up on my toes, I let my lips linger just in front of his. Trae's body stiffens, as if he doesn't know what to do.

He may seem older—he may *be* older—but he's still Trae. *My* Trae.

I close the gap, kissing him deeply and letting our connection take over. Guiding his lips, he finally releases the tension in his shoulders and takes me in his arms. He presses me against his body, his lips crushing down on mine until mine tingle and my heart races. His kiss is fervent, passionate, and hungry. My mind blurs and my pulse purrs.

It's only been weeks since our last kiss for me, but for him—it's been so much longer. I can only imagine what that was like for him, not knowing if I'd ever return. Not knowing if I was alive.

After a long moment, he finally breaks the kiss, resting his forehead against mine. His breath is jagged, and his hands tremble on my neck.

"I've missed you so much," he whispers.

"That makes two of us. Thinking of our first kiss—it's what got me through some of the tougher days when I first went through the Tree," I say, sighing.

"So, how does it feel kissing an old man?" he chuckles.

"You're still you. That hasn't changed."

I grin, lifting my hand and letting my fingertip trace his left eyebrow.

"Not as much as you are," he says, a hint of a smile drawing across his lips and making his dimples shine.

"Well, not for long. I'm going to find my Caudex and get back to you. Do you hear me?"

"How are you going to get back? What about the trials you've been talking about? Don't you have to finish—" he says.

"Not at the expense of those I care about," I say, shaking my head.

Nothing—not even finishing the trials is worth the loss of my friends. I take his hand, leading us the rest of the way to the small cabin.

Opening the door, Ammon stands in front of the large table, a smile beaming from ear to ear.

"What's going on?" I ask, suddenly suspicious.

"Oh, nuthin'," he says, rocking back and forth on his heels.

It's the first time, his poor bruised face has been able to break into a full smile. He's finally starting to heal, but the swelling around his eyes seems to be the last to go back to normal.

I cock my head to the side, "It doesn't seem like nothing."

"Well, how much do you love me?" he asks.

I look at Traeton, who shrugs in return.

"Er—I don't know. Is this a trick question?" I ask laughing to myself.

Unable to hide his excitement, Ammon steps aside, revealing my Caudex resting on the table behind him.

"Unbelievable—Ammon, where was it? I was just telling Traeton that I was going to make it my mission to find the Caudex and get us out of here," I say, rushing to the little boy.

I scoop him up in my arms, giving him a great big hug and twirling him around in a circle.

He giggles, and as I release him, he says, "I didn't find it anywhere. Sometime after the two of you went off galavanting to wherever, I was sitting here wondering what I could do, and all of a sudden this bright light filled the room. Next thing I knew, the book was sitting on the table like it'd always been there."

"Well, this is fantastic," I say, sitting down and pulling the aquamarine stone out from under my NanoTech jacket and undershirt. I wave it in front of the Caudex, opening it up.

Trae walks up and stands behind me, peering over my shoulder.

"So this is the Caudex thing, huh? Looks pretty...old," he says, "and vacant."

I flip through the book, searching for any new passages that may have been added to the tome. Of course, it's as empty as it's always been.

"Tell me about it," I say, sighing.

"Is there anything in there that's gonna help you get back?" Trae asks.

"Nothing so far," I say, raking my hands through my hair.

I don't get it. Why bring the book to me, why have all this crypticness surrounding what I can and can't know? Why can't *I* determine when I'm ready for the next lot of information?

This is ridiculous.

"*Ugh—*" I say, slamming the book shut. "This is so frustrating. I need to find a way out of here, but this book never wants to give up its secrets."

"How so?" Trae asks.

"It seems like whenever I want information, it's never available. Then, when I'm about ready to give up, it will finally show up—just in the nick of time. I don't understand it. Why can't I just be given the access I need? Why can't I be the one to determine when I'm ready for new details?"

"Maybe it's not about you?" Trae suggests.

"What do you mean?"

"What if it's about the people around you, the lesson you're learning, or even the elements you're surrounded in?" he suggests.

"Like the kind of light I see the book in? Or—" I ask, eyeing the book.

"Maybe? Has there been any time where it consistently reveals more information?"

I think for a moment, "Not really."

"Well, there has to be something. Don't you think? What about the Tree itself? When did it reveal itself to you?"

"Not until I had my sight."

"Okay, and you're certain your sight is working—erm— the way it was before?" he asks, narrowing his eyes.

"Yes, I—I think so?"

Suddenly, I'm unsure. When was the last time I saw the orbs of light? Or anything that wasn't immediately obvious?

How on Pendomus did I not notice this sooner?

"Wait a minute—you might be on to something," I say, getting up to pace.

"I am?" Trae says, following me with his eyes.

"Yeah, he is?" Ammon repeats, scratching his head.

"We'll find out."

I reach down and reopen the book. I flip to the first page I find with writing on it.

"Can you read this?" I ask, pointing to the passage.

"In the age of the elders, the Acropolis served as the source of foundation for all of Pendomus—long before the invasion of dying Earth. The structure was the most beautiful in the world, truly a spectacular sight. Inhabitants of Pendomus..." Trae says.

"Okay, see what I mean? Anyone can read this. So what if —" I break off, my mind racing, "—what if my sight is missing and didn't even realize it? What if this is another trial?"

"What good's the other sight gonna do?" Ammon asks, craning around to look closer at the Caudex.

"Runa can see things we can't. Her blue eye can somehow make out stuff—magical stuff all around us. Stuff you and I would have no idea was even there," Trae says.

Ammon's eyes widen, and Trae's eyebrows pull in as he takes a step forward.

"Ammon, can you do that again?" he asks.

"Do what again?" Ammon says, backing away.

"You haven't done anything wrong. I just want to see something," Trae says, reaching out for him.

"Trae—what are you?" I begin, but Trae holds up a finger to wait.

"Where did you say you knew Ammon from again, Runa?" he asks, his voice curious and slightly amused.

"I found him bound in a cave on the desert side of Pendomus. Well, at least I think it was. Now, who knows. Why?"

"Ammon, can you widen your eyes again for me?" Trae asks.

I stand up, walking closer, trying to figure out what Trae's looking for, or what he's seeing.

Ammon shifts his gaze from Trae to me, and when I nod, he tries to widen his eyes as best he can. The swollen puffiness has gone down tremendously, but you can tell it's still difficult for him to do.

"What is it?" I ask, "What did you see?"

"Runa, look at the color of his eyes," Trae says.

Moving in closer, I take a look. Under the heavy lids of his swollen eyes, I distinctly see a color similar to my own—a deep, vibrant amber in both eyes.

Ammon watches me as I watch him.

"Whoa—I've never noticed before. You've got—hey, what's going on here?" Ammon says, reaching for my face.

"I know, I have two different colored eyes—" I begin.

"No, it's not that, I could kinda see you had two different colored eyes before. You're right eye, it's the same color as mine. No one ever has the same color, not even my mum from what my dad told me," he says. "I liked being different."

"My eyes were always this amber color. Well, before I was attacked. No one has ever had the same eye color as me, either," I say, turning to Trae. "What do you think this means?"

"I was hoping you were gonna be able to tell me," Trae says, scratching the back of his head.

"I honestly don't know what to think. Could Videus have been tracking us down because of the eye color?" I suggest.

"Could be? Is there anything special about it?" Trae says, shrugging.

"Not as far as I'm aware. It's just...different."

"Well, in Videus' eyes, that may have been just enough to hunt for. Remember the kinda guy he is. At least, I think he's a guy," Trae says, making a face. "He's after anyone who may threaten his creation. Or his way of life. If he thinks he's found a link of some sort, he'd go after it."

"True," I say, blinking furiously as I try to make sense of this new revelation. "Why would Ammon be beaten to the point where we couldn't see his eyes? Is that relevant? Or even important? Or was it just happenstance due to what Videus was doing?"

"I think it could be important. Then again, it could all be

one big coincidence," Trae says. "There are too many variables."

I make a face, and shake my head. "You of all people should know there aren't coincidences when it involves me."

"Well, I don't know about that. You and I meeting was a coincidence," he says.

"You're different," I say, getting up and walking away.

"Not really. The only difference was you were saving him," Trae points at Ammon, "and I was saving *you*."

"Yeah, but you were in an area you were typically in. You...you being where you were wasn't unusual. I was teleported—or something—to his location. Or close to it, anyway," I say, trying to reason out my thoughts.

"You weren't teleported right to me, though. You said you had to get a bit lost first," Ammon says, trying to be helpful.

Trae grins, shrugging slightly.

"Oh, don't be so smug," I say, sticking out my tongue and smirking.

"Not smug, just...happily validated."

"Okay, regardless, I think we should be wary of it. My instincts are telling me to be cautious. Videus doesn't seem to do things without a lot of thought. In some ways, he seems infinitely more advanced than we are. Like he's been preparing for centuries and we're just learning to crawl."

"I'll give you that," Trae says, nodding. "There's obviously been a lot going on behind the scenes. More than anyone was ever aware. Hell, until I met you, I thought the biggest problem we faced on Pendomus was not wanting to live in the Helix."

"Until I was attacked, that was my biggest problem, too," I say, beginning to pace.

"Nothing is ever easy around you, Runa."

"That's putting things mildly. Okay," I say, eyeing

Ammon's grinning face, "so going back to my sight. What if I'm in the middle of a trial and didn't have any idea? From the trends I've seen happening, they're going along my senses or integral parts of me. The things that make me, *me*. Or keep me alive. Thirst, hunger, hearing...I don't know. Maybe I'm reading too much into it?"

"Until you have reason to believe otherwise, your hunch sounds pretty accurate," Trae says.

I nod, but bite my lip.

"The only trouble is, if my supernatural sight isn't working, how do I get it to come back?"

14

TRAETON

I'VE NEVER SEEN KANI like this before. She's completely left the building and a blank slate appears to have taken residence in her head.

"Are you going to be able to get her back?" I ask, "This is getting creepy."

"Trae, she's in shock. She'll come out of it when and if she's ready. Not before," Landry says, rolling his eyes and lowering his eyebrows. "Since when did you get so impatient?"

"I'm not impatient. I'm just—I need to know what happened to her. To *us,*" I say, sinking back and taking a seat on the couch.

"And we'll get there," Landry says, his tone taking a deeply serious one I've only heard my father use when I was a kid.

I nod, keeping my distance from Landry as he tries for the third time to coax Kani out of a fetal position.

For whatever reason, seeing her this way puts me more on edge than I'd like. There's something seriously not right with it. I mean, even after she had to—well, after *Fenton*— she was okay. Not perfect, but okay. What could be worse than that? What in the hell happened down in the Archives?

"What was the last thing she said to you? Do you remember?" Landry asks for the second time.

"Landry, we've been over this and to be perfectly honest, who cares? She wasn't making any damn sense. And we need sense to be made."

"Fine. What about you? You said you were outside? How'd that happen? Did you sleep walk or something?" he asks.

"No idea," I shrug, then run my hand through my hair. "If I knew, things would probably be a bit simpler, don't you think? I don't even remember what I was doing right before —well, before blacking out."

"Whatever happened, it had to have been big. Either psychologically or physically. Maybe a bio-explosion? If I can figure out what it was, I can treat it more effectively."

"You mean like a bomb or something?" I ask.

"Sure," he says, nodding, "Could be anything."

"Well, it did kinda seem like a bomb went off—just not the standard kind. Sure, there was stuff all over the place, but no incendiary evidence."

"Could be a different kind of device, though. Could have been of biological origin or even one designed to only affect the humans in a room. Like an EMP for people's brains. You and Kani both have the eLink embedded. Could be something tied to that?" Landry mutters, shifting over to his holographic screens.

"Sure, I guess— But that's way your area of expertise. Besides, if it were an EMP, why would Kani be like this? Wouldn't she just be as confused as I am? Not completely mental?"

"Unless it malfunctioned," Landry says.

"Right. Didn't think of that. Ugh, I'm way outta my depth here."

I don't know how to put it into words, but there's something I feel like I'm forgetting—something important.

What in the hell was it?

"Okay, right. I'm gonna—" Landry taps the center of his forehead with his fingertip.

"You okay?" I ask.

Landry hasn't quite been himself since he met up with us. I can't put my finger on it; he's just—*off*. Not a ton, but enough. I take a step toward him, but he raises his hand.

"No, Trae," he shakes his head, "I don't know when I'll be okay. Shit sucks and I've been better—but I know you get that."

I nod. Nobody has gotten over what's happened to Fenton and I don't imagine it'll happen any time soon. Losing people, especially those who you care deeply about— it stays with you. But we need to find a way to make it mean something. If we don't, then what's any of it for?

"Trae, how about I make you something to eat? This could take a while and to be honest, it's probably best for Landry to work on Kani alone," Alina says, entering the main room from the allayroom.

For the first time in ages, I entertain the thought of food. I lurched up anything that had been in my stomach, so it's probably a wise idea. Food hasn't had the same appeal without Fenton. He was the one who could make a meal out of damn near anything and was always making sure no one went hungry.

I actually have no idea when I last ate.

"Yeah, that sounds nice, Alina. Thanks," I say, nodding.

Getting up, I follow her into the small kitchen area in Landry's home.

"What can I help with?" I ask.

Alina points to a chair at the table and smirks.

"No offense, Trae, but the last time you offered to help and I accepted, we ended up with burnt mushrooms and a hockey puck out of our meat. I'll handle this one alone."

She winks at me, and continues to take out the utensils, pots, pans, and ingredients she plans on using.

"Hey, I could at least hand you stuff. Right?" I say, chuckling.

"I doubt that's wise. You have a way of trying to interject yourself and it never turns out well," she laughs. "Remember that time when you and Fenton—"

Alina stops short, her fingertips brushing her lips as she holds onto her memory.

"It's okay, I don't mind you talking about him, you know," I say, my eyes flitting to my interwoven fingers on the table in front of me.

"It's not you I'm worried about," Alina says, her eyes flitting to Landry not more than a couple meters away.

Whether or not Landry heard Fenton's name, it's hard to tell. He continues to flit between working on coaxing Kani out of her catatonic state and his holographic screens. His eyes are squinted and his nose scrunched as he searches for something in the jumbled mess on the screen.

Something niggles at the back of my mind every time I think about what happened, and how I woke up. I feel like there's more I should be able to recall, or something I need to remember. Well, clearly, there should be. But as hard as I try, the feeling slips further and further out of my reach. It's like there's something on the tip of my tongue and I can't spit it out. I hate it.

"What's going on with him?" I ask in a hush, and nodding toward Landry, "I mean, don't get me wrong, I know

Fenton's loss hit him hard. It's hit us all hard. But is he okay —or will he be?"

Alina's eyes flit to Landry, then back to me.

"Trae, it looks like we're missing some of the ingredients we need. Wanna come to my place and help me grab them?" Alina says, her voice raised slightly. "At least that's something you can help with."

She laughs, a small, forced chuckle.

I take the hint, and nod, "Sure. Whatever you need."

Alina drops the spatula in her hand onto the table and walks over to Landry, placing a hand on his back, and leaning in to speak quietly in his ear.

"Okay. Be careful and come right back, both of you. Alright?" Landry says, concern filtering though his eyes. "We don't know what did this. Or if they can do it again."

"Of course, we'll be right back," she nods.

"Good, good," he says, nodding to himself and turning back to Kani.

Alina tilts her head to the door and I follow behind her.

"See ya in a minute, Landry. Good luck with Kani," I say, tipping my head in acknowledgment.

"Sure," he says, continuing to take Kani's pulse.

"Bye Kani. We're getting stuff for supper, but we'll be right back," I say, trying to include her—make her feel like she's still got some stake in coming back to us. "You won't wanna miss it. Alina's cooking, so you know it'll be good."

I turn and walk out the door, a few steps behind Alina. Her shoulder length brown hair sways back and forth as she walks, reminding me almost of Kani.

"Hold up," I call out.

Alina pauses, allowing me time to catch up, but only barely.

"Thanks," I mutter as I reach her.

She nods her head, but doesn't say anything.

"So, I assume you wanted to talk to me out of earshot?" I say, as we continue back to her house.

"How'd you guess?" she says, raising an eyebrow and smirking, "Astute. That's what I'd call you."

"So, let's have it. Is he okay?" I reiterate my question from earlier.

Alina sighs, but keeps walking, "I honestly don't know, Trae. I've never seen him so—ugh—it's hard to explain."

"Try," I urge.

"Volatile. Unpredictable," she says, biting her lip, "He's kept it together pretty well for the past few minutes. I've been impressed, actually. It's almost like he's come back to us. But honestly, I don't know how much longer he'll be able to keep it up. Maybe having something to do—Kani—I don't know, maybe it keeps his mind off of things."

"How do you mean? He seems pretty stable to me."

Alina shoots me a sideways glance and shakes her head.

"He's showing you the face he wants you to see right now. But he's not okay. Not even remotely. Sometimes, he's so —*angry*. I've never seen him like this before. It scares me."

"Has he tried to hurt you?" I say, concern rising.

"No—god, no. But I think he could hurt someone else. Sometimes I worry about him trying to hurt himself," she says.

"He wouldn't—surely?"

"Trae, there have been times where I had absolutely no doubt," she says, her expression dark. "I've been mentally preparing myself for weeks."

We reach the front to her house, and she opens the door wide, allowing me to head inside. The main room is pitch black, all of the windows are covered, and when we enter, the auto-lights are already preset to dimmed.

"Is it always so dark in here?" I ask, stepping inside and taking a closer look around.

"Yeah, he doesn't usually like the bright lights. I'm surprised he hasn't shut them all off at his place. Something about the light has started giving him migraines."

I spin around, "Migraines?"

"Debilitating ones. He's been out for days with the last round. They're not good."

I lick my bottom lip, wondering if Landry's migraines could be tied in any way to mine. Could there be a correlation? It never occurred to me someone else could be getting headaches. What could be causing them?

"How long have the migraines been affecting him?" I ask.

"Since shortly after," Alina says, stuffing some food into a bag to bring back with us.

"Do you think that's been causing the disregulated moods?"

"Maybe. All I know is he hasn't been the same. There's something rising in him—something I don't like. Which is why I've been trying to stay with him. I guess it's a protective thing. Even though—"

She stops, and sighs.

"Even though?" I ask, trying to prod her to continue.

"Even though we're not together," she finishes, raising her eyes to mine.

My eyebrows rise, and say, "Oh—I thought you'd been able to work through—"

"No. We're just friends, Trae. We can't be anything more than that. Not after—" she turns away, shaking her head and stuffing more into the bag. "I'm saying way too much. It's just been so hard these past couple weeks. I don't have anyone I can talk to."

"What happened between the two of you? No one knows.

It's like this great big mystery to everyone, including Fenton. We figured something intense musta happened since no one wants to talk about it," I say, trying to continue our dialogue to understand things better.

"The only reason no one knows is because it's hard to talk about. Landry and I—we were—well, I was—" she begins, scratching her head.

"Oh," I mutter, recognition dawning, "you were pregnant."

Alina bites her lip again, tears threaten to emerge as she turns away.

"Yeah," she whispers, "but it didn't work out. We, uh, lost him before we had the chance to tell anyone. I was nearly five months. Just about to show, so we knew we'd be telling everyone soon."

"We would have supported you both. You could have trusted us," I say, walking toward her.

"We know we could have, but when I found out, well—we wanted the news to be just ours for a bit. Our little gorgeous secret. Then when we lost him—well, it was devastating. We'd hoped to try again. To have another chance. Somehow, it didn't work out that way, either. We couldn't get over what had happened. Landry couldn't get past it; he felt like it was all his fault. We tried for a number of months afterward, but we never—well, obviously."

"Alina, I hope you know we're here for you. Is there anything I can do?" I ask, raking my fingertips through my hair. It's such an odd revelation. Landry as a dad? Fenton was almost an uncle?

Runa would be so much better at this than I am. What do you say to something like this? How do you help your friends cope?

The sudden pangs that arise from the automatic thought about Runa, makes me realize how easily this type of thing can debilitate you. My stomach plummets and guilt arises because I'm not doing what I should be to help her, either. Runa and I—we haven't even come close to this kinda relationship, to babies. Hell, I don't even think Runa knows how babies really happen. But I'd hoped, for a moment or two, to be able to one day have a future that could open up the possibility with her. She's awoken a place in my heart I didn't even know existed. A life I'd never considered possible.

"There's nothing, Trae. It's been a year since we ended things. We're as healed as we're going to be for now. The worst is over between us."

"Well, if you need anything, you let me know, okay?" I say, grabbing the bag Alina has packed full of foods and spices she wants to bring back to Landry's.

"Of course I will, Trae. Thank you for your friendship and loyalty. It means a lot to both of us," she says, trying to smile. "Are you ready to head back?"

"Sure," I say.

There's more I was hoping to ask—about Landry and the way he's been acting. The migraines. But somehow, I feel like the moment has passed. I don't want to keep inundating Alina with more questions after such an exposed confession.

I open the door leading out to the cobbled street, and Alina nods.

"Thanks," she says, stepping out in front.

I follow along with her in silence, my thoughts straying back to Runa. About what she means to me. Wondering where she is—what she's doing. If she's okay. If I'll ever see her again. There's gotta be more I can do to help her.

I swear, we were at the Archives for that reason—

As if on queue, my head starts to gently throb and I can tell the headaches that have burdened me are starting to return. Interestingly enough, it's been a while since I had the last one. In fact, not since before the blackout.

I rub my temple.

"You're not getting the headaches, too? Are you?" Alina says, stopping in mid-stride.

I blink back, unsure of what to say. Instead, I opt out of saying anything and instead, simply nod.

"What's going on with these lately?" Alina says, shaking her head. Her eyes take on a distant quality, but her jaw tightens.

"I don't know what it is. Probably just stress," I shrug.

"Yeah, maybe," she agrees, "but you should mention it to Landry. He may find it interesting enough to look into why it's happening to the both of you."

"I'll let him focus on Kani for now. I don't want to inundate him. My headaches are manageable and by no means migraine quality. They're just…annoying."

Alina nods, "Don't wait too long to talk to him."

"I won't. Just wanna wait for the right time," I say.

"Okay," she says. "I know we might not get much out of Kani, but were you guys able to find what you were looking for in the Archives? You know, before all the weirdness happened?"

I lick my bottom lip, trying to think. What *were* we looking for at the Archives again?

"I'm gonna take it that perplexed look means no?" she laughs.

"Actually," I start, but stop to take a moment to rummage through my mind. For the life of me I can't recall what we were doing there. I know it was important, though.

"Actually?" Alina repeats.

"I—I can't remember why we were there," I mutter,

tapping the side of my head as if it will make a damn bit of difference.

Alina chuckles, but stops when she sees my expression.

"Oh—you're serious."

"Yeah, I am," I say. "How in the hell could that be? I mean, did something happen to me, too? Why would I not remember why we were there?"

"Maybe whatever attacked Kani also attacked you?" Alina suggests, "Like that EMP idea I heard Landry suggest... But maybe with you, it wasn't as traumatic?"

"Yeah, I guess," I say, unsure.

I suppose it's as good of a guess as any.

"We need to get back to Landry. If he's having trouble getting information out of Kani, maybe he should start with me," I offer, picking up speed as we near Landry's house.

Alina nods, jaunting out in front and opening the door before I can reach the doorway. She's always been a quick one. Opening the door, she stops just inside the entry.

"Landry, we're back—"

Alina's voice stops dead in her tracks and as I enter the main space of Landry's home I see why.

"Hi guys, where ya been?" Kani says, waving from the kitchen. "I'm starving."

15

RUNA

I CAN'T JUST SIT HERE waiting for my sight to come back. There has to be an answer to this riddle. Something in plain sight, so to speak. Everything else has almost come easy. Perhaps *too easy.*

"I've been thinking," Ammon says.

Both Trae and I turn to face him. He sits crosslegged in the middle of the main room, his back turned to us as he faces out toward the windows.

"What if—" he stands up, his head cocked to the side, "what if your sight isn't working because you're out of whack. Like, physically something is up with you?"

"Like what?" I ask.

"Like a cold? Or a virus? Maybe you've been implanted with something? Or maybe all the transporting, or teleporting stuff messed around with you," Ammon offers.

"Or maybe, there's not a real use for it out here?" Trae suggests.

I sit with all of these musings for a moment, thinking about what I'd do if I were putting someone through a trial of readiness. Would I take away their sight arbitrarily? I honestly don't think so.

"You may be on to something, Ammon," I say, thinking things through.

"I am?" Ammon smiles, "I mean, of course I am. What was I onto?"

"You said something about the teleporting or transporting messing with it. What if that's only part of the answer? We already know we're not in our own timeline. What if I don't have my sight because I'm not meant to be here at this time? What if it won't return until I'm back in my own timeline?"

As soon as I say the words, something inside me resonates with the message. My instincts are telling me I'm on to something, I just need to keep unraveling the ball of thread.

"When was the last time you remember seeing with your special vision?" Trae asks.

"You know, truthfully, the last time I know without a doubt was when we were transported out of the cavern where Ammon was held. A TerraDweller helped us to escape."

"Are you sure?" Trae says.

"No, I'm not sure of anything any more. But Ammon said he couldn't see it—so, that's something. Right Ammon?"

Ammon nods, then scrunches his face.

"Then again, I can't overly see much."

"Well, regardless of whether it's the timeline, or the next trial, we need to figure out what needs to be done to get you back where you belong. We can start there. Should be easy enough, right?" Trae laughs.

The impossible task, in truth.

"Yeah, totally easy," I laugh. "Any chance you have a time machine in this room?"

"Nope, nothing like that here. I can dye my hair back to blue, but that's as close to a time machine as you're gonna get outta me."

We both laugh for a moment, but something catches my imagination. I pause, my eyebrows tugging in.

"You can dye your hair? I would have thought the process is—well, old. I guess."

"It is," Trae chuckles. "Then again, so am I. Wanna try it?"

For a moment, I take in Traeton's expression. It's strange, but I've already forgotten he's not my Trae. Not the man I'm in love with, not the man I know. He's older; wiser now.

His expression hardens, but he takes my hand gently and walks me to the allayroom.

"Will you help me?" he asks. "It's been years since I've done this."

"Of course. But I think you should know, I've never done this before," I say, unsure of what to expect.

"That's okay. I'll walk you through it."

Trae reaches across the counter, taking hold of the vial of blue liquid I noticed the first day I was here. I bite my lip and my spirits lift.

Of course, it was there all along—I just didn't know what it was. In fact, I wouldn't have had any idea it was for Trae at the time, though.

"What are you smiling at?" Traeton asks, his dark eyebrows pulling in, but a hint of his dimples emerge.

"Nothing—no, that's not true. I just think we're on to something," I say, taking the vial from him and turning it over in my palm.

"And why's that? Do you think the powers that be have

always wanted me blue-haired?" he laughs, watching me intensely.

"Maybe," I say, "or maybe it has more to do with setting things right and this is the first step."

Trae takes a moment to consider.

"Who am I to argue with that?" he finally says.

Trae steps around me, reaching for the door handle to the allayroom. A set of eyes appear around the door frame, just as Trae goes to close it.

"We'll be out in a few minutes, Ammon," Trae says as the door latches shut.

"Doing something top secret in there?" Ammon says from the other side of the metal door.

"Something like that," Trae says, smirking at me. This time, his dimples cut deep.

I shake my head, but something in his broad smile makes my heart skip a beat.

In a swift movement, he tugs at the back of his shirt and it lands in a crumpled heap on the floor. His bare chest is still muscular, and strong—reminding me of just days ago when a younger version of him was standing naked beside me. I shiver at the thought, brushing the memory away because I don't know what to do with the feelings it arouses. It wasn't really Trae—and that means this man wouldn't have any recollection.

"Why are you blushing?" Trae asks, stepping closer.

"I—I am?" I say, trying to sound calm and collected. My hand automatically raises to my cheek, as if I could feel for redness.

"Yeah, you kinda are," he says from inches away.

"Well, you are standing in front of me without a shirt," I say, pointing to his bare chest.

"It would be difficult to dye my hair with a shirt on. Wouldn't want to turn it blue," he grins.

I back up slightly, his proximity makes me light-headed.

"That makes—perfect sense," I nod.

"I thought it might," he laughs. "I'm nothing if not reasonable. Well, unless I'm not."

I clutch the vial in my hand tighter, but look up into his dark, mysterious eyes. There's so many years of secrets hiding in their depths now. They've seen so much more than the Trae of my time. Part of me wants to stay here, learn all that he's witnessed; hear his stories.

"Well, it's a combination of that, and honestly, I like the way your innocence makes you blush. It's been a long time since I've gotten to see it," he grins. "There's so much I miss. So much I wished I woulda—Well, I'm sure you can imagine."

I blink rapidly, trying to center myself and understand what he's trying to say without actually saying it. I suppose I do understand, in a sense. There's a lot I'd wish I'd told him too and I'm sure there'd be even more if I hadn't gotten the chance to see him again.

"So, how do we—ah—How can I help you with this process?" I ask, trying to bring us back to where we were headed.

"It's easy really. For someone else to do, anyway. I'll need you to use this device," he says reaching into a drawer, and pulling out what looks like a small handheld phaser, but flatter. On the side of the silver device is an opening about the size of the small blue vial I hold.

Trae reaches his hand out, taking the little vial and slotting into the side. The device lights up, turning a bright blue, and making a low, barely audible humming sound.

"What do I do?" I ask, taking the device from him.

"As simple as it sounds, you just point and shoot. The device registers the difference between the hair on my head and the tiny hairs on a human body. It dyes the ones on your head by reading the variance in size of the hair and current pigmentation. So don't worry about getting it on anything else. I was kidding before about it getting on my shirt. It is however, damned hard to get the backside of your own head."

"How will I know if it's working?" I ask.

"You'll know. It takes effect immediately," Trae says, watching my every move.

I nod.

"Seems simple enough. Are you ready?" I ask.

"As I'll ever be, I suppose. Part of me's wanted to do this for a while, that's why the vial was lying around in the first place. The other part of me, I guess, always felt like it was a bit of lie trying to be the man I was before—" his eyes meet mine, and his brows tug downward. "You know what I mean?"

"I think so, yeah."

"Alright," he nods, "so where do you want me?"

"Wherever's easiest. Can you bring in a chair?" I ask, looking around for the best location to have him sit.

"It honestly doesn't take long. No point in getting a chair involved. I'll just kneel."

Dropping down in front of me, Trae kneels on the floor facing me. He looks up expectantly.

Taking a deep breath, I walk over to him and tip his chin upward with the crook of my left pointer finger, then pull the trigger of the device. Instantly, the dark brown hair with flecks of gray begins to turn the bright color blue I've associated as Traeton Revasco. It doesn't color anything beyond the hair on the top of his head, just as he said. I fluff up different sections of his locks, with my fingertips, and Trae closes his eyes, grinning to himself.

"Your hands feel nice," he whispers.

A smile creeps across my lips as well, and somewhere in the middle of my chest, my heart swells. If this man, so many years in the future can still find it in himself to feel this way about me—I know how the one in my timeline feels about me. I need to get home to him. I can't let this alternate version of reality exist where Trae ends up alone and without those he really cares about.

I walk around Trae, dying his hair until every strand looks the way I remember it. When I'm satisfied, I place my hand on his shoulder and smile.

"You're all done," I whisper.

Trae's dark brown eyes widen, and his dimples emerge deeper with the years of experience now carved on his face.

"Thank you, Runa. How do I look?" he asks.

I grin.

"You look like you."

"Well, I'd be concerned if I looked like someone else," he laughs.

Standing up, Trae brushes off his knees and takes the device. The blue light glows dimly on the side, but as he takes the vial out, it goes completely dormant again.

"Trae, do you have any other colors for this?" I ask, watching as he throws the vial into the trash incinerator.

"What do you mean?"

"Do you have any other vials. Any other colors?"

Surprise filters into his face, and he shrugs, "I—I don't think so. The last time anyone dyed their hair it was ages ago when Kani was still here. I could check?"

He begins to open drawers, rummaging inside to look for

another vial. After a moment, he pulls out a purple vial, and holds it up for me.

"Looks like she left one behind. It's not green, but then again, she really liked that color. I can't say I've ever seen Kani have purple streaks," he says.

"Perfect," I say, taking the purple vial. "So the room with the two beds, it was for Kani and Fenton?" I ask.

Trae flinches imperceptibly.

"Trae?" I ask, concern creeping into my voice.

"Kani was here, but—"

A realization begins to dawn and for some reason it makes me feel sick. I should have guessed he wasn't alone all these years. He would have had to find companionship somehow.

"So you and Kani were a thing, then? When did she break up with Fenton?"

Trae's eyes widen and he shakes his head, his hands fly up in front of his body, "Oh, no—no, no, no. It wasn't anything like that. Kani was here, for a while. She didn't want to be on her own. Fenton, though...he didn't..." his eyes take on a distant quality as he searches for words.

"Why wouldn't he come out here, too?" I ask, trying to understand.

"Fenton didn't come because he was dead, Runa," Trae says, clearing his throat.

My body feels like it's sinking, or stuck in thick viscous mud.

"How? When? How?" I repeat.

Trae scratches at the top of his newly blue head.

"There's something you should know about when you left through the tree... Fenton, well, Videus—he took Kani hostage just after you entered the portal. We—there was no other way..." Trae's sentences are fragmented. I can tell it's hard for him to get everything out.

"That long?" I say. It's not really a question, it's a statement.

It happened just after I left.

Trae nods.

"We weren't able to recover Fenton from Videus' control. Kani—she had to—" Trae says, shrugging.

"I see. I—Traeton, I'm so sorry," I say, stepping forward and taking him into my arms.

"It's not your fault, Runa."

"Of course it is. You wouldn't have ever been there if it wasn't for me. Videus would never have used Fenton, if it wasn't for me," I say, burying my face in his chest. "I never should have involved you."

"Everyone did what they wanted to do out of their own volition. No one made us help you. The one to blame for Fenton's death is Videus. He's the one who took free will out of the equation, forcing Fenton to do things he would never do," he says, tipping my chin up and forcing me to look into his eyes.

I hear what he's saying, I do. But a part of me feels like I should have known. Or I should have been able to prevent it somehow. There was no need for any of this to happen.

How dare Videus do this? How dare he take someone like Fenton from us? As if taking my brother wasn't enough? Destroying people's lives in the Helix—

"Videus is going to pay, I promise you, Trae. This will not go unpunished."

"Runa, it was a very long time ago. And there isn't much left of anyone now. You saw the Lateral; the Haven. Every-one's gone. It's not just Fenton. What would you do, avenge them all?"

"Trae, I'm in the future somehow with you. I'm not even in my own timeline. There *has* to be something I can do. I won't accept anything less," I say through gritted teeth.

"Just don't put yourself into more danger than you're already in," he says squeezing me tighter.

"I'd like to say I could keep that promise, but you and I both know who we're dealing with. I need to get back to my timeline, find out more about the prophecy, and put an end to Videus once and for all. That's the whole point of being the Daughter of Five, right? Setting things right?"

"I sure as hell hope so," he says.

"So do I," I say, clutching the little purple vial in my hand. It burns in my palm, and even though I don't have the sight to tell me this vial was meant for me, I can feel it.

"Trae, I'd like you to do me a favor—" I begin.

16

RUNA

I TAKE ONE LAST LOOK in the mirror, satisfied with my new appearance. Not only is my hair much shorter now, but the bottom half of what used to be a white-blonde is now a deep, beautiful purple. In a sense, I can see why Kani never used it. The color is so deep, adding it to her already black hair would have gotten lost. Besides, the bright neon green suited her personality so much better.

"What do you think?" Trae asks, throwing the used vial away.

"I love it," I say, nodding. "It's different, but good different."

Trae stands behind me and places his hands on my shoulders. For a moment, he doesn't say a word, just watches me through the mirror. The feeling is oddly ominous as I look into his worn, aged expression. His eyes are slightly sad, but they have a hint of amused sparkle to them.

"Guys, are you ever gonna come out of there?" Ammon says, pounding on the door.

Torn from my relatively small bubble with Trae, I smile. I'd almost forgotten Ammon was with us. In a weird sort of way, it was as if I was a part of the future with Trae now. A small piece of me wishes I could stay, but then, I'd have lost so much and this expression on Trae's face would remain a part of his reality. If I can change it, I will. He deserves so much more.

"Yes, we're coming out now," I say.

"Good, because your book's getting a little crazy out here," he says in a higher pitch than normal.

I throw a concerned glance at Trae as we both reach for the door. When we enter the hallway, Ammon jumps up and down, pointing toward the table where we last left the Caudex.

"Has it ever done this before?" he asks, excitedly, then does a double take at my hair. "Nice color, by the way. Both of you."

Trae nods, and I reach for my hair, instinctively.

"Yeah, it was sorta last minute, I guess."

Ammon's eyes shift from me to Trae again in an oddly suspicious manner. There are some instances where I swear, he's sizing Traeton up.

Turning to the Caudex, it glows brightly, telling me there's new information I need to be aware of. Does this mean I'll be able to see it?

I turn to look at Trae, who nods at me to carry on.

Reaching for the little crystal on the end of my necklace, I wave it in front of the book, making the locks disengage.

I give one last once over around the room, take a deep breath, and open the book.

Quickly, Trae places his hand over mine and slams the cover shut.

"Trae?" I say, surprised as I look up at him.

"Before you read this, I need to tell you something," he says, suddenly serious.

"You can tell me after— " I begin.

"No, I can't. This is important and I..." his eyes go distant, and he licks his upper lip before continuing. "We never know when things will change. If the book whisks you away from me the way it brought you here, I have to know I said my piece. Do you understand?"

I nod, unable to blink my wide eyes.

He breathes a sigh of relief and nods, "I need you to tell me, I mean the other me, to figure out what's going on with my headaches. This needs to be done *before* any of you move forward with the Vassalage."

"Sure, I can do that. But...I don't understand. Why are you telling me this now?"

"I don't know. I got an intense feeling in the pit of my stomach and I knew you needed to know," Trae says, shrugging.

"What's so important about these headaches you're talking about?" I ask.

"They, uh...they cause a lot of problems moving forward. I can't elaborate on it because it could really mess with things. All I can say is you'll need to figure out why on your own. Don't involve anyone else," he says.

I laugh. "You can't be serious? I don't know anything about headaches or neurology."

"Runa, it's critical or I wouldn't tell you. Trust no one. Not even Landry," he says, his eyes burning into mine. "Promise me."

"Okay, I promise," I whisper.

"Good. That's good," Trae says, nodding. "One last thing."

"Anything," I whisper.

"Keep a close eye on me," he says.

"I'll— "

Suddenly, the Caudex sears a bright, crystalline white and

the pages burst open, unable to be held back any longer. The light takes over every ounce of my vision. I can't see anything, or anyone else beyond the brightness of it. Oddly enough, though, it feels like home—as if this light is something I've always been a part of.

For a moment, there are no questions floating around in my head, no wondering about what's happening, where I'm going, or how I'm going to get back. I don't even think about Trae or Ammon, or even regard myself.

Slowly, however, all of the thoughts begin to pull back into my awareness and my vision begins to take in more of my surroundings. Just as he'd suspected, I'm no longer in Trae's cabin on the edge of what used to be the frozen tundra—but instead, I'm standing inside the Tree of Burden. Only, this time, the Tree is a frozen, crystalline mass and beside me, is Ammon. On the floor by my feet is the Caudex.

I claw at my wrist as the fourth petal is seared into my skin, leaving only one petal remaining.

"Was that your tattoo?" Ammon asks.

I nod, rubbing at my wrist.

"Yeah, looks like I passed my third test. Whatever that was about."

"Where are we now?" Ammon asks, trying to hide an edge of terror in his tone.

"From what I can tell, we're inside the Tree of Burden," I say, reaching out to touch the frozen water.

"We're in the whaaa?"

Ammon makes a face and I realize I haven't given him some of my backstory. When I have time, I'll have to fill him in.

"It's an important part of who I am," I say, picking the Caudex up from the floor.

"Okay, but why are we in here. And how do we get back out?" he asks, knocking on the tree.

From this vantage point, the Tree no longer looks like a tree, but rather a clear, crystalline, circular fortress. Looking up, I can see the whole sky through its branches and deep into the earth through its roots. When I look to the trees beyond, it's almost as if we're inside Tethys' shield, as everything is magnified and pushed outward.

I think back, trying to retrace my memories to see if I know how we'd get out—and where we'd even be in our timelines. Trae from the future told me the Tree had been destroyed, burned down by Videus and the Salamanders. However, when Tethys had put me in the Tree—it had been hollow and full of water. So narrowing down the timeframe by what Tracton had told me, about it filling with ice and spitting us out...

"I think we're nearly back to our own timeline, Ammon," I say, glee bubbling up inside me. We're so close, now. I'm not far from Traeton and my friends.

"How on Pendomus do you know that?" he asks, giving me a funny look.

"Because this Tree has a history, and a specific timeline," I say.

"Great for it. How do we get *out?*" he reiterates.

I clutch the Caudex to my side, but instinctively know the Tree will let us out. In a weird way, it's an extension of me. Walking to where the doorway was when I entered the Tree the very first time, I step right through the ice as if it wasn't even there. Ammon, immediately follows, swiping at his hair and looking around wildly.

"That was the strangest thing I've ever done. It didn't even get my hair wet, or anything," he says, his eyes open wide with wonder.

He walks back the way he came and runs into the wall of ice.

"What the?" he says, rubbing his nose.

"One way door, I guess," I laugh.

"Swell," he says, sticking out his tongue.

Beside us, a familiar snort makes me abruptly turn to my left. Once again, my sight has returned as I take in the beautiful spectacle that is Tethys. I've missed her so much. Her invisible, iridescent body shimmers in the light in so many colors I can't even label—all distinctly her own. Magnificent in every way.

"What was that sound? Did you hear it?" Ammon asks, his eyes wildly searching for something he can't see.

I reach out, resting my hand on Tethys' head, as she takes a step closer and leans into my touch. Every fiber of her being is thrilled beyond measure that we've returned. She's waited only a short period of time for my revival through the Tree—and that's what she calls it, *a revival*.

What an odd word to use.

"I need more details, Tethys. *When* are we?" I ask out loud, still resting my hand on her head.

Moments after, is the only answer I receive.

"Moments after what?" I question. "Moments after I left?"

"Uh—who are you talking to?" Ammon asks, eyeing my hand, that to him must look like it's resting in mid-air.

Tethys guides me through her mind, allowing me to see the events of recent past for her, and suddenly it all makes sense. She means sometime after her attempt at opening my sight—and sometime after Trae ran off to bring me to the Haven. Beyond that, the timing is anyone's best guess because she couldn't go with me underground.

I'm not exactly in our timeline, but much closer than I was before.

"Thank you, dear friend. Hopefully this means there's still time," I mutter, running through so many different options in my mind.

I could save Fenton, protect the Lateral. I could even save Baxten before he was taken by the Salamanders, if the timing holds true.

I try to prioritize where I'm needed most.

"Ah, Runa—" Ammon says, tapping my shoulder.

"Hang on, Ammon, I'm trying to think about our next move."

"Yeah, but Runa—you might wanna see this," he says, continuing to tap my shoulder.

I turn to face him and he extends his right arm out as he points to a descending darkness in the distance.

"We need to go, Ammon. Now " I exclaim, grabbing hold of his extended arm and pulling him toward Tethys.

Still too far away for Ammon to truly get a good look, but I'd know that movement of darkness anywhere. The herd of Salamanders are coming our way fast. Their bodies darken the snow, making it undulate in strange ways as they move close, burning away the snow as they race forward.

I crawl up on to Tethys' back, and turn to reach for Ammon. His amber eyes widen further, sparkling more than I've ever seen them before. It's almost like looking into a mirror of a younger version of myself—had I been born a boy, anyway.

"What are you doing?" he asks, pulling his hand back.

"Ammon, you have to trust me. We don't have time for an explanation right now," I say, holding my hand out for him.

"But—"

"Now, Ammon. Trust me, what's coming from out there is far worse than taking my hand."

Ammon takes one last look at the incoming Salamanders

and takes my offering. I lift him up quickly so he rests in front of me. I place his hands on Tethys' neck and he tightens his grip into her fur, despite not being able to see it. I wrap one of my arms around him.

Instantly, Tethys' shield goes up, protecting us from the onslaught as best she can. The ground around us shakes, as she pulls in as much moisture from the snow on the ground and in the air. Then, she shoots forward, taking us away from the incoming darkness.

"What is this thing?" Ammon says. "Is it like an invisible rocket or something?"

It must be strange staring at his hands, clearly holding onto something, resting on its back, but unable to see anything.

"Ammon, this is Tethys. She's my guardian," I say, hoping the two short sentences are enough of an explanation because we're about to come into trouble.

"It's a she—" he begins, "—*where* is she?"

I open my mouth to answer, but one of the Salamanders slinks up nearby, closing in on us far more quickly than anticipated. Tethys thrusts us forward through her connection to the snow, trying to put distance between us and the Salamander. We veer away from the Tree of Burden and off into the vast woods around us.

The Salamanders continue to advance in a strange semicircle, herding us closer to the Helix. Ironically, the path leads us right on top of the Lateral and Safe Haven. A pack of them breaks off, running over the top of what is the cavern system, if they only knew. Blue electricity sparks between their toes and arcs back and forth between each of them as they spread out in front of us.

Tethys grunts, as she shifts to the right. Her energy wants to draw them away from the cavern system as quickly as possible, not confront them right on top of it. Unfortunately, the Salamanders have other things in mind. The other half swings around, trying to box us in and take a stand.

Tethys maneuvers away, gliding between a handful of them just as one of their electricity nets goes up.

"What in the—what are those things now?" Ammon says, his voice nearly a screech.

"They're trouble," I say, trying to focus on Tethys' intentions and helping to guide her with my own.

"They look like—I don't even know what they look like. Well, other than creep-tastic."

"You're not kidding," I mutter, still focusing on our surroundings.

Far off in the horizon, coming from way of the Helix is a dark cloud   most likely the juncos. This isn't good.

~We need to leave, Tethys. This is going to get worse and the others are in the cavern system below the Salamanders. If we're not careful, their energy could set off a—

My thoughts get interrupted as recognition takes over.

We've done this before. This is what was happening when the Haven experienced the local seismic activity. Fenton could never place where it was coming from, or why it had happened.

Now I know why.

~Tethys, we have to draw them away. Fast. The other me—and my friends will be emerging soon. The Salamanders are already causing seismic activity in the cavern below.

Understanding exactly what I mean, Tethys heads straight toward an opening to the far right of the clearing. It's tiny, but it could give us enough of an opportunity to draw the Salamanders away from the Haven's entrance.

"Ah—why are we heading straight towards that big group of scary black things? They don't look like they're friendly,

Runa," Ammon says, gripping Tethys' fur tighter and closing his eyes.

"Hang on Ammon, I can explain everything once we're outta this mess."

Tethys picks up speed, drawing as much moisture from the snow as she can to fuel our escape. Half of the added energy extends to her shield, the other half to thrusting us as quickly as we can through the fray. The maneuver seems to have had the effect we were hoping for, as the Salamanders on top of the Haven take pursuit.

It's good timing, too. In the distance, I barely catch a glimpse of Trae, Fenton, Kani—and a different version of myself run out of the cavern entrance that leads to the Haven.

I can't tell from this angle if we're far enough out of my line of vision, but we must be, because I don't recall ever seeing the Salamanders until one captures—

No, no, no—Baxten!

"Tethys, we have to turn around. We need to go back for my brother," I exclaim.

He's priority number one, now that I know where in time I am.

"Your brother? Since when is your brother here?" Ammon asks, twisting around to see.

"He's not here, but I know where he is. And he's about to be—*attacked.*"

Ammon makes a face, "How do you—? Oh, right."

He nods, understanding I've been here before and know where we are in our own timeline.

Tethys, however, ignores my pleas. Instead, she makes it clear I'm not to meddle in the workings of the past. Even if that's where I may currently be stuck.

Shaking my head, I tear at her fur. What good is being

here if we can't change some of what went wrong in the first place?

"Are you kidding me? We have to go back for Baxten. He's in trouble," I say, trying to force her with my thoughts—get into her mind the way I had with Fenton at the Tree.

Instead, she practically chuckles, and continues to lead the Salamanders away from my friends and the Haven.

A small group of Salamanders edges nearer, slinking in and out of the snow, but barely touching it. A small gray bird with a white beak has joined them, flying along side.

~Tethys, be careful. Caelum is here.

Taking a quick direction change to the left, Tethys pulls further away from the assailants as she continues to put distance between us and the past version of me and the others. Our direction change led us directly into a large group of Salamanders as they creep out of the trees, blocking the way in front of us. Tethys gears up, deciding which direction to take next, but her momentary pause is enough time for the vultures to swoop in from the trees, beginning their attack against her shield. I know from experience, she can't take much of this.

Their talons scrape against the bubble that keeps us safe, causing the edges to crackle and buckle.

"Whoa, what in the—?" Ammon screams, ducking his head and as he tries to cover his eyes. "What are those things? Why is everything attacking?"

"They're a part of Videus' army. If they get inside Tethys' shield, we'll have to fight them off on our own."

"Well, that's super. How do we do that? I'm lucky to have clothes, let alone something to fend off crazed birds and monster-sized reptiles," he says, breathlessly.

"Your guess is as good as mine. Let's hope it doesn't come to that. I don't feel any closer to being able to protect

Pendomus—or anyone else—than I was before," I say, realizing the mark I've been given hasn't translated to much of anything.

A surge of despair bubbles up at my utter lack of advancement.

"Wasn't that the point of those trial thingies?" Ammon says, ducking again as another vulture swoops in, right in front of his face.

"I'm not finished," I mutter. "So it looks like we have to fend for ourselves."

17

RUNA

$\mathcal{I}$F SOMETHING DOESN'T CHANGE QUICKLY, this could be the reason I never make it back to help my friends. The reason Trae was out in the middle of nowhere and the Lateral was decimated.

I can't let that happen.

I have to do something. I can't sit here while everything is destroyed. Giving up the reigns of control to Tethys, I close my eyes to center myself.

All the sounds around me, the birds, the jagged breath of Tethys, the frightened inhalations of Ammon—it flitters away like snowflakes in the wind. For a moment, everything is completely silent. Then, a string of energy explodes from my chest, painting the air in pink light behind my closed eyelids. The string flows from myself, to the nearest Salamander, then the next, as it splits itself in every direction and touching each and every dark body. The energy enters the Salamanders, calming the electrical storms and fills their own energy with calm.

I focus on the feeling the string resonates—*love*. Why

love, I don't really know. But love is all I feel, I'm consumed by it. And so are they.

The Salamanders begin to back off. Some in the front drop, as if bowing their heads in reverence.

"What the—?" Ammon begins.

Once connected, I feel each and every Salamander's inner essence as if they're an extension of myself. They don't really want to be here. They don't want to be attacking—but they must if I let go of my embrace. It's out of their control. Without needing to ask, they give way, granting safe passage to us. The vultures and juncos circle, clearly disrupted in their attack plan and left confused by their cohorts.

My heart widens, and I understand something I never really grasped before. The Salamanders aren't evil. The birds probably aren't either, but they were made that way. They're made to fight. To be the minions of a madman.

Once there's enough space between us and the Salamanders, Tethys bolts forward. She moves so swiftly I can't feel any exertion from her. Ammon and I hang on tight as she glides along the snow, acting as one with her element.

The route is up to her as trees blur by and scenery shifts. Holding on just a little longer, I try to use my connection with the Salamanders to send a message.

Please, don't hurt Baxten. Don't hurt Baxten. Please.

The message is broadcast through the pink energy stream and into each of them. There's no doubt they received the plea, but now it's up to them if they can hold onto the message once I let go.

I try to search their minds, to find the one who will be nearing him soon. Glimpses of snow flash through my mind, pieces of clothing, people nearby. Through the support of the other Salamanders, I narrow in on the one with the mission.

In his mind, only one thing is on repeat. As if he's not allowed to think anything else.

Take him. Take him. Take him.

Trying to enter his mind is like trying to pick an incredibly difficult lock. Without proximity, my energy thread isn't able to connect to him the way I'd like, even though I can still feel him.

Releasing my energy string to the rest of the Salamanders, I focus solely on him. I can sense he's getting closer to Baxten and I need to act fast. I push the pink cord from my chest, forcing it to find him and disrupt his orders.

The Salamander falters for a moment, temporarily overcome by the sensations of connection and love. He remembers his mission, but can't remember why it's necessary. As if on automatic, he continues toward Baxten. Through his own eyes, I see him slinking nearby, trying not to be seen.

~Let him be. He's no harm to you.

The Salamander isn't interested in harm. Not to himself or to Baxten. Yet, he struggles against his programming and my intentions. Despite our connection, he wraps himself around Baxten's feet. I'm not strong enough to stop him. My connection with him is weak, as my energy slips, depleting.

I feel light-headed, but force myself to focus. There has to be a way. I'm so close. I reach out again, but flames burst from the Salamander's feet, consuming them both. In the distance, I can hear screaming—my own screams from before.

My energy and connection to the Salamander fails, and I'm falling... falling. Then, suddenly back in my body, limp and consumed.

"Are you okay?" Ammon asks, turning around.

My eyelids droop and my limbs feel so heavy.

I've failed. I was so close to saving Baxten and I've failed.

SOMETHING DOESN'T FEEL RIGHT. My insides are twisting and turning, like they've been chewed up and spat back together. Whatever I did, whatever power I drew on, it's potent and isn't easily controlled.

"Are you okay, Runa? What happened?" Ammon asks, his eyes filled with worry.

"I was trying to— " I sigh. What do I say? "I was trying to do too much at once, I think."

"Well, whatever you did, at least it helped bust us out of that tight spot," he says. "Do we have a plan now? What to do next?"

My mind is fuzzy; the texture of chalk that's soaked too long in water.

"I'm—I'm not sure yet."

Tethys offers her suggestion, letting me know she believes we should lay low. Rebuild our strength for another time.

Baxten. He's still taken.

I shake my head.

~No, Tethys. We have to get to Baxten. I need to find out what my friends know.

It becomes painfully obvious that I can't connect to them now. Not in this timeline. I need to find a way to gather the information I need, without them realizing I'm here. Who knows what kind of cataclysmic event I could cause, or disruption to the timeline they're on.

Tethys tries to sway me against going to the Helix, but a part of her knows I won't let this go. Even if I have to go alone, I'm going to get him back.

Tethys huffs, giving in. She knows I have to try.

She turns, using the snow to glide us on our new trek. After a few moments, I realize we're veering too far off to the western horizon. The Helix is more east than this.

Where is she going?

Tethys is serious, and quiet. Her mission is driving her, even if I'm not sure of the route.

The area is remote, the trees giving way to a large, open field of blowing snow. In the distance, huge rocky outcroppings become apparent. It's beautiful, as the low sunlight filters through the purplish sky. Random, natural birds fly across the sky in their oblivious voyage to wherever they're going.

Suddenly, the ground appears to be coming to an abrupt end in front of us. My pulse picks up as much speed as Tethys does.

What is she doing?

Gravity takes a moment to catch up with us as Tethys launches the three of us into the air, shooting straight off the ledge. Suspended inside her shield and barely latching on to her body, my muscles tense, bracing for the impact. Ammon screams, ducking his head down as we drop. I dig my ankles in to her sides and squeeze, hoping not to lose contact as we hit the bottom.

I can't take my eyes off the way the sunlight streams from behind me as it hits the tops of the snowy mountains in the horizon. The sky has pulled in a brilliant spectrum of orange to deep blue and mixes of purples. I'm mesmerized by the absolute stillness and serenity of the moment. Right now, right here, it feels like time stands still. But it only lasts for that moment.

The explosion of ice and snow slams my body against hers and Ammon, but miraculously, we maintain our position on her back. The impact opens a gigantic crater in the ground, and we slip quickly into the black abyss of running water deep below. Tethys' shield keeps us safe, bound by her protection, despite the suffocatingly close quarters.

My eyes take far too long to adjust to the extreme difference in light and dark as we dive deeper into the water. The sun's rays penetrate in strange pockets of light, illuminating a part of Pendomus I'd never even known existed. And so close to where I lived my whole life. After a few moments of gliding along to gather her strength, Tethys takes off like a rocket as she connects fully to the water around us. Just like on the snow, the water reacts to her, propelling us forward as much as her will is.

Perhaps more.

Everything is different here, magical. As if *time* has frozen instead of the water. Stone pillars and enormous outcroppings surround us, but so far, no other signs of life. As we move deeper, carved in the outcroppings, a large hand appears to be bidding us forward. A second later, we pass a monolithic face hidden in the depths. My body is barely the size of one of the enormous stone eyeballs staring blankly back as us. Mesmerized, I notice an everblossom carved in the pupil and glowing faintly.

From somewhere to our left, the sounds of singing filters to my ears. Softly at first, but rising until the voice becomes distinctly human and tremendously loud. Tethys doesn't seem bothered as she weaves in and out of the outcroppings with ease.

"Do you hear that?" I ask Ammon.

"Hear—hear what?" he says, trembling. For the first time, I realize his eyes are still shut and he's practically crouched in a ball.

"Everything's okay now, Ammon. We're safe," I say, trying to reassure him.

"If it's the same to you, I'm going to just keep my eyes closed from here on out. Let me know when we're back on solid ground."

I place a hand on his back, rubbing a small circle between his shoulder blades. The tension he's holding releases a little bit.

Tethys glides through the water, not even slowing down when she has to dodge things my human eyes can't make out. She has a sight I simply don't have.

~*Where are we going, Tethys? I need to go to the Helix—to the Vassalage. Why are we underwater? Shouldn't we be—*

Without warning, four of the rock outcroppings move of their own accord, boxing us inside an underwater cage of rock. Tethys slams against the containment, a surprised squeal emanating from her.

She wasn't expecting this. So much for being safe.

Tethys fights against the containment, and worry replaces all of our previous efforts to calm down. Her shield isn't very big and there are two of us consuming the remaining oxygen inside. It won't be long until it runs out. She may be able to filter the oxygen from the water for us, but if the stones remove the water—

Or worse, squash us in...

I shudder.

"Runa, what's going on?" Ammon asks, his eyes still shut.

"Hang on, Ammon—just hang on," I mutter, searching for a way to help. Something I can do. But what can I manage from here and inside her shield?

I can't go out and try to use brute force on the stones. There's nothing to mentally connect with like the Salamanders.

Time is running out as the rocks edge closer and closer.

Tethys pulls the remaining swells of water to her, trying to force her way through the stone, but to no avail. It continues to advance on us, mechanically and without remorse.

My brain feels frozen.

What can I do? I can't come all this way only to be squashed.

How can this even be happening?

Frenzied thoughts race through my mind as I grasp for answers—searching for a way out.

"What's going on?" Ammon repeats, his voice an octave higher. His eyes are open wide now and his mouth is gaped open. "I thought we were safe," he squeals.

"I did, too," I say, my voice quivering.

Ammon covers his head, his arms reaching up and around his ears.

"Nothing is safe with you," he says, trembling.

Tethys is trapped, no longer able to move between the four pillars as they squeeze tighter. Her shield is threatening to burst, and Ammon begins to rock back and forth like a small child. He mutters to himself with his arms still covering his head as if he's protecting himself from a blow.

Tethys howls, and every hair on my body stands on end.

This time, there's no where to go. No one to help. I don't have any power over any of this. I'm just a human. A girl with no way of helping in this ridiculous situation.

I bury my face in Ammon's back, hugging him close around the waist.

"I'm so sorry, Ammon," I whisper to him, "so, so sorry."

Throwing down his arms, as if he's had enough of everything, Ammon screams. It's a deep, animalistic snarl. All around us, the rock shatters into millions of pieces—bursting like an exploding star as it sets a galaxy into motion. Water comes rushing back in at us, thrusting us from side to side as Tethys equalizes in the commotion.

I close my mouth, and try to speak. Only to find it drop open again without a sound. This wasn't me—it was *him*. Tiny little Ammon. The little boy who I've had by my side. Who's been abused and hurt. The one who never once thought I was strange for having abilities or training to be this — Daughter of Five. All along, he's had his own set of powers.

"How did you *do* that?" I ask, bewildered and amazed.

Ammon releases a long, slow breath.

"I don't...really know," he says. "It sorta just—happened. I've always been able to manipulate rocks. But just little ones. Nothing like this. I just couldn't let us get squashed," Ammon's voice trails off.

I'd wager everything this is why Videus wanted him. He has abilities beyond the norm. The cavern was an experiment —testing to see what he could do, or how far he could be pushed before he snapped and used his power to try to escape.

I lean back a bit, letting the realization sink in. All the possibilities of what Videus could manage if he could manip-ulate stone and rock. Ammon would be the perfect weapon.

A weapon against—the Lateral or the Haven. Against the rest of humanity.

Against me.

The memory of the crater left behind from the Lateral in the future flashes in the back of my mind. I never realized how important Ammon really was. I figured he was just someone else Videus was toying with... I should have known it was bigger than I guessed.

I need to keep Ammon safe—

Tethys begins to move forward again, slowly pushing through the debris field and onward to our destination. The pit of my stomach starts to swell, making me feel as if I'm doing something terribly wrong.

Maybe heading to the Helix now isn't the answer. It isn't safe for *Ammon.*

Tethys maneuvers us through more tunnels of water and darkness, then picks up speed. We enter a larger underwater cavern and light shines through the rock above us. It streams through what looks like cracks in the ceiling, but with more geometry and patterns than should be. As I look up, the ceiling is supported by what appears to be five spokes shooting outward from the center of a main hub. It almost looks like a spider web.

Tethys slows down, then hovers in one location. The water around us begins to boil, surrounding us and her shield. It gives her more power as she catapults us straight up.

I grab onto Ammon, who buries his face into Tethys' invisible back. Once again, I brace for impact as we head toward the streaming light and rock up above. Breaking through the levels of stone, we come to a halt in the middle of an empty street.

As the debris settles, I get a good look around.

We're in the middle of the Lateral.

It only takes a moment to realize that I know this street. I know this house. I've been here before, but it feels like it's been so long...

We're right outside Landry's door.

As much as I wish I could run inside, trepidation begins to fill my body. As amazing as this is, we can't stay. I can't explain it—but being here isn't safe for anyone. My eyes rest on Landry's door. I wish I could go inside—maybe my friends are here. Then again, maybe the *other me is.*

As the reverberations from our blast settle, people pop their heads out windows and doors. Their expressions of shock and bewilderment transform into concern and upset as they take in the mess of the street.

Feeling terribly exposed, I stay put on Tethys' back, staying hidden behind her shield.

~Tethys, I know you meant well, but we can't stay here. We'd be putting everyone in danger. We have to go. We need to go from here, now.

For once, she heeds my warning. Just as she drops back into the depths below, the door to Landry's swings open.

I capture the slightest glimpse of Traeton—*my Traeton*— as we sink back into oblivion. Ammon's hands raise toward the light, squeezing his fingertips into a small fist. The gaping hole left by our arrival vanishes as quickly as it was made, cutting off the light as we descend. All evidence we were there, quickly extinguishes.

"That was easier than I thought," Ammon says. "I don't know why, but it's like I've passed my own trial. Or maybe I'm just getting the hang of it now."

I consider his words for a moment—his own trial. It certainly feels that way. It's awoken me to a new realization of the gravity of Videus' plans. This extends much further than just being the behind the scenes string puller. What does this mean? Are there more like him? Like *us*?

Now that I'm aware of Ammon's abilities, no where feels safe enough.

Where in the world are we supposed to go now?

My mind races through a million ideas as it scenario-builds.

What if there are many of us who can do things with our

minds? Or have special powers? How then, does that make me any different from them? I'm just another person who can fall in line. There has to be more to all of this.

~Tethys, take us to the Archives. We need to get there before the other version of me does. I need some answers.

*G*AINING ENTRY TO THE ARCHIVES was surprisingly easy. Tethys knew precisely where to go, as if she's been here a thousand times. We leave her standing guard, our invisible lookout. With Ammon's special powers, we didn't need the key to open the door. It slid along easily with the wave of his hand.

"Ammon, I have to know—have you always been able to do this?" I ask, unable to contain myself.

He makes a face.

"Not exactly. It's been getting stronger the older I get," he says. "And obviously, today."

"How did you know? When did it first happen?"

My questions come flooding out, and I'm unsure how to stop myself. I need to know everything if I'm going to figure this out. It's like pulling a string in the middle of a tangled mess to find out where it leads.

"The first time it happened was a couple of years ago. I was playing with my Dad..." Ammon eyes drop to the ground and his lips turn downward. "Anyway, we were playing with a ball at the Lateral, but it hit some rocks above his head. They were about to crash down on him and I covered my face because I couldn't watch him get hurt. Only, the rocks never hit the ground."

"What do you mean?" I asked.

"When I realized there wasn't a crash, I looked up. My Dad's face turned upward and—well, above him, all the rocks were floating in mid-air. Only—" Ammon sighs, swallowing hard.

"Only what?" I prod.

"Only, when I stopped to look at them, it must have broken my concentration. I was too surprised about the whole thing. Plus, I didn't know it was me. At least, not really. I suppose a part of me did," he says, his eyes distant.

Tears well up, and he bites his lower lip.

"Oh, Ammon—" I whisper, taking him into my arms, "I'm so sorry."

"I didn't know," he says, trying to restrain a sob, "Had I just learned sooner. Or realized it was me… I mean, he was safe. For a moment, he was safe. He could easily have walked away before I dropped the rocks. But we were both just too shocked, I guess. I've never tried to use it. Well, until today. I was too mad about it. Like it was a curse or something."

"Is that why you didn't tell me about it?"

He nods, and says, "It's why I wasn't scared of what you can do. I knew we weren't all that different."

"We aren't," I say, messing up his hair. "In all the commotion, I didn't get the chance to thank you. What you did was incredibly brave. I wish I had the ability to move stone."

"How do you know you don't?" Ammon asks, raising his eyes to mine.

"I guess I don't, but everything I've been able to do so far is more mental. At least, that's how it feels when I connect to it," I say, thinking back. There have been a few times when it felt like there was more I could do, hidden under the surface. But it has never really transpired into much.

"Well, we make a good team then," Ammon says, trying to smile.

"We sure do," I say, nodding. "C'mon, we need to see if we can get more details about us. I need to know if there are more children like us who have powers. If so, where are they?"

"Who's Baxten?" Ammon asks as we head to the small mainframe Fenton and Trae used—or will use soon, considering.

"He's my brother, the one I was talking about before. He was taken by the Salamanders and I have to get him back."

"Hey, at least now we have a mission. Well, beyond just getting weird tattoos that glow."

"Very true," I say, sitting down in front of the mainframe.

"Wow—I've never seen one of these so old," Ammon laughs, leaning in. "How long has this been sitting here?"

"I honestly have no idea. It could be centuries. My friends said it's left over stuff from the colonization," I say, placing the Caudex beside me as I take a seat.

Ammon's amber eyes widen.

I turn to the holographic screen, then back to Ammon. "Any chance you'd know how to use one of these?"

Apprehensively, Ammon shakes his head.

"Not even a little bit. If it was a Physics simulator, I'm your guy. But then again, how hard can it be? I think between the two of us, we can figure it out."

AMMON and I have sat in the Archives for what feels like forever. So far, with Ammon's help, we've been able to get inside the Helix. Unfortunately, we've come up empty handed on the few searches I've been able to manage. There's no indication there are children like me, let alone others— like Ammon. Either the information is here and hidden in a different format, or there isn't anything to be found.

"Can I try something?" Ammon asks, pointing toward the holographic screen.

"Be my guest."

I back out of the way and let him take control for a bit.

"Runa, do you mind if I look up your hProfile from the Helix?"

"No, go for it," I say, pacing behind him.

"I thought it might be a good place to start, just to see how the Helix classified you and your brother. Did you know this?" his little finger points at the screen.

MOTHER: Absala Cophem
    FATHER: Genetic Match Unknown

"What in the—?" I lean in closer. "This makes no sense. I was there when my father died."

"That's odd? Wonder why it says this?"

"It must be a glitch. Or maybe when someone dies, they erase them so they're no longer in the database?" I say, trying to make sense of it.

"Could be, I guess," Ammon shrugs. "But you'd think they'd keep better records of the stuff."

"I agree."

I suddenly get a mental warning from Tethys. The others are coming. I barely have time to log out of everything on the mainframe before I hear the heavy metal hatch slam shut at the other end of the long hallway.

"Ammon, we have to hide. *Now*—"

Picking up the Caudex and racing to another section of the Archives, we hide behind a large shelving unit out of the way just in time to see the large round door roll to the side. One by one, my friends, walk into the entry—followed by a different version of me.

"Whoa," Ammon mutters under his breath. "I've gotten used to your short hair with the purple underneath. Almost forgot you used to look like that."

He points toward the other me as she says, "This place...is beautiful."

I didn't notice before, but the entire time, Trae had his eyes trained on me—not the Archives. He mutters something under his breath, but we can't hear from here. I vaguely remember him agreeing with me at the time, but now I'm not so sure.

"We can't stay here, Runa," Ammon whispers.

Watching my friends, knowing all that's about to transpire is a strange experience. Everyone was on edge, humming with a tension I couldn't place at the time. I've learned so much since this moment. For instance, Trae was pushing me away because he was afraid to get too close to me.

Glancing back at Ammon, I see little orbs dancing along the walls...bobbing up and down as if leading me in another direction. It's been a while since I experienced the orbs. So long since I've seen them. I'd almost forgotten about them.

I poke Ammon, just to be sure.

"Do you see those?" I ask.

Ammon turns around, looking over his shoulder cautiously, "See what?"

He turns back, his eyebrows pulling in.

"I see little orbs of light dancing down that dark hallway. I think they want us to follow them."

"Of course they do," Ammon mutters, a hint of consternation fleshing out his meaning.

"We can't stay here anyway. The others will be all over this place soon, digging through books and artifacts. We need to give them some space to work or we'll be caught. Maybe the orbs are trying to lead us out of here?"

Standing up, I start following the dancing light as they lead the way to a deeper, darker extension of the Archives. I never made it down this far, but there was enough to look at where we were. The large open hallways go on for a long ways, and in many smaller side halls.

"Runa, where are we going? What are the orbs doing now?" Ammon continues to whisper, as he slides his arm under mine, linking them together.

"Just stay with me and I'll lead the way. Trust me, we'll be okay."

I have never been able to put a finger on why I trust the orbs, even when I first saw them. I just always have. There's a peacefulness around them. *Serenity.*

The orbs lead us from the dark hallway to a smaller opening, then to a doorway at the end of a tiny circular room. If I had been looking at the space without guidance, I'm not even sure if I'd notice it was here. The walls are adorned with paintings of landscapes, flowers, and sunlight. In the center is a circular table covered in ancient looking books, not unlike the one in my arms. I pick one of the smaller ones up out of habit, blowing off the dust and running my hand along its cover as I set it back down.

"Well, so much for your orbs. They've led us to a dead end," Ammon scratches the top of his head, and for the first time, I realize his dark hair is starting to grow out. A thin light blonde line has appeared at his roots.

Pushing the book back in place, I smile.

"Actually," I tip my head toward the little door, "you may be mistaken."

He turns his head, following me as I head to the door. The faintest outline of its existence is hidden between the paintings with no handle or obvious way to open it. The orbs settle along the surface, spreading out like a blanket over the entirety. Their light grows brighter and as the rays interconnect, the doorway begins to dissolve in front of my eyes. I can clearly see into a hidden area beyond.

Reaching for Ammon's hand, I say, "C'mon, let's go."

My smile falters as he makes a face and jabs a finger toward the doorway, "Go where? Through the wall?"

His eyes are wide as his eyebrows shift upward.

Turning back to the entry, nothing has changed for me.

"Are you saying you can't see the next room?"

"There's a room?" he snorts.

"Hmmm..." I walk forward, my hand out in front of my body. I extend it beyond the space where the door or wall should be, and it easily continues on.

Ammon inhales quickly, "That's the most bizarre thing I've ever seen."

"What is it?" I ask.

"Your hand just disappeared. Like, it's gone. Or more like your hand's stuck in the wall and you're protruding out of it."

Returning my hand to my side, I bite my lip.

"Ammon, try touching the wall. Maybe this is a Daughter of Five sight thing."

He drops my other hand and walks to the door. He raises his hand, as if to knock on it, then waits. Taking a deep breath, he proceeds to tap the door.

"It's solid," Ammon says.

Ammon's lips tug downward as he looks around the room.

"Guess I have to stay here," he mutters, taking a seat on the floor. "Just hurry, would ya. I don't want to be out here all alone."

I nod, then walk over to him. Dropping to one knee, I kiss the top of his head.

"I'll just be a minute."

"I sure hope so," he says, then points at the large tome in my arms. "Want me to watch your book?"

"That would be great. I'll hurry."

I hand him the Caudex, and he hugs it in tight. Messing up his hair, I stand up and walk through the open doorway without any problems. As I enter the hidden room, bright light streams in, illuminating the entirety of the space, and flooding in from every direction. A white, see-through curtain flows from the ceiling on either side of a large stone directly in front of me. Stepping forward, I push through the curtain to fully take in the location. It's a large, pentagonal shaped room. Decorations, etchings, paintings, and more flowing see-through curtains adorn the room. There are vases with white flowers—real, *live* flowers—set on tables throughout the space, though they're wilting and clearly past their prime. On every window is a frosted, etched design of what I can only describe as the Everblossom. I walk to the center of the room, taking it all in.

What was this place for? Why is it here?

There's something both magical and mysterious about the aura here. Powerful.

I turn, realizing the large stone I walked past is actually an ornately designed chair made of white marble—or something very similar. Jewels and gems of all shapes, sizes, and colors adorn the whole thing from the very top, down to the armrests, and on to the floor. In the center of the backrest is a delicate, five-petaled flower. Again, the Everblossom.

"What is this place?" I say aloud. My voice carries, echoing against the walls.

I can't be sure—but I'd swear the light dances with my voice. It vibrated somehow, and the energy of the room amped up to a level of...*anticipation?* Though I'm not sure who or what's anticipating something.

I thought this was simply the Archives—or a place for knowledge. At least, that's what my friends had told me. But this—it's like being in a different world entirely. As unusual as it is, there's something familiar about this place I can't quite put my finger on. Almost as if I've been here before, though I don't know how I could have. We never ventured this far into the Archives when I was with my friends. Besides, the feeling of this place is different. As if it looks similar, but not the *same*.

I trace my hand along one of the stone arms, letting my fingers caress the gems and stones. Each of them glows faintly upon my touch. Then, as if noticing sounds for the first time, I hear a low, soft humming. It touches at the edge of my cognition, but gets louder the longer I focus on it.

Drawn by the sound, I find myself walking toward a small, round table illuminated in a beam of light as it pours in through the window. In the middle of the table is my Caudex, the one that should have been outside with Ammon. Its binding is open wide as it displays delicate writing which scrolls along slowly and simply:

Locked within space and buried in blood, the keys to creation anew bide time. They linger in wait for when the wheels of Pendomus are set in motion and the threads of existence begin to unravel. Through intentions and fear, safeguards become the Captor's demise. The Daughter's deliberate agreement to deliver her life's Burden will liberate the Five and reconstruct time in its accordance. Through human blood and ultimate sacrifice, the Acropolis will rise and all balance shall be restored.

Without any second thoughts or doubts, I know what this is.

The Prophecy.

I stare at the words, partly dumbfounded, partly in awe. The words make no sense, yet I know they mean everything. It's what I've been waiting for. The direction I've needed to know my next move. Only, nothing is any clearer.

I read and reread the words over and over again. One sentence stands out above all others.

The Daughter's deliberate agreement to deliver her life's Burden will liberate the Five and reconstruct time in its accordance.

All of this, being out of my timeline—Videus' attempts to stop the prophecy—it's all here. I'm in it. *We're* in it already.

"Deliberate agreement to deliver her life's Burden," I whisper. "Blood and sacrifice."

My heart sinks. Does this mean what I think it means?

I can't bear to bring myself to say the words, or even think them. It's too much.

Grabbing the Caudex, I take a final look around the room and rush back the way I came—through the wall and into the small alcove where Ammon stands, befuddled. The Caudex still clutched in his hands.

"Well?" he asks, "Whatcha find?"

I look down, realizing the Caudex I had in my arms is gone. Was it ever really there?

"I—uh, let's go," I mutter, grabbing his hand and pulling him behind me.

"Wait, what about the other you?" he asks, dragging his feet.

I need to get out of here. I need fresh air to think properly. Being trapped inside the Archives with another version of myself suddenly makes me want to crawl out of my skin. The prophecy swirls in my mind, making me realize everything I'm doing is leading me on a suicide mission.

"We need to go. Now— "

As we edge nearer to the way out, and the other version of myself and friends, the less I care about being seen or caught by them. At this point, I'm not sure I care what happens. My emotions and thoughts are swirling up into a potent, angry mixture and it's threatening to bubble over.

Is this all I am? A sacrifice?

The thought invades my mind and I bite my lip. Rushing toward the door, I let go of Ammon, instinctively knowing how this all plays out. I've been here before, after all.

As I get to the door, Ammon uses his ability to move the rock aside as we rush past. I know a few seconds behind us, the other me is about to follow through—heading toward the Helix as I try to escape Trae's insinuations.

I've been here, in this time, before. Ammon and I were the reason the other me had such tremendous luck when I wanted to get away. It was all in the timing. I continue on in whatever direction I feel pulled, knowing the other me never once had any inclination we were here. Instinctively, I know it will be the same now as history—or future—repeats.

I throw open the hatch, and the cold winter air assaults my senses. Tethys is instantly at our side, ready for whatever is necessary.

Shaking my head, I run my hand along her face.

~Not this time. You need to be ready for me. The other *me. You have to make yourself known. It's time.*

Knowing there's a minute at most between us and the other me, I continue onward with Ammon's hand interlocked in mine. I yank him behind a tree, just in time to see myself escape the Archives to head to the Helix. I witness the moment when I realize Tethys isn't the monster I thought she was. The epiphany hits my eyes and cascades through my entire being as I remember my guardian for who she was. Then, I vanish before my own eyes as her shields engage.

"Whoa. Is that what we look like?" Ammon stutters.

I nod, "I suppose so."

"Weird."

"Yeah," I say, crumpling down in the snow.

"What's going on, Runa? What happened back there?" Ammon asks. "Are you okay?"

Without a word, I flip open the Caudex to check if the prophecy is still here. When I find the page, and see the words written in black and white—I spin the book around for him to read. He reads silently, his face solemn and still until the very end.

"Through blood and sacrifice?" he whispers.

"Yeah."

"What does that mean?"

I raise my eyebrows, "Exactly what we're both thinking, I'm guessing."

"That can't be right. I mean, what's the point of all this trial stuff if it's just to sacrifice yourself at the end of it? Why not just open a big hole and ask you to jump in it?"

"Maybe there was never a point, other than to serve the purpose of the prophecy."

Ammon sits quietly for a minute.

"What if you didn't do it?" he asks, finally breaking the silence.

I look up into his serious face.

"What do you mean?"

"I mean, what if you called it quits? Like, okay, 'I've had a good run, but I'm done now' sorta thing," he says, closing the Caudex and handing it back to me.

I shrug. It's not something I considered because everything that's happening feels out of my control. As if it's all playing out the way it's meant to and there's nothing I can do to change it.

"I don't know if it works that way, Ammon," I whisper.

"Why not? You're the Daughter of Five, right? It says right here you have to deliberately agree to deliver your life—or whatever. What if you *deliberately* didn't?"

Suddenly, Trae lunges out of the hatch, scanning wildly around. I tug Ammon against me, covering his mouth so we sit silently together and wait.

When Trae is nothing but a small dot in the distance, I release his mouth.

"Was that—?" he says without finishing.

I nod.

"He looks young."

I smirk slightly at the obviousness. It's a welcome relief in the midst of my inner turmoil.

"It's not like I was always in love with someone old enough to be my father."

Being with Trae and everything we share feels so right, yet so far away. Like it was a fleeting moment in my short life and I may never get that back.

I may never get him back.

I swear, if it's the last thing I do, I will find a way to get back to him and let him know how much I love him.

With that thought, the Caudex bursts open and white light consumes us both.

19

RUNA

WHEN THE LIGHT PULLS BACK, my brain can't process what to take in first. The visual information is brutal. From the strange way the light penetrates, to the heavy ironworks around us, to the way the stone walls, floors, and ceilings are full of etchings that make no sense—it's all too much.

"Where are we now?" Ammon asks, edging close to me so he can slide his hand in mine. I shift the Caudex to my left hand, propping it against my hip.

This shifting back and forth is starting to weigh on him.

For the first time, I'm taken aback at both his strength and willingness to join me on this strange mission I seem to be on. It's not his burden, yet, he's come along so willingly.

"I don't know," I whisper.

Walking to the nearest wall, I trace some of the etchings with my fingertip. I've never seen this type of drawing before. Perhaps it's writing. I'm not even sure.

Every time I feel like I know where my mission is and my next plan, the Caudex seems to have a different one for me. As if everything I'm experiencing isn't even for my own benefit. It's more like I'm merely an observer, rather than a participant.

The room is relatively small, and cold. Gripping Ammon's hand, we walk tentatively down a short hallway to a larger, open room. The etchings are gone, but the stone walls and strange decor remain.

I've never seen a room built quite like this, but in some strange way, it reminds me of the cavern system of the Haven and Lateral. Its dark, stone encasing is similar, I suppose. To the far end of the larger room is a broad, wooden and iron door. Without a word, we walk to it and I push the door open.

Instantly, my senses are assaulted by the cold, bitter wind of winter and intensity of the sun's light on snow. Though the sun isn't nearly as high in the sky as it was on the desert side, it's still higher than what I'm used to.

Taking slow, deliberate steps, Ammon and I wordlessly consume our surroundings. Completely treeless, and devoid of life, the stone walkway in front of us opens to a large courtyard of crimson colored statues. They appear to rise out of the pure white snow, red blemishes that don't belong. As we edge closer, I stand at the foot of one and look up into its wide open eyes and gaping mouth.

"How peculiar," I whisper to myself.

"Are those what I think they are?" Ammon says, backing up.

I turn to face him. His eyes are open wide and he steps back.

"What do you think they are?"

"They look like people sculpted in blood," he says.

I shake my head.

"No, that can't be right. I'm sure they're just colored red—"

I reach out, touching one of the ice sculptures with my fingertip. The crimson ice melts at my touch, painting my skin red. It crackles between my fingers, sending off sparks of blue light. Smoothing the liquid between my thumb and pointer finger, I bring my fingers to my nose. The sweet, oddly metallic smell of blood is evident.

"It is, isn't it?" Ammon asks, then biting his lower lip.

I nod.

"Knew it."

"Why on Pendomus would anyone do something like this? Why use blood to create ice sculptures?"

"Who knows. Probably sick and sadistic, by the looks of it," he mumbles, taking a step back.

There's only one person I know who's this sick and sadistic. Only one whose moral compass is clearly broken in this sick kind of way. It just so happens he's also the reason I'm being transported through time.

"We need to get out of here," I say, turning to Ammon.

"Well, thank the planet for that," he sighs. "How do we get outta here?"

"You don't," a voice calls out.

Stepping out from behind one of the statues, a tall, dark skinned woman with long wavy hair emerges. Her eyes glow with a tinge of purple around the edges, but beyond that, they're completely white—matching the color of the soft flowing gown that contrasts her skin.

"Your destiny is deeply tied to this location. Before anything else, you must first understand the meaning behind this place," the woman continues.

"Who—who are you?" the words stumble out.

She smiles softly.

"This form is one that's borrowed. It's taken me a while to

get it in the right place and time to follow you. The fabric of space and time is unraveling, and it won't hold for long."

"I don't understand?" I blink, trying to place why her demeanor is so familiar.

"You know me by Adrian, Runa. Though I was in my natural form when we last spoke. Please, both of you, walk with me. I don't have much time," she says, grabbing both my free hand and Ammon's.

With each of us on either side, we walk back the way we came, passing the crimson sculptures. Their gaping mouths and eyes a bit more ominous.

"So, you're like, what? Runa's guardian?" Ammon asks.

Adrian laughs, "No my child. I don't have the form to protect Runa. That's Tethys' job. I am merely a guide. I have waited millennia for her."

"Oh," Ammon says.

"And for *you*."

"Huh?" Ammon sputters, stopping in mid-stride.

Adrian smiles, squeezes my hand and turns to him, "Have you not wondered why you've been brought along with Runa this whole time? Why you were the first encounter she had when her quest began?"

"Well, yeah, I guess. Sorta. I just figured she was protective of me. Or that she didn't have time to—"

Adrian touches his cheek, then turns to me, "And you, Daughter of Five. Has it never occurred to you why Ammon has been your companion through all of this?"

"I—well, I've been grateful for him. I guess I've never looked at it as something to question," I say, my thoughts flickering to all the things we've been through together.

"Runa, darling, when we last spoke, you had a mission that was going to be higher than the rest. This little boy, he's the one you were meant to be searching for. He's the one you were meant to recover."

Adrian waits, letting this revelation set in a moment.

"What are you talking about?" I finally sputter. "You told me I needed to save my brother. That his link to me would make things dangerous if he wasn't found. I haven't even had the chance to find Baxten yet. Every time I get close, I'm shifted away. Ammon here, he can't possibly—"

"I'm afraid Baxten's course is his own, my dear Runa. It's best to consider him gone," she says.

My heart sinks.

"You, you're saying he's—?" I sob.

"It's what Videus does. Look around you," she waves a hand in front of her, motioning toward the statues.

All this time, I thought I could actually save him. All this time I thought I was put on a mission to bring him back.

"What you're implying, though— it's preposterous. Ammon isn't my brother."

I look into Ammon's amber colored eyes. His dark dyed hair growing out, revealing a half-inch of light blond roots.

"He...he can't be. Can he? How—" my voice drops off as my entire world spins inside my head.

Not Baxten—Ammon?

Adrian's expression softens, as she waits for me to process.

"If Ammon's my—" I say, flicking my glance to his face and giving it another once over, "then why all this? Why continue on with the trials? With everything? Why drag him with? I got him away from Videus."

Adrian smiles softly, making her glowing eyes look slightly ominous.

"Not everything makes sense simply because it's explained. Sometimes, it needs to be experienced to fully grasp its magnitude. You needed to continue on your mission for many reasons. It needed to play itself out. To draw out your abilities, to draw out his. To bring you and Ammon together. To give you glimpses of what was and what is yet to pass. To show you you're not alone in the power you hold."

She rests her final word, letting it linger on her lips like something needed to be consumed slowly.

Ammon blinks at me, cocking his head to the side. His eyes pierce my own, as if it's the first time he's really, truly taken me in.

His eyes narrow, but he exhales and says, "I remember my dad once talking about my sister. It was before the accident. He'd had a rough day and wasn't making much sense. He was talking as though I needed to find her. That she and Mom should never have left. At the time, I thought he'd just drank some of Selphior's home concoction again—and maybe he did. But now…"

He bites his lip, blinking rapidly.

"Runa, I've always felt comfortable with you. In a way, it was like having Dad back. I always sorta knew with you I was safe. At first, I thought it was because you saved me," he whispers.

I turn to Adrian, "How could this have happened? How could Ammon be my brother? I grew up with my mother. With my brother Baxten. I remember my father. He died when I was four."

"Much will be revealed, but this is as much as I can tell you. Videus has been tracing your bloodline back for ages, trying to uncover your lineage. He's hunted centuries for the one who he believes would set everything into motion for his downfall. Look around you. This is his trophy hall. The place where he keeps the pieces of the puzzle to his survival. With their own blood, these statues have been sculpted in the likeness of those he's eliminated on his way to you. They're drained completely, and their shells destroyed in the flames of the Crematorium. Your family knew the risks and did what they thought was their only option. Your mother and father separated to keep you and Ammon concealed."

My mind is swirling in a sea of too much information. It's as though everything I've ever known about myself, my family, and life has always been a mirage.

"Has anything about my family ever been true?" I ask, my stomach suddenly feeling uneasy.

Adrian nods, "Your mother is your own."

"Well, that's a relief," I mutter.

"But she is also Ammon's," Adrian finishes.

"How—how on Pendomus did Ammon happen? My mother and I were never in the Lateral. He's younger than me, I think I'd know if my Mom got pregnant when I was seven."

Adrian takes my hands into hers, folding them in prayer, "Runa, if you've learned anything on your recent voyages, it should be that time is irrelevant. You are both outside your normal times, but exactly where you should be at this moment."

"What's that supposed to mean?" I ask, more confused than ever. Everything is beginning to feel surreal, as though part of a dream.

"If time were a line, Ammon would be the same age as you. But because Videus found a way to pluck him from his timeline to dispose of him, we had to put you on target to find the younger version of himself before he died of starvation and thirst. It took us many tries before we knew exactly where and when he was."

Ammon's head snaps up, "You mean—I've been dead?"

Adrian nods ominously.

He scrunches his face. "Wow, that sucks."

"Indeed," Adrian says, "it put the rest of the prophecy in jeopardy. We knew you must be found at all costs."

"The same age?" I finally whisper.

Adrian watches me closely with those glowing eyes, "Yes."

"Does that mean—we're?" I glance at Ammon again, his face a painting of confusion.

"Twins, yes," Adrian acknowledges.

"Whoa," we both say in unison.

"If we're twins—then what makes me so special? Why not a Son of Five?" I ask, turning to her.

"Though you may have similar genetic makeup, it was foretold that a daughter would be the one to save us. Your experiences Runa, your choices are what make you who you are. Not chance, not genetics. Ammon is important because of his blood tie to you, but he can't replace you."

"What about Baxten?" I say.

"He was your half brother. While he still held some importance by way of blood, his loss spurred you to keep pushing forward. It was an unfortunate necessity."

"Who gives you the right to play with our lives like this? Deciding who lives and dies." I sputter. "Baxten was still my brother. He was the only brother I've ever known."

"And you would have lost both of them. At least one could be saved," Adrian says softly.

A thunderous crack makes Ammon and I both jump. Before our eyes, as though massive claws are ripping open the curtain of reality, the sky tears in two.

Adrian calmly looks over her shoulder, "My time with you is coming to a close."

"Not yet. I have so many questions. What happens next? What do I do with all of this information? I feel so—"

"What you need to do now, Runa, is in your blood. Now that you know who and what you are—and that there are others, you need to find them all," Adrian says as the vortex begins to pull her backward. "Once you do, you will be unstoppable. Videus will be thrown out of existence and Pendomus will be saved."

"How will I even find the others? It's not like there's a special alarm that goes off, telling me they have powers. I didn't even know Ammon—"

With a soft pop, the tear closes itself and Adrian is gone.

"Dammit," I mutter. It feels as though a heavy weight has been placed on my chest.

I can't breathe.

How do I do this? How do I find the others Adrian is talking about? What makes her think any of it will matter once I do? All of this seems to hinge on me being this special Daughter of Five, but right now, I feel anything but.

Ammon grabs my hand, "Runa, it's time you do what you've done since I've known you."

Taking a deep breath, I look down at his wide eyes, "And what's that?"

"Consult your big book there and keep moving forward," he says.

Glancing at my white knuckles as I clench the binding of the Caudex, I nod in agreement.

"You're right, Ammon," I say. "Thank you."

I nod, giving him a hug. My twin—

My mind is a blur of unintelligible thoughts. We need to get out of here. Away from the blood sculptures. Away from anything remotely associated to Videus. I need to get Ammon to a safer place and I need to figure out how to find the others.

Dusting off a spot on the frozen walkway, I kneel down

and open the tome. Flipping through the book this time reveals pages and pages of new information. More than I could even consider reading in one go. Especially here.

"Wow, it's nearly filled up," Ammon says in surprise.

"I'm not seeing what we need, though. We have to know how to get out of here."

Half expecting the right page to jump out and consume us, I continue flipping the pages relentlessly. Nothing happens.

I shut the Caudex, clutching it to my chest as I look up into the snow covered hills in the distance. I have no idea how far away from the Lateral and Haven we are. Or if I'm even in a timeline that matters.

"We need to go," I say, standing back up.

"Go where?" Ammon asks.

"Anywhere is better than here. This is Videus'—I don't know, lair? Sanctuary? All I know is, this isn't our territory and if we don't get moving, things could get far, far worse for us."

"Okay, then I'm more than with you. Let's get outta here," he says.

Grabbing his hand again, I take a final glance at the sculptures all around us. Videus has captured and killed so many people in his search for me. Or my blood line. I wish I understood why. What are his motives for any of this? My brain simply can't wrap around the desire of one man to want to destroy the lives of so many people, the entire planet, in fact. For what? Power? Because he can?

We follow the row of statues to the furthest end of the walkway as it leads out over the undisturbed snow drifts. Glancing up at the final two sculptures, my mouth drops open. On one side is a man, his face stern, and eyes wide. But on the other side, the woman's face is all too familiar. The way the bloody snow shapes the curls that line her face, and the perfectly mimicked badge for a RationCap Chemist.

My hand instinctively flies to my mouth.

"What is it? Runa? What's going on?" Ammon asks, tugging at my arm.

I blink wildly.

The last time I saw my mother, she'd been transformed into a Labot. Perhaps she'd always been one, I don't honestly know. Even though we'd never had the best of relationships, I'd never wish this for her. Never—

Ammon looks from me to the sculpture again.

"Is this…? Your mum?" he whispers.

Unable to speak, or remove my eyes from her crimson gaze, I simply nod.

Of course he'd do this. It makes perfect sense. Once he knew for sure I was the Daughter of Five, he had his lineage to go after.

Deep inside, lamentation takes root.

Unable to stop myself, I step forward, reaching out for her. I never meant for any of this to happen. More than anything, I wish I could undo it all. Bring her and Baxten back. Make Videus pay.

I place my hand on the curve where her hand meets her wrist, sliding my fingertips in the cold palm. The warmth from my hand begins melting hers on contact.

Even in death, she recoils at my touch.

Pulling my hand back, I stare into my palm as her blood pools in the center. As if a drain has been pulled, the blood soaks into my palm and light shoots out of my fingertips.

Ammon sucks in a breath and steps back.

"Whoa," he whispers.

Very slowly, the light pulls back into each one of my

fingers. Lingering behind is a new sense of serenity. And an odd sense of power.

I turn to Ammon, seeing the wonder and fear hidden in his features. But it's more than that—across the iris of his amber colored eyes is the lighted outline of a five-petaled flower. I inhale quickly, taking a step back. Blinking once, I look back to find the flower has all but dimmed. With my right eye closed, however, and focusing on it with my left—I still see it there. Hiding in plain sight.

Literally.

"Well, my little Everblossom and her pet. It's wonderful of you to join me," Videus says from beside us. "Just the two people I've been looking all over time and space for. You have no idea how difficult it's been to track you down. And here you've come to me. Who could ask for anything more?"

*M*Y JAW DROPS OPEN and both Alina and I stare at Kani for longer than we should.

"Guys, why the hell are you staring at me like that? It's giving me a complex," Kani says, running her hand through her hair.

"They're just surprised to see you feeling better, Kani," Landry says, entering from the allayroom down the hall.

"Understatement of the year," I say, glancing at Alina. Her eyes are wide, but she doesn't say anything. Instead, she turns to Landry and tips her head toward the bedroom.

Kani notices the exchange and snorts.

"It's okay. Alina and I just need to talk a minute. Trae, you'll stay here with her, right?" Landry says.

Blinking away my own confusion, I nod, hoping to hell Landry plans on filling me in, too.

"Sure," I hear myself saying.

I scratch the top of my head and take a seat on the sofa and try to act normal.

Kani sits down next to me once the two of them close the door.

"What in the hell is that all about?" she asks, clearly unaware of the precarious situation she was in only moments ago.

I lick my lip.

"C'mon Trae. Really? It can't be that bad," she glances at the door and back to me. "Can it?" she adds.

"Well, I—" I begin. I honestly don't know what to tell her. How much is too much? What does she think is going on? "What's the last thing you remember?" I offer.

"What kind of stupid question is that?" she snickers. But after a moment, her expression fades as her eyebrows knit together. "You know, I have no idea. I mean, it's all kind of fuzzy. I remember being here and being safe, though."

That's an odd thing to say, even for Kani.

Safe.

It must be an implanted emotion from Landry in an attempt to keep her calm.

"Good. Safe is good," I mutter, nodding.

"Yeah, except I'm getting the distinct impression there's something going on. So spill it, Traeton. I don't have all day."

I shake my head, "Kani, I would if I knew what was going on myself. I'm kinda in the dark here, too."

Creeping slowly up the back of my neck, like a snake uncoiling and ready to strike, I sense my headache surging. I wish to hell I could get rid of these damn things. They're coming with more frequency and the NeuroWand isn't doing a damn thing to stave them off anymore.

I rub my temple, willing it to fade away.

"Headache? Do you need a NeuroWand?" Kani offers.

"I, uh—" I stop myself. How far back are Kani's memories fuzzy? "I better not," I mutter.

"Suit yourself," she shrugs.

Landry and Alina open the door and Alina's expression is stone cold. Not a single emotion is readable and I stand up.

"Alina, I need to—"

She nods without hesitation and points to the bedroom.

"Thanks," I say, giving Landry a what-the-phug is going on glance.

Once inside, he closes the door behind us.

"Sorry, I didn't know she'd take the reframing so easily," Landry begins.

"What's going on with her? She doesn't remember anything and is acting completely—normal. Well, kinda," I say.

"That's the point, Trae. I was able to pinpoint some of the memories, well, more accurately, the timeline in her memory. I restructured it, trying to erase the emotional drama that surrounded whatever happened. Very complicated stuff," he says.

I run my hand through my hair and give it a tug, wishing it could alleviate some of the pressure building up in the back of my skull.

"Landry, as happy as I am to have Kani up and operational…should we be messing with her mind like that? I mean, hell, I didn't even know you could get in there and do that sorta thing. Were you able to see what freaked her out?"

Too many questions are flooding in all at once.

"Nah, it's not like that," he shakes his head.

"What is it like then?"

Landry paces from one end of the small room to the other.

"It's kinda like hunting for a thread that's linked to a series of memories in her timeline and then, unraveling the way it's housed in her brain. There are pathways that disintegrate, though, and you have to be careful to pick the right

ones. I just got lucky, really. I pinpointed the area and sorta…
scrambled it."

"Scrambled it?" my eyes widen as I picture an egg and
whisk situation happening inside her brain.

"Well, more like muted it, I guess. I had to blank out the
section so she could let go of the trauma."

"Will her memories ever go back to normal?" I ask, not
sure if it would be a good thing or not if it did. "Will they
ever come back?"

He shakes his head.

"Oh," I mutter.

"Look, it wasn't invasive. It was just a slight reframe so
she feels safe and secure. In a way, it's like she was in one of
those meditation sessions with Jordan—even though Kani
wouldn't have been caught dead in one. It just relaxed her
mind enough to reset and forget about whatever trauma she
just went through."

"But we still don't know what happened. What if whatever's out there decides to—"

"We weren't going to get anything out of her regardless.
Our best bet to uncover all that is you."

"Does she remember anything? Fenton?" I say, pacing
now, too.

"I don't know yet. I haven't had much time with her to
find out where her memories are at. Or how far back the
muted memories go."

"Well, then let's go find out before we freak her out with
something we say," I mutter, shaking my head and walking
out.

Sometimes, the things Landry can do are borderline
frightening. I know it's a good thing in this case, but in some
ways, it's not far off from the way the Helix handles situa-
tions like this.

"How's everything going out here?" I ask as we walk back into the main open space of Landry's small abode.

"Gettin' weirder by the minute," Kani says, side-eyeing everyone.

"Look Kani, we need to talk," Landry begins.

"No, really?" she says, thick with sarcasm.

I exchange a glance with Alina, who shrugs.

Landry takes a deep breath and says, "There's no easy way to say this, so here goes. You and Trae were recently out to the Archives and something…happened."

Kani's expression turns grim. "Happened?"

I nod.

"Like?" she asks.

"Well, we don't really know," I say. "I blacked out and found myself outside when I came to. When I got back to the Archives, the place was a mess. Like someone or something had attacked us. You were hiding and…well, kinda out of it."

"We needed to sedate the memories so we could get you back," Landry finishes.

"Mkay," Kani's eyebrows could touch the tip of her nose if they drop any further.

"What do you remember? About anything recently? Do you remember Runa?" I ask, trying to prod some of the memories from her without actually bringing up Fenton.

Kani's face scrunches, "Well, duh. I'm not lobotomized."

"Then you start us off. What do you remember?"

"Runa's gone. We've been…she's—" Kani's eyes go distant as she tries to recall the details.

There's a moment of awkward silence as we wait.

Landry takes a deep breath, "What about Fenton?"

"What about him?" Kani asks.

We all exchange a significant look. *Here we go.*

Landry clears his throat as he walks to her and says,

"Well, he's on a mission. We're not sure when he's going to be back."

I shoot a glance at Alina, who pins her lips together in a thin line. She doesn't approve.

Can't say I blame her.

"Where in the hell did he go now?" Kani sighs.

"Not sure. We just know it's important," Landry says. He turns around and widens his eyes, hinting that we need to play along.

If we lie to her and she finds out what really happened... she's likely to kill us. It would devastate her all over again. Is this really wise? It seems like a dangerous line to cross.

Instead of playing it out, I stand up and walk to the allay-room for the NeuroWand. My head is pounding now and I know there's no amount of discussion I can add that will make this situation better.

Everything feels so messed up. Confused and muddled. Wrong.

I know there's stuff missing from my mind, too, and it worries me. There's something I'm supposed to be doing and now I'm not sure what the hell it was. Did I have my mind messed with, too? If so, who's had their fingers in it and why?

"Everything okay?" Alina asks, nodding at the Neuro-Wand in my hand.

"Yeah, headache. Just gotta get rid of it so I can focus on what to do next," I say.

"Do you need to lie down?" she asks, nodding toward the bedroom again.

"Yeah, I think laying down is a good idea. Thanks, Alina. Let me know if you need me," I mutter, taking the Neuro-Wand and closing the bedroom door behind me.

Something's not right here. With all of it. Me, Kani—the Archives. I shouldn't be this confused. Maybe a little sleep will help me regain some focus. Hell, even if all it does is get rid of this thumping headache, I'd be happy.

I hear Alina and Landry continue the conversation with Kani, but I can't seem to muster the strength to care what's being said. Or how they're handling it. White searing light is filtering into my vision, despite the pitch-black room. I flip the NeuroWand to transmit the medicine, rub it across my forehead, and lie down. My back sinks into the comfort of the bed's embrace and I let go.

My last thoughts before I drift off surround the missing time, all the missing moments before the attack on us. I wish I could remember something; anything. I need to figure out what I was meant to be doing—or where I should be going. I feel like there's an urgency to it, but I can't place where. Or why. I know if I can unlock that piece, the rest will come.

THE AIR RUSHES IN and around my body as I fly above the trees. There's a freeing relief when you're so far above the fray. Part of me knows this isn't normal for me, but I feel like I've done it a thousand times before. It's natural. Innate.

I circle the sun and its halo, dancing in the sky as if I own the entirety of the space.

Life is simpler here. It's beautiful. Even if I know I have to reengage eventually. Part of me wants to stay here, in the air, forever. Letting the pains of humanity flood the world below, leaving me untouched all the way up here. But I know there's so much more I need to do. More that has to happen before letting go is truly possible.

Deep below the tree line, I sense the girl somewhere buried in the underground. I don't know why I can sense her, but I can. She's important, but I can't place a reason on why. There have been hundreds of girls who have come and gone over the years. But she has power. More than she realizes even. I'm unsure if this is for good or bad. In more ways than one, I feel drawn to her.

Suddenly, I feel myself being called back. A muscle memory buried somewhere deep in my mind. He doesn't have a name, I only know I must answer. If I don't, unspeakable things will happen.

My body shifts, taking me to where the pull draws me. To where I'm meant to be. The call is powerful and even if I wanted to, I know I couldn't ignore it.

The structure rising in and out of the ground floods the horizon and I'm soaring towards it. I enter the narrow gate near the upper arch. Darkness surrounds me as I continue my descent into the depths of his lair.

I perch upon the door of the human boy most recently captured. His dark hair is matted to his head in this heat and I find myself wishing I could escape it myself. I'm meant to check on him. Ensure he's still where he's meant to be.

My mind relays the information without my own effort, and I'm released from my mission as quickly as it came. Relief foods my body and I retrace my flight and escape the heat as swiftly as I can. I know I'll be called again. I always am.

But for now, I'll go see the girl. For some reason, I need to see the girl.

It takes only a few moments and I enter the small cavern system to wait. I go in as far as I dare. The TerraDwellers wouldn't be happy of my presence if they knew.

I need to see her.

I claw my way deeper, but my powers of flight are diminished the further I go. I can feel myself getting disoriented.

Then, suddenly, miraculously, I'm in her gentle hands.

A dark-haired girl nearby says, "Don't you even tell me this is the bird you were delirious over when we first got here."

My eyes pop open and the contentment of being in Runa's hands dissipates. I shiver, still feeling the immensely powerful urge to remain there forever. Her hands had given off an energy, a power of love and joy. Peace. The sensation was so strong I didn't even know I could feel those emotions so powerfully.

Now I feel disjointed. As though I was really there, really flying. My mind doesn't completely feel like my own, as I integrate the dream into the memories I already own.

I'm not sure what to believe anymore. Am I losing my mind?

On the upside, I remember what it was we were looking for and why it was urgent.

The sweaty face of Runa's brother Baxten lingers in my memory. I'd remember it anywhere. After he'd perished, we'd even looked him up and discovered information about Videus' Vassalage.

Perhaps the odd dream was an answer to my silent prayers as I fell asleep. That has to be it, right? I wanted to remember what I was doing and why. This is what Kani and I were working on. That's about the only thing I'm certain of.

I'm not sure why my brain would twist everything around in the way it did, but I'm grateful for the guidance. In a weird, abstract kinda way, it felt natural for me.

The headache I laid down with is thankfully gone and I sit up on the bed, stretching. Landry's home is silent, except for the rhythmic breathing of someone on the other side of the door.

The rest of them must have gone to sleep, too.

I open the door to find Kani asleep on the sofa. Neither Landry or Alina are in the house, which leads me to believe they've gone back to Alina's. Suits me just fine. I have to collect my thoughts anyway.

Shaking the sensations of the dream is harder than it should be. I pace the floor in front of the kitchen counter. What starts as retracing my steps, or flight as it were, starts to morph into formulating a plan. I don't remember what happened to us in the Archives, but knowing where we were heading is the next best thing.

"What are you doing?" Kani asks, rolling onto her side.

Startled, I let out a quick gasp.

"Wow, there's a first," she laughs. "Never thought I'd ever get a girly squeak outta Traeton Revasco."

She chuckles, and sits up.

"I remember what we were trying to do at the Archives," I say, taking a seat across from her.

"Which is?" she asks, flipping her hair behind her back.

"With Runa gone, and Fenton—er, you know. We were there to do the one thing we knew would help everyone. We were searching for more information on the Vassalage. And I think before we got attacked, we'd stumbled on where the Vassalage is located."

Kani sits up straighter, her eyes wide as she waits for me to continue.

I bite my lip, hoping to hell I'm right.

"We need to break into the Helix. The Vassalage is a part of the Crematorium. I vaguely remember some information about why Runa may have been given the role she was before she left. They were trying to eliminate her."

"Wait, what? Are you saying the people who were Cremators are actually marked for death?"

"I didn't think of it like that," I say, "but yeah, I think some of them are."

"Where did you get this information?"

"Well, before, I think it was information we found on the mainframe at the Archives. But I just had a dream about everything, and it sorta reminded me where the Vassalage was. I know it sounds shifty, so I get it if you don't—I just know what I need to do. Where I need to go."

I tap my head, still trying to release the dream's memories enough to be present.

"Look, Trae, I trust you. But if we're headed to the Helix, we're gonna need to be sure. And to be honest, if we were both attacked after you found out this little detail, aren't you at least a little bit concerned this could be why?"

I blink, surprised. The thought hadn't occurred to me yet.

"You're right. This could be the reason. Which lends even more credibility, don't you think?"

"Maybe?" she shrugs.

"Then, let's be sure. We need to sneak into the Helix, tonight. We'll have a look around and one way or another, we'll know for sure. You with me?"

21

TRAETON

*I*F THE CREMATORIUM houses the Vassalage, then that makes life a helluva lot easier.

"All we need to do is blow the Helix up," I say, pushing back from the holographic screen.

"Suuuuure," Kani mocks, "once we know it's truly the Vassalage, something has to be done. But as much as I hate the place, I'm not about to go in there and kill a bunch of innocent people. And what about tonight? How do you propose we go forward? It's not like we can just waltz in and say, 'Excuse me, never mind us. We're just here to hunt for your hidden prison you've got buried in the Crematorium.' We need to have a reason to be there. Hell, for all we know, you're flagged from the last time you broke in. The moment we get within a meter of the place, alarms are probably going to go off."

With my middle finger, I tap the space in the center of my forehead.

Think, think.

"Do we have plans or blueprints for the Helix?" I ask. My dream showed me a possible entrance that lead from the top, but the space wasn't much wider than a single person. It was barely enough for a small bird's flight to make it in and out of. I shudder at the thought of trying to use that as our path.

"How the hell would I know? I'm not Fenton. Stupid man. I can't believe he's not here." Her words hang in midair and we lock eyes.

"I know, I was just…" I mutter.

"Yeah, well, I have no clue," Kani recovers, turning her back to me.

"Well, let's see what we can dig up here. There has to be a weakness in the structure, or a way to get into the Crematorium that doesn't involve waltzing through the thick of the Helix."

"And if there's not?"

"Then we deal with the scenario as it plays out," I offer, as my fingertips command the search on Landry's mainframe. He's always held a fascination for the Helix. Maybe he has details we're not aware of for the structure?

"Fine by me," Kani mutters, walking away. "I'm gonna go for a walk. Been cooped up here too long."

"Don't go too far," I say, "we'll need to head out soon."

"For phug sake, should I just take one of Landry's ComLinks so you can stay in touch?" she says, walking back and snatching a ComLink from the desk. She throws her black curtain of hair over her shoulder and places the link against the flesh behind her right ear.

I pause, unsure if it's wise, considering what happened to Fenton. But I can't bring myself to say anything. I nod, picking up the other link and doing the same. The electrical tickle of the device connecting to the electrical impulse of my body always makes me want to itch at it. I resist the urge and go back to hunting for something that will give us a more detailed plan.

Kani reaches for her safety blanket of choice, her knives, but her hand hovers over the table where they rest. I pretend not to notice, but we briefly share a glance.

"Not sure why, but I don't feel right about these today," Kani says, clutching at the smallest blade and shoving it in her hip holster.

My eyes flick to the ground. I know exactly why, but I can't bring myself to tell her.

"Be careful," I offer instead.

She nods and taps her ear, "If anything comes up, let me know. I'll come back and we can get started."

"Alright," I say, but she's already out the door.

I start the search, locating a few sketches and diagrams Landry has. They're not very detailed, but they offer a glimpse into ways to get in. I notice some areas where the information of the Helix is incorrect, as if whoever drew it was given old, outdated schematics. Even I could have given better details than this, if anyone had ever asked.

After what feels like days of searching, it becomes pretty clear there's no good way to get into the Helix's Cremato- rium. It's heavily fortified, and secured. According to every- thing I know and the diagrams I could find, there's only the one way in.

I wonder if the best way in may be by attempting the descent from my dream—assuming the tunnel even exists. I start flicking through images and recon photos of the outside of the building, hunting for the small opening.

The more I think about it, the more idiotic it sounds, to be honest. It was a dream. A really vivid dream, but a dream nonetheless. And I was flying, as if I wasn't human. Yeah, not strange at all.

Absently, I flick through the photos, not really paying attention. Instead, I'm more in my head, focusing on the location and how it looked in my dream. It felt so real. Everything did.

I rub my temple, realizing the headache has been silently creeping back in. I wish I could figure out what's causing them, but I'm almost afraid to find out. There are so many things that could go wrong with a person's brain and body. We're really such fragile creatures.

My mind flits to my sister Ava and the way her mind deteriorated. What if it runs in the family? What if it's something more serious?

I shudder, pushing the worry from my mind. No good will come from that line of thought. What matters now, is trying to do as much good as I can while Runa's still gone.

"Whoa," I mutter, flipping past a photo, then returning to it.

There, in an image clear as day, is a bird flying toward the Helix. Any other time, I wouldn't have even cared or noticed it in the picture. They were always around. But this time, it's the location in which it's heading that makes me sit upright. The little black dot is on a mission, heading straight toward the Helix—and the tiny opening on the upper side.

The location looks exactly like it did in my dream.

"Gotcha," I whisper. "I may be taking crazy leaps, but at least they seem to still pan out."

Standing up, I walk to Landry's closet and grab anything resembling climbing equipment. Getting into the Helix from off the ground won't be easy. Hell, it could be damn near impossible not to be seen. But at least we'll have equipment —and we'll be outside and away from the Labots.

Once I feel satisfied I've packed as much as I can, I take a moment to call on Kani through the ComLink. Once she accepts the exchange, something inside me clenches.

Should I even be taking her? Could she jeopardize the mission with her scrambled mind?

~Trae, you there?

Why didn't I think this through? I suppose she'll have to come with now.

~Yeah, sorry. Was looking for a carabiner.

~So, I assume that means you're ready, then?

~Should be. Wanna get back here so I can fill you in?

~On my way

She abruptly ends the exchange and opens the door.

"Guess you weren't that far, eh?" I laugh.

"Nah. I was just sitting on the step outside," she says. "Couldn't think of anywhere to go."

I scratch my head, "Well, you coulda just stayed in here."

"I suppose," she mutters, her eyebrows knitting together.

"What's up?" I ask, taking a seat next to her.

Kani shakes her head and sighs, "I don't know. I feel off. I know you and Landry said something happened and I needed to have my brain unscrambled or something. But I feel like a whole big piece of me is missing or something. Does that sound stupid?"

"Not at all. Look, maybe it's best not to go digging through your mind anyway. Whatever happened, it didn't leave you too well off. It messed with you in a way I've never seen."

"What do you mean?" she asks, her narrow eyes meeting mine.

"Well, I don't know if incoherent is the word, but close. We couldn't get anything to make sense. You just kept repeating 'Gone, gone, gone' over and over again."

"Don't you think that's scary, though? I mean, whatever it was—it was bad. Like, *way* bad," Kani whispers. "Do you know when Fenton's supposed to be back?"

I make a face before I can stop myself, then try to recover, "You know, I'm not sure—"

"What was that?" she asks, pointing at my face.

"What was what?" I ask, innocently.

"Don't give me that shit, Traeton. What was the wince for?"

I don't honestly know why Landry didn't tell Kani about Fenton. To me, it feels like something that could seriously come back to bite us in the ass. Especially if she finds out it was something we kept from her.

I press my fingertips to my mouth, waging an internal civil war.

"Spit it out, Trae. Don't make me get my knives," she says.

Again, I wince without trying. Her eyes narrow further.

On the upside, when everything went down, she handled it. I can't say it was easy, but knowing she was the one who put a stop to Fenton didn't throw her over the edge.

"Look Kani, I'm sure Landry had his reasons—" I start.

Kani opens her mouth to protest, but I hold a finger up, silently asking her to allow me to finish.

My right temple throbs, and I place a finger to it, pushing in hard. My vision feels off—as though it's gone almost telescopic.

"We—we struggled with," I start again, "Fenton wasn't meant to…"

As if shifting from the front seat of my mind, to the forgotten and unused back seat, I witness myself continuing. But oddly, I'm acutely aware that I'm no longer the driver of the bus.

My neck crooks to the side briefly, as if stretching itself into new bones.

"The yellow-haired boy is gone," I hear myself say.

I can see through my eyes, hear the words and my

surroundings, but as much as I struggle, I'm not in control. Everything is tinted an odd wilted color, as if all hues are slowly being leached out.

"Yellow-haired boy?" Kani snickers. "What the hell, Trae? Why are you being so cryptic? This isn't funny."

"You put an end to his life," my hand reaches forward, tapping the knife strapped to her thigh.

Kani's face goes from open, to irritated, to horror in a few microseconds.

"What are you talking about?" Kani whispers, her eyes distant as she tries to hunt for information in her clouded memories.

"Truth," I hear myself say, "and now we need to get you to the Helix to rectify it."

Tears well in Kani's eyes as she tries to reprocess this new information. I want to break out of this mental cage, reach for her. Tell her everything is okay. Tell her this isn't me—it's not how I'd handle it. I want to tell her it wasn't her fault and no one blames her. Inside, I'm screaming all of it—but it doesn't seem to matter at all. I'm completely locked out of myself.

How in the hell did this happen? And what do I do now?

"I knew there was something I was forgetting. I could feel it, down deep. I just didn't think it was this—" Kani says, tears steadily streaming now. "I remember now—the Tree. The fight. Oh god—"

She didn't even cry the first time.

Why hasn't she slapped me? Or told me to go to hell? Why isn't Kani fighting?

Kani—don't you dare let this slide. Don't lose the spark. You have to fight this. Fight me. Everything is all wrong, and you're the only one who can stop it! Can't you tell this isn't me?

I scream in my head, trying to force my way out. Force my thoughts to spill into words.

"There is nothing you can do now. We need to get to the Helix. Then we can sort everything out," my voice says.

Kani takes a moment, allowing the sadness to consume her, before she sits up a bit straighter.

"Alright. You're right, Trae. Let's find the Vassalage and put an end to this," Kani says. "Who cares how we get in. Without Fenton, none of it matters anyway."

"Very well," I hear myself say.

Her eyebrows pull in, and she makes a face.

"Can you knock off the stoic crap. I get what I did hurt you, too. So this should make you happy," she says.

"I very much doubt there's anything you can do or say that will make amends."

Kani takes a deep breath.

"I suppose not."

Whoever—or whatever—has possession of me stops to take a beat. It's an awkward kind of silence, and annoying at the lack of control I have. It's as if there's a wall between whatever it is and me. I sense they're in here running the show, but I can't hear their thoughts or interact at all. It's as though I'm enclosed in a panic room where no sound I make can escape—and nothing from their side can enter.

After a moment, I hear myself say, "Let us go to the Helix. We shall worry about the rest later."

Stumped for a moment at the almost calm and detached manner my captor is delivering, I wait for the next shoe to drop. Instead, I start to feel an enclosing sensation—as if the box I'm in is being shut. I can't tell if it's a deliberate door being closed, or if it's simply the way things work when you're not in charge of your own mind. Before I have the opportunity to travel that train of thought, everything goes completely dark.

SELF-AWARENESS IS A TRICKY THING. I never questioned it well enough before. I didn't know my actual consciousness was separate from my body until being forced to take a back seat. Who would, I suppose?

It feels like ages since I was last attached to anything. Sometimes this nothingness is overwhelming and I have to escape. I have to find a new *home*. If I don't find an attachment somewhere, I know I'll go mad. I have to be —Something.

Maybe I've already lost my damn mind.

There are moments...moments when I feel connected, other times when I feel so very lost. Without my body, I keep slipping out of self-recognition. Like I'm melding into a universal energy. Or maybe I'm just being erased. Maybe both.

As hard as I try, I can't always hold on. Sometimes, I relax into the abyss and let go. Who knows how long it's been. Then, something always pulls me back. I don't know why. Could be myself, hunting for a way back in. To take back control. Or maybe it's just the way a soul searches until it's able to inhabit a body. I don't know anymore.

Glimpses of speaking with Runa—finding her beside a fire in the dead of night rushes into my mind and it pulls me from my slumber in the abyss. I can't tell if the conversation with her was real or an illusion. I guess I'm not sure of anything anymore. I just know I needed to feel safe. I needed to be home. Then, magically, there she was. I could see her as if I was standing right beside her. How does that work? Am I a ghost?

I never gave much thought to ghosts before, but I suppose it's as good a description as any. I keep forgetting who I am. Where I am. What I am. Did I think that already?

See what I mean?

A tug slowly pulls me from the darkness of the abyss, drawing me closer to the forefront of consciousness. Once again, I regain a sense of purpose. I regain some of my orientation, even if only momentarily. These are the moments I cling to, otherwise, what else is there?

Like waking up groggy, I can suddenly see through my own eyes—but I'm still not in the driver's seat. Whoever's taken over my body still has control. Either they've granted me awareness, or I've somehow found a way back to myself.

Either way, the situation is now the same. I'm locked out of my own body, and watching the world through a viewer's eyes only.

Almost as if pushing my way through a series of satin curtains, I finally understand my surroundings. No longer in the Lateral, instead, I'm nearing the Helix. By my side is Kani.

Her lips are moving, but my senses haven't caught up yet —I have no idea what she's saying.

Dread pours into my awareness, and I realize she's trusting someone—she's trusting me on a mission that will not have the results we originally intended. For all I know, it's Videus himself who's taken over my body. He did it with Fenton, after all.

How the hell does Kani not realize?

Pieces of my personality, my passions, the simple way I am start to thread back into my being and I feel more complete than I have for a long time. Almost as though, I have a chance at taking myself over again.

I focus intently, trying to get an idea of what's happening. Of what Kani's even saying. Locked out of my own body is a torture I never imaged enduring. Especially when you can see the imminent threats, but can't hear or speak to warn anyone.

Oh my god. I'm trapped in my own body.

The realization slams against me with such force, I feel I'd be knocked over if I was actually the one standing.

"Kani, Kani—you need to get away. You can't trust him— uh, me. You need to go," I scream in my head.

It's no use, there's no voice to connect it to.

I watch as my own hand points to the main access point of the Helix, the doorway on the side of the building.

They aren't going to just walk up to the Helix, are they?

Memories flood my consciousness—though I'm not sure how that even works. But we were looking for the Vassalage. I can tell you, whoever's using my body isn't doing it for the fun of it. Or to help Kani find the Vassalage. They're leading her to something far more nefarious.

Suddenly, it occurs to me. All this time, all the headaches —the blackout at the Archives.

Holy shit.

Did *I* attack Kani? Well, not me—but whoever this thing is? No, it can't be—can it?

How long has this been happening?

I search my memories, but they're dark. Abyss dark.

As quickly as it came, the awareness to my body slips away again. Darkness descends, consuming everything as I lose grasp on everything I'm clinging to.

Remember this thought process, Trae. Hang onto it.

Remember.

22

RUNA

*E*NERGY SPARKS IN MY HANDS as I open them wide. Without overthinking it, I embrace the surge, allowing it to wash over me like a collective storm. Turning around, Ammon and I face Videus again.

For the second time, I come face to face with the man himself. His bird-inspired headdress once again shields us from his face, and he's alone, for now. A solitary man, dressed in blacks and reds and in deep contrast with the snow outside. His cloak drapes majestically over his shoulders and caresses the ground.

Alone, and dressed this way, he doesn't look as intimidating as he did taking over Fenton. Or even as he did in the cavern where I found Ammon. Instead, he looks as though he could be easily overwhelmed under our capabilities.

Perhaps I could end this. Right here, right now?

There are a great many things I've been in the past—naive, inexperienced, incapable. Now doesn't feel like one of those moments. The travels I've been through, the things I've seen so far—they've all led me to a place where I know I can make a difference. If Videus thinks he'll take me or Ammon without a fight—well, he's in for a rude awakening.

Ammon stands straighter, his shoulders mimicking my own. Whatever I feel or think about my new sibling revelation, I'm so happy he's here. And proud to have him by my side. I know what he's capable of, and I hope we can use that knowledge to our advantage.

"I'm going to take a wager and guess you understand more of where you fit into all this," Videus starts, his usual toying manner, as he tries to put us on edge.

Without a doubt, his minions won't be far behind and if we're to make a difference, we have to strike fast.

"It's starting to make sense," I say, matching his passive, nonchalant tone.

"Oh, I highly doubt that," he mocks.

His voice reminds me of something, though I can't put my finger on exactly what. It's a strange combination of tech and humanity. But it's almost lost between the two.

I feel the power of this place coursing through my veins. It could be coincidence. Or it could be truly the connection I have to all these people. The bloodlines.

Turning to Ammon, I swear he feels it too. His eyes are glowing again with a bright, five petaled everblossom.

"Well, if there's more I should know, feel free to enlighten me," I say, calmer than I should.

Videus watches us silently for a moment. Perhaps sizing the situation up. Perhaps biding his time.

"What makes you so special?" he finally asks.

"You should know," I say. "It's because of you the Daughter of Five prophecy even came into being."

Videus waves a hand dismissively.

"I don't care about old literature and misunderstood dialogues."

"Then what do you care about? What in the hell does any of this matter?"

"It wasn't personal, you know. But now— You think everything should magically work for you, don't you? That the world revolves around what you think and do. But I'd like to know why you think you could possibly save any of them."

"Any of who?"

"Humanity. Your friends. Your brothers. Take your pick."

Involuntarily I flinch at *brothers* and clutch the Caudex to my body.

Pulling Ammon behind me, I step forward, "My brothers are none of your business."

Videus laughs. His deep, near maniacal chuckle.

"Oh, Runa. Dear, disturbed, confused Runa. It's been my sole purpose to make your brothers my business," he says.

For the first time since he arrived, a shudder creeps up my spine.

"I thought your sole purpose was to screw up the planet. To mess with the natural order of things," I spit.

"Yes, of course you would see it that way," he says, taking to a slow, deliberate pace in front of us.

"What else should I be thinking?"

"I'd expect nothing more of you, Daughter of Five. Still so naive. So unobservant. Everything I've done has always been for a sole purpose. For one desire and one desire only," Videus says, turning to me and getting right up into my space.

He's inches from my face, but I hold my ground, peering into his mask's bloody face. I wish I could see what's really hidden behind it. Look into the face of the man who hates me so much. Hates us all.

"To control all of humanity," I say.

Taking a step back, Videus snorts.

"Humanity is not my concern. Not in the least. It's a means to an end, that's all," he says. "No, ironically, my desire is exactly as yours. So why should you matter? Why should your desires trump my own? Why should you be offered salvation, or the opportunity to save your brothers when I have never been able to save my own?"

His words linger in the air. A strange mixture of truth and trepidation.

For the first time since I left the Helix—since I started this journey, I feel as though Videus has been honest. Exposed.

He's lost his brother, and this is what's become of him.

Suddenly, the ground beneath Videus begins to rumble. Confused, I look for the source of the commotion—and find Ammon focusing on the ground with his eyes, his hands splaying open. I've seen this look before.

"What are you—?" I begin, but before I can finish my sentence, the ground splits, opening up a crevasse of split rocks around Videus' feet.

Videus stumbles, straddling the broken fragments of earth as they break apart in large chunks, shifting forward and back—upward and down. I watch him intently, surprised by his own humanity. His natural ability to be hurt, or lose his balance. It doesn't seem like something he should be capable of.

Ammon's hands fly outward, and with it, the stones beside Videus' feet open up into a chasm. For a split second, I swear, Videus is completely caught off guard as he tries to regain his balance without falling in.

I try to shake off my own surprise, but instead, realize what Ammon's done is the absolute right thing. I let my guard down and Videus was toying with it. I let him appeal to my own humanity and it could cost both of us our lives. What was I thinking? He probably wasn't even telling the truth. Just luring me in until I couldn't act.

Inhaling, I join in, commanding the power and energy I felt moments before. I allow the presence of the bloodlines to meld into me as I pull on their weight and send the snow and sculptures crashing inward. They meld into one powerful, crimson snow serpent, throwing Videus aside as though he was composed of nothing more than air.

The blood serpent pushes him down, forcing him into the opening Ammon's created. Within microseconds, Videus reclaims his composure—commanding some power of his own as he bursts into flames and disappears before the chasm can collect him.

Stepping back, I release my connection and the serpent bursts into a flurry of red flakes that blanket the ground.

Ammon slams his hands together, closing the chasm.

Turning to him, I say, "Thank you, Ammon. I—I don't know why I hesitated."

"Because he knows what makes you tick," Ammon says. "That's what makes him so dangerous."

For a child, he understands more about people and their motivations than I ever have. I don't know if it's the difference in his upbringing, being raised in the Lateral—or the fact he was Videus' captive for so long.

I nod, "You're right. I just—I wasn't expecting him to seem so—"

"Normal?" Ammon finishes.

"Yes, exactly. He's always been so illusive—superhuman almost. As though he's untouchable. I wasn't expecting him to appeal to my humanity by showing his own."

"Well, whatever he's done in the past is apparently not working. He's gotta try something else, right?"

"Yeah, probably," I say. "We better get out of here. There's no telling what's on its way, or if he'll be back to finish the job."

"Think you can command the snow like that again?" Ammon says, looking out over the vast sea of snow in front of us. We have two choices. Move through Videus' building, or continue on through the landscape. It's pretty clear which one Ammon's chosen.

"I'm not sure, but I can try," I say.

Tethys has always been my answer in the snow—she's fast and capable. Her protection has always been unwavering.

I stop, holding my breath for a moment.

Where is Tethys? Whenever she could, she's always been where I needed her. We've been linked, she and I. Since the very beginning, before I knew about any of this. She was there to have my back.

I peer out over the undulating snow, but there's no sign of her. Only drifting flurries and the sky-locked sun.

Taking a deep breath, I focus on the snow, spreading out my consciousness the way I've felt Tethys do so many times before. At first, nothing happens, but as I focus on the crimson snow at my feet, it begins to resonate. Ammon steps closer, grabbing hold of my arm as if he's afraid he'll be left behind.

For the first time, I engage with something deeply innate within myself. The ability to connect to the snow—or water —floods me, making me realize this power has been here all along. I'd simply never tapped into it.

"Let's get out of here," I say, taking Ammon's hand as the snow melds into a shield around us, exactly as Tethys' does.

Before we know it, I used the energy of the snow to propel us forward. Connecting to the snow myself feels both familiar, but far more powerful. Every particle, every snowflake makes up the whole as though it's connected directly to me.

In a way, it's as though it has its own collective conscious-ness. Or its own sense of direction. With my thoughts I'm able to send out the visualization of where I need to go, where I want to be, and effortlessly, our course begins to alter. Like the way birds always know which direction to fly, even if they stray too far.

There's a lot at stake and if I'm meant to find the others like Ammon and myself, there's only one place I want to start. Once place with a connection to both Ammon and myself.

The Lateral.

Being there will put everyone in danger—but we already are. Videus will be back and he won't stop. I need my friends by my side. I need Trae.

The moment I think it, the crystal around my neck burns brightly. Still clutched under my left arm, the Caudex bursts open dropping to the floor of our shield. Both Ammon and myself, along with the shield around us gets sucked into it. It's like being minimized to the size of a keyhole, then expanded back out to normal, all within a matter of microseconds.

As the expansion to our normal size ceases, a shockwave spreads out over the snow. The trees tremble, causing snowflakes clinging to the branches to flitter to the ground. Disengaging the shield, I take a look around. We're not at the Lateral, but I know exactly where we are.

Standing in a pool of ashes, the Tree of Burden is at my feet. The Caudex suddenly fuzes itself together and drops to the ground. Grabbing Ammon's hand, we move back as the book morphs from the large tome, to a seedling, to a small tree, to the magnificent, ancient tree it was before—with one exception.

For the first time, tiny buds have appeared on the ends of its branches. Tightly bound, they cling to themselves as if huddling for warmth.

It's a sign from Pendomus.

We're on the right path now, and back where we belong.

"Wow—" Ammon whispers, "Did you see the way your big book just turned into a Tree?"

I smile to myself.

"Yes, Ammon, I certainly did," I say.

"Whew, that was cool. But where are you going to get all your information now?" he asks.

I don't even need to worry, I already know the answer. Ever since being in the presence of my bloodlines, information, energy, and power course through me. In a way, they've passed on their own knowledge. The Tree of Burden obviously felt the Caudex was no longer needed.

"I think I have all the information I need, Ammon," I say.

"Really? What about the trials? You still have one more left?"

"I can't worry about the trials right now. Besides, we both know I'm meant to help the others like us. Adrian herself told me. We don't have time to stop and contemplate another trial anymore. Now, it's time to take a final stand against Videus," I say.

Ammon frowns, but shrugs. His bruised face looks so much better now, but his skin is still so discolored and his eyes are still so puffy.

Stepping forward, I take his face in my hands.

"I know we both had an enormous revelation dropped on us. And I want you to know, I don't take any of it lightly. From the moment we met, I felt immediately bonded with you—" I sigh. "Now I know why. We also know why Videus took you, why he did *this* to you."

I rub my thumb across his cheek.

"I never expected to become this Daughter of Five. And I certainly never expected to find out I had a twin. But—in this weird twist of fate, I'm actually really grateful. I would never have known you otherwise."

Ammon's amber eyes are large and tears threaten to spill. He bites his quivering lip, but keeps silent. Instead, he nods—his silent agreement.

"Whatever happens next—whatever we come up against, it's not going to be easy. I want you by my side," I say. "Not only for your abilities, but so I can learn from you. I want to know what our father was like."

I smile.

"I'd like to know about Mum," he whispers.

"And I'll tell you everything I know," I say.

Ammon takes a deep inhalation, blowing it out in a puff of air. He scratches the top of his head and looks around.

"So, where to next?" he asks.

"We're in my normal timeline now, I can feel it. In order to launch an attack on Videus, I'm going to need help. The Vassalage is inside the Helix and I want to be as prepared as possible," I say.

"We're heading to the Lateral for the blue-haired guy, aren't we?" he says, smirking.

"Yeah, yeah we are," I nod.

"Well, he's not in the Lateral," Ammon says, his eyebrows raised.

"And how on Pendomus would you know that?"

He raises his hand and points.

"Isn't that him?"

I turn around, looking toward the direction of his finger.

He's right. Off in the distance, a man with bright blue hair trudges through the blaring white snow and trees.

"What's he doing ya think?" Ammon asks.

I shake my head, and say, "I'm not sure. Beyond the tree line that way is the Helix. I don't know why he'd be coming from there. Maybe he was doing recon? Let's go find out," I say, grabbing Ammon's hand.

Ammon and I tread carefully through the snow and trees. We both keep watchful eyes, to make sure there are no birds or Salamanders in the vicinity, or tracking Trae.

As we get closer, something is off about Trae's stature. His mannerisms are stiff, and jarring. Almost as if his knees and elbows are in pain. He walks with purpose, but also in an oddly zoned out kinda way.

"What's up with him?" Ammon asks, throwing the words out of the side of his mouth.

"I was just wondering the same thing. He doesn't look right, does he?" I say.

"He looks like he has a stick crammed up his—"

Suddenly, Trae's body drops. First to his knees, then face down into the snow. The entire time, his arms remain at his side, as if he has no intention of bracing his fall.

Releasing Ammon's hand, I race forward to Trae. Behind me, I hear Ammon calling my name, but I can't take it in—I can't respond. There's something really wrong with Trae and I need to help him.

As I reach Trae's side, I slide to my knees, rolling him over in the snow. Clumps of ice cling to his face and hair and his eyes are wide open.

Letting out a squeal, I fall back in the snow.

"What is it? What's happened?" Ammon says, dropping down beside me. As he looks at Trae, he shivers. "Eeeesh. Why are his eyes open?"

Regaining my composure, I get back up and shake Trae's shoulder.

"Trae, Trae—are you okay? Can you hear me?" I say, watching for signs from him.

Resting my head on his chest, I listen for his heartbeat.

"Is he—? You know. Is he—" Ammon asks, standing up and backing away.

I hold up a finger, asking him to give me a second.

I can't hear with him talking.

Through his clothing and the wind, it's near impossible to make out a thing. But I do feel my head bobbing up and down with Trae's shallow breaths.

"He's alive," I say, sitting up and exhaling in relief.

"Oh, thank god. I thought things were really gonna start going screwy with the timelines," Ammon says.

"Help me get him up. We need to get him back to the Lateral. Landry will know how to help him," I say, grabbing one of Trae's arms.

As I pull Trae up, Ammon slides beneath his other arm and we get him to his knees.

"How on Pendomus are we going to get him to the Lateral?" Ammon asks. "He's too heavy and awkward for the both of us to carry there."

"You're right, but luckily, we won't have to," I say.

"Huh?" Ammon asks, quirking his face.

Right beside him, Tethys snorts, making Ammon scream.

23

TRAETON

'VE ALWAYS WANTED to know what it felt like to fly. To soar incredibly high above the trees, no cares in the world. Riding the currents and clouds, knowing I was able to rise above it all.

I find myself floating and flying with such speed there's no way I could be disconnected from the air. I *am* the air. The colors and sights below make complete sense, greens and blues intermixed with the white of the clouds as I disappear through them.

When I have spent enough time in the clouds, I swoop in lower, enjoying the fragrance in the air of the Everblossoms as the scent mixes with the dew on the grass. Settling myself on a sturdy branch, I see a woman below; her feet kicking playfully at the waterside.

Beside her sits a large animal with brilliantly colored light fragmenting in every direction as the sunlight passes through it. There's a name for this animal, but my mind can't seem to recall it as easily as it did with the flowers. I know its my friend though. A fellow creature of this planet.

Sensing my presence, the woman turns to me, her

shoulder length hair with deep blue and purple streaks on the underside blows about in the breeze. Her eyes light up with joy as she sees me and I find myself floating down to her to take in her face more clearly.

Getting lost in her gaze, I realize there's more to this woman than I can recall. More than I can even describe. She's unimaginably gifted and has a radiance not unlike that of the creature beside her.

Reaching through the depths of the atmosphere, I hear her thoughts as if they were my own. As if I were somehow a part of her.

I missed you.

I realize I feel the same. This woman and who she is belongs to me as I do to her. Bound by something more powerful than time and space.

She strokes my chest as I lean closer to her. Her touch sparks something inside me. The memory of a cold, barren place where this one should be. It jolts me from this beautiful world where I can fly and anything is possible.

I MUST STILL BE DREAMING.

The weight of someone next to me, their rhythmic breathing, it's jarring. I open my eyes. Beside me, Runa is curled, beautifully—blissfully asleep. As if these past few weeks have only been a dream. Or perhaps a nightmare.

I try to recall what happened before this. What I'd been doing, or why I don't remember her return.

As I slowly regain consciousness, I realize we're back at Landry's and laying on his bed. Runa's resting beside me, just as she had before in the cavern, with one exception. I'm a bit more exposed than I was before. For some reason, my Nano-

Tech jacket and shirt are open and she's laying directly on my skin, her right hand resting over my heart.

Curiosity of how I got into this situation plays at the edge of my mind, but I can't keep my focus. My memories are so fuzzy and jumbled. I can't seem to hold onto my thoughts for very long. Partly because of the intense headache shooting through the back of my skull and partly because of Runa.

"You'd better be careful. I might get used to waking up like this," I whisper, trying not to wake her.

I squeeze her tight and lift my right hand, playing with the ends of her hair. It's shorter now. Didn't I dream that? Again, something I need to figure out. When did she cut it? My insides twist and my heart clenches.

Despite the confusion, I smile to myself. Here she is again, resting with me, so oblivious to what her touch does to me.

Even something as simple as this.

But this is a different day. We are different people now. It feels like forever since I last saw her. Since I last felt her body near mine. I'd forgotten how reassuring her presence is.

Her eyes open, eyelashes gently brushing my skin before she lifts herself and props on her elbow.

Relief flashes through her eyes and her face lights up. The next thing I know, she's kissing me as she flings one leg over and straddles my body. Both her hands press against my chest as she bends forward. The spot where our skin touches feels like it melds together, and I like it. I shudder in response, lifting slightly as I return her kiss.

Scratch the previous thought. I could get used to waking up like *this*.

All at once, a number of things happen. I'm suddenly blinded by an insanely bright light just as Landry comes rushing into the room. Runa abruptly sits up while Landry surveys our situation, but shrugs it off. He continues forward, medical instruments of some kind in his hands. An annoying beeping off to the left enters my consciousness and I realize I have electrodes connected to my body and the alarms are sounding.

That explains my chest being exposed. One question answered.

Oddly enough, my headache feels better than it had when I first woke up. A little laugh escapes before I can stifle it.

Must be the endorphins.

"Well, that worked better than I expected," Landry half-chuckles, shifting his gaze to me and raising his eyebrows in approval. Taking a seat, he turns to watch my vitals on the screen. "Your pulse is a bit erratic, though."

Thus the alarms.

Still straddled across my body, hands still burning into my chest, Runa holds my gaze surveying me closely. Her face is a beautiful shade of crimson and I can't help but laugh.

She looks more embarrassed now than when her mother walked in on us.

Clearing her throat quietly, she asks Landry, "What worked, exactly?"

Landry turns around and answers with a smirk, "I knew I'd be occupied with Ammon for a while and I needed to know as soon as Trae *was up*. Figured the heart monitor would alarm if you were nearby."

His grin deepens as he meets my eyes, cocking his head slightly to the side.

I can't help but roll my eyes at his double entendre.

He's just like Fenton. Only with ten years more experience.

She misses his double meaning, as he knew she would. Thank the stars for that.

Sliding off me slowly, as if it wasn't a choice she wanted to make, she takes a seat to my right.

"Will he be okay? It's a good thing, right? That he's finally woken up?" Runa says.

Landry and Runa exchange a significant glance before Landry nods.

"Yeah, of course it's a good thing," he says, returning to the monitor.

"Finally? How long was I out? And who's Ammon?" I ask.

The two of them exchange another round of glances. Concern creeps in, and I shift to a seated position.

"I'm sure you'll be fine," Landry reassures me, but worry is hidden behind his eyes. He leans forward and removes the electrodes from my skin.

"Okay…" I say slowly.

Evidently, something's not right with me.

Runa places her hand over mine and whispers, "We aren't quite sure what's happened to you. You've been out of it for a while. And Kani's—well, she's missing."

"What do you mean? Missing? How could Kani go missing?" I say, lowering my eyebrows.

"We're hoping you could tell us. You'd both gone through some stuff, but seemed to be better. You lost time, she lost— well, she had issues that needed to be resolved. Do you remember any of this?" Landry asks.

Everything he says rings a vague bell, so I nod.

"Yeah, I think so. I remember Landry had to wipe pieces of her mind," I say, rubbing the back of my neck.

"Well, we're wondering if not all the pieces were put back together properly. You were found out in the woods, but no one knows where she went. Do you have any idea?" Runa says.

For the life of me, I can't remember much after Kani's memory restructure.

I shake my head, "Nah. Everything is pretty muddled after that."

"Landry thinks he may have a theory about that," Runa says.

"Oh yeah?" I say, my gaze shifting to him.

"What did you call it again?" Runa says, turning to Landry.

"I think it may have been the Seize Scanner," he says, eyebrows pinched.

"Right. *Seize Scanner*," she frowns before meeting my eyes again. "I keep forgetting."

"Why would you think my loss of time stems from that?" I ask, confused.

It's been ages since I was attacked by the Labots inside the Helix.

"Because you've been off since then. Headaches and whatnot. I figure that's when it all started. It's likely a side effect or a deliberate defense mechanism the Helix cooked up to make sure there were lasting effects of those they seized. For instance, if they got away, they'd at least be sure to cause lasting neurologic damage."

He's right. The headaches started after Runa and the Helix. After the Tree and—after Fenton.

Landry meets my stare and adds with a shrug, "It's what I would do if I were inventing it."

Shocked, I ask, "What does that mean? You'd want people to suffer?"

"No, not that," he shakes his head. "If I felt the need to stop someone, or protect myself, I'd want to put in a fail safe. Not all people behave, think, or physically operate the same. So I'd want assurances."

"You know, man. I can't tell if it's awesome or creepy that you can make sense of the crazy shit the Helix does," I say.

Landry, shrugs again, accepting the burden of being dangerously smart.

I take a breath, and pinch the bridge of my nose. My eyes are sore, but my head feels like it's beginning to clear.

"Anyway, no one has seen Kani for a while. Ammon and I found you unconscious in the woods. Near the Tree of Burden. We brought you back here to get help. You've been out for days. When Landry and Alina told me what happened before, I went to the Archives to see if there was anything there I could make sense of. But everything was a mess. Tables knocked over, stuff everywhere. The mainframe has been destroyed."

My eyes wide, "Wait—what?"

Memories of what happened at the Archives are still fuzzy. I remember getting Kani out of the box and getting her to Landry. I remember the mess—but not the mainframe. Then again, I guess I never really took a moment to take in the extent of the damage.

Landry interjects, "The way Runa tells it, the mainframe is in a million pieces. Doubt we'll be able to get it operational again. On the upside, I'm close to being able to untangle the memories I extracted from Kani on the the event. We should be able to get to the bottom of things soon."

"You can do that?" I say, astounded. "Do you think Kani'd be happy with this?"

Kani was always the one against Landry's fascination with meddling in the mind. From the beginning, she fought him, trying to get him to reconsider his techniques. I suppose it was the inner medic in her.

But if she knew Landry had removed memories and was going through them, she'd be pissed.

Landry makes a face but says, "I don't think she was really in a place to argue. Right now, they're our only lead."

"Do you think this is a good idea?" I ask, turning to Runa.

She takes a moment, her multicolored eyes going a bit distant as she considers, "At this point, I think Landry's right. We need answers. But more than that—if you were attacked by Videus, which is the likeliest of explanations, then we need to know what was worth attacking Kani, or destroying the mainframe over. Or even hurting you."

Suddenly, the memories about the vassalage, Baxten, and the strange feeling of possession come flooding back.

My eyes widen and I lick my lower lip, "I think I know exactly what was so important."

Both of them turn to me with quizzical expressions.

I take a moment, weighing what to tell them and what to leave out. Until I know what's going on for sure, I don't want to worry anyone. Hell if I want to become Landry's next lab rat.

"It's the Vassalage. I found out where it is."

"It's in the Helix," Runa says.

"How'd you—?"

"It's not important," she says, dismissively.

"Well, if we can get inside, I think I can find Baxten," I say.

Runa slides off the bed, standing with her hands on her hips. Her face is ashen, and her eyebrows tug in.

"What do you mean?" she asks, frowning. "That's not going to be possible, Trae."

"Why's that?"

"I've been told he's gone."

"By who?" I ask, indignantly. Deep in my bones, I know there's more to the Helix and the Crematorium than any of us thought.

"It doesn't matter. He's gone."

My heart breaks for her as her sorrow becomes palpable in this small room. I know how she must feel, taking the responsibility onto your shoulders. It's a heavy load to carry.

"Listen to me. We need to be sure," I say. "And like you said, you need a place to start. Kani and I talked about the Crematorium before all this happened. Maybe she went there looking for answers—or vengeance."

Something flickers in Runa's eyes and I see a hint of determination creeping in as she stands a little straighter.

Landry sighs, "We'll get this all figured out soon. But no one is going anywhere anytime soon. You need to rest and get your health back. I want to watch your brain scans for a bit to make sure you're not still suffering any of the effects of the scanner."

"How long?" I ask, suddenly agitated and antsy.

"Trae, your vitals look good for now. But even Runa needs some rest. She hasn't slept much since she got you all back here."

"You all? There's someone else?" I say, vaguely remembering them talk about someone else.

Confused, I throw my legs over the edge of the bed and walk into the kitchen. Curled up on the couch is a small boy, no more than eleven years old.

"Who's this?" I ask, pointing in the direction of the sleeping child.

Runa shifts slightly, her eyes wide, "Traeton, this is my brother, Ammon."

Silence falls for a few moments as I take in her words.

"You have *another* brother?" I finally say.

She nods.

Thinking back to the information Fenton and I discovered about Runa, I'm suddenly not surprised. There was something off about her family. The Helix didn't have her father's information down. I've always thought that was a bit odd.

"There's a lot I need to tell you, just not right now. We really should—" she begins.

I step forward, placing my hand along her jaw and my thumb against her lips, silencing her words.

"Okay, Runa. I trust you. We'll figure this out—tomorrow," I sigh.

I reach my arm around her back to pull her closer. I kiss her forehead and she sighs as she relaxes into my body. It feels so good to finally hold her in my arms again and I find myself wondering why I ever fought this.

Because it's what I've always done.

As I release her from my embrace, I take her hand, "Landry's right. We should both rest. You need your sleep. We'll be better prepared to take on whatever comes next."

"I'll get out of your hair and go see Alina. Come get me when you're ready and we can work out a plan of action," Landry says, making his way to the front door.

With all that's happened today, my brain is working overtime to make sense of it all, shifting the data around. I'm sure the Seize Scanner hasn't helped. If that's what the weird feelings of possession are, then it's far worse than even Landry believes. Maybe it was just a dream? That has to be it, right?

With Runa's hand in mine, I walk with her back to the bedroom and take a seat on the edge of the bed. I'm suddenly so tired.

Together, we curl back up in bed. I know after days of being asleep, I should be sick of it, but my brain feels like sludge. A little deliberate sleep might be exactly what we both need.

Runa rests her hand over my heart again, and I allow my body to meld together with hers. There's so much to discuss. So much to sort out and make sense of. Not only will I have some explaining to do, but I want to know where she's been. How she got back. Tomorrow will be a full day.

I allow the mixture of memories, thoughts, and desires to wash over me as I settle into a restless sleep.

The dreams that ordinarily fill my headspace turn ominous.

I meander a hallway so hot and stifling I can barely breathe. In the rooms branching off on either side, there are people held captive to the walls. Some are huddled in the corners, hiding their heads. Somehow, I'm unconcerned. Almost as if it's a normal, everyday occurrence. Like it's a good thing.

There's a loathing that washes over me and I find I can't stand any of them. They're all so pitiful and weak. So incapable of redeeming themselves, utilizing their innate ability—it makes them easy to control and it makes me sick.

I turn into one of the rooms, moving swiftly to the latest prisoner. Kani's face is gray and her body depleting. When we've achieved the outcome we're looking for, she will be assimilated into our legion. This I know for a fact, and I am again, unconcerned.

As she slowly raises her head, struggling to lift it level—I let out a laugh. Her suffering amuses me. Beside her, in the same room is the boy we took earlier. The Daughter of Five's brother.

"We've located her," I cackle. "When she comes, and she will— everything will finally be over."

Abruptly, I'm pulled from my sleep, cold sweat dripping off my body. Runa has shifted slightly, but is still curled up beside me.

I can't stop shaking. My insides are coiling tight, making me feel sick. There's a deja vu in this dream, in the events, and even in the feelings everything aroused. I can't shake the suspicion I've been to this place. That this was no dream, it was a memory resurfacing. If that's the case, then I know what happened to Kani. I was the one—

What the hell is wrong with me?

TO BE CONCLUDED...

NEXT UP—

Revolutions

The Pendomus Chronicles: Book 3

AFTERWORD

Did you love **Polarities**? If so, please kindly leave a review wherever you love to find books. It helps others like you stumble on this crazy, beautiful series.
You Rock!
Carissa

NEXT UP—
Revolutions
The Pendomus Chronicles: Book 3

CONCLUDE THE TRILOGY...

To conclude Runa's quest to save Pendomus and embrace her destiny as the Daughter of Five, continue on with...

Revolutions: Book 3 of the Pendomus Chronicles

ALSO BY CARISSA ANDREWS

THE PENDOMUS CHRONICLES

Pendomus: *Book 1 of the Pendomus Chronicles*

Revolutions: *Book 3 of the Pendomus Chronicles*

THE 8TH DIMENSION NOVELS

The Final Five

Oracle: *A Diana Hawthorne Supernatural Thriller*

Awakening: *Rise as the Fall Unfolds*

Love is a Merciless God

THE WINDHAVEN WITCHES

Secret Legacy *(Sept 8, 2020)*

Soul Legacy *(Oct 6, 2020)*

Haunted Legacy *(Nov 3, 2020)*

Cursed Legacy *(Dec 1, 2020)*

ABOUT THE AUTHOR

Carissa Andrews
Sci-fi/Fantasy is my pen of choice.

 Carissa Andrews is an international bestselling indie author from central Minnesota who writes a combination of science fiction, fantasy, and dystopia. Her plans for 2020 include publication of her highly anticipated **Windhaven Witches** series. As a publishing powerhouse, she keeps sane by chilling with her husband, five kids, and their two insane husky puppies Aztec and Pharaoh.

To find out what Carissa's up to, head over to her website and sign up for her newsletter:
www.carissaandrews.com

facebook.com/authorcarissaandrews

twitter.com/CarissaAndrews

instagram.com/carissa_andrews_mn

amazon.com/author/carissaandrews

bookbub.com/authors/carissa-andrews

goodreads.com/Carissa_Andrews